Somebody's Baby

DONNA ALWARD

St. Martin's Paperbacks

3 5942 00108 1720

This is a work of fiction. All of the characters, organizations, and events portrayed in this novel are either products of the author's imagination or are used fictitiously.

SOMEBODY'S BABY

Copyright © 2017 by Donna Alward.

All rights reserved.

For information address St. Martin's Press, 175 Fifth Avenue, New York, NY 10010.

ISBN: 978-1-250-09268-7

Our books may be purchased in bulk for promotional, educational, or business use. Please contact your local bookseller or the Macmillan Corporate and Premium Sales Department at 1-800-221-7945, ext. 5442, or by e-mail at MacmillanSpecialMarkets@macmillan.com.

Printed in the United States of America

St. Martin's Paperbacks edition / April 2017

St. Martin's Paperbacks are published by St. Martin's Press, 175 Fifth Avenue, New York, NY 10010.

10 9 8 7 6 5 4 3 2 1

CHAPTER 1

Oaklee Collier was so sick of attending bridal and baby showers she was thinking of developing a chronic and convenient illness just so she wouldn't have to go.

Saying no just wasn't an option. Not for sunny and upbeat Oaklee, who ran the town of Darling's social media and knew exactly what was going on, where, and when. She'd been present at so many events that she'd been given the office nickname—unoriginal at that—of Social Butterfly. Of course she'd been naïve back a few years ago when she'd started interning with the Darling Town Office during the summers. And oh, so smug, like she had the world by the proverbial tail. Flitting from event to event had suited her just fine. Brides and babies had her oohing and aaahing appropriately, because she'd figured she was well on her way to both events, and in that order.

She wasn't smug anymore. And she was sick and tired

of pasting on a smile when faced with happy ever after when she knew for a fact such a thing didn't exist.

She hit the gas and turned onto a backroad, heading toward the lake just outside the town. This last shower had been a double whammy. The bride was a coworker, and she was also expecting a baby. Double the celebration, since the wedding would happen in September and the baby was due in February. Rebecca was blissfully happy with her blissful husband-to-be and their blissful home, and in six and a half months she'd give birth to a blissful little baby Becky or Darren.

Blech.

And it might have been easier to stay cynical and annoyed if she hadn't felt the sting of tears at the back of her eyes, clogging her throat.

Damn Jeff anyway. Damn him for ripping out her heart by leaving her standing at the chapel altar. The only consolation was that they'd been eloping in Vegas, so her humiliation hadn't been witnessed by a church full of family and friends. It was one of the best-kept secrets in Darling—no small feat.

Thank God for small miracles. Being left at the altar was not an event that would ever have been forgotten in a town the size of Darling. Especially not when the bride was a former Homecoming Queen and the groom was her high school sweetheart, and both were at the tender age of twenty-two. Thankfully Jeff had disappeared across the country to a new job and she didn't have to face him ever again.

She was twenty-four; young, just embarking on her career and with a world of options ahead of her. But tonight, at the fifth or six shower since spring, she'd felt much, much older. And tired.

The lake never failed to make her feel better, though. It was mid-August, and the brash heat of July had faded just a bit, taking the humidity with it. Days were hot with a clear, blue sky; evenings were cool and peach and purple, all soft around the edges. She parked away from the public beach, wanting to avoid people. Instead she took off her flimsy sandals and walked away from the evening stragglers who marred the smooth sapphire surface with their splashing. She followed the slightly more rocky shore a few hundred yards east, and then stopped and stepped into the cool water.

It surrounded her toes, curled around her ankles, washing away the hectic pace of the day and the constant ache from her impossibly high heels. She let out a sigh and waded deeper, but not up past her calves. She didn't want to get her hem wet, then have it itch the whole way home. Instead she stood there, soaking in the last of the sun's rays, letting the lake water wash away the stress of her daily performance. Oaklee Collier. Good for a laugh, plays on the Internet as her job, never has to worry about money because her brother's a big shot. Oaklee Collier who has it all. And oh, by the way, how's your love life? The reality was far more boring, so she never bothered to set anyone straight. The truth was, she worked damned hard, and she refused to let her big-shot hockey-playing brother pay her way. Her love life? Hah. Nonexistent.

A powerboat sped by, quite a way from shore, but close enough she heard the catcalls from the guys on board. In a few minutes the wake would create gentle rocking waves that made the lake sound remarkably like the ocean. Oaklee waited, and smiled a little as the first little curl chased her calves. The rhythmic laps of the waves broke on the gravelly beach, and Oaklee took a step back. When she did, her foot landed on a rock—a slippery rock that put her off balance. She stumbled and instinctively reached out to steady herself, only there was nothing to grab on to. Instead she took half a dozen awkward steps, splashing in the waves and soaking her skirt in the process.

"Dammit!"

She made her way back to the dry shoreline and assessed the damage. The back of her skirt wasn't too bad, just a little damp. But the front, where she'd tipped forward, was soaked halfway up her thighs. It was a white skirt, and she supposed she should be grateful that it hadn't got wet farther north. She still had to walk back to her car. The last thing she needed was to be practically exposed. No one needed to see what she was wearing beneath her skirt.

So much for peace and quiet and equilibrium.

Still out of sorts, she started for Darling and home. Home consisted of an apartment, the end unit of a four-plex in a new development close to the golf course. She lived there alone. Her folks lived across town in the same house they'd lived in when she was growing up. There were days she seriously considered taking her talents and moving elsewhere, but she had a good job and in the current economy that wasn't anything to sniff at. Besides, Darling was home. Maybe it wasn't perfect, but there was still something comforting about it. She could always count on Darling to stay exactly as it had always been.

She was halfway back to town in the purple twilight when her phone buzzed. She ignored the sound, but a few seconds later it buzzed again, and then again. Sighing, she reached over to the passenger seat and grabbed it. She hit the power button and looked down, only for a second, and when she glanced up again she gasped and hit the brakes as hard as she could.

But it was too late.

Her heart pounded as she sat for a few moments, numb. Oh God. She'd hit . . . something. Had it been a raccoon? A bear cub? A dog? She didn't want to go look, but knew she must. Throat tight, chest cramped, she got out of her car and ventured carefully toward the front of the vehicle.

It was a dog, and it lay on the road, chest heaving, head resting on the dirt. His—or her—tongue lolled out of its mouth, and tears spurted into Oaklee's eyes. "Oh God," she said, stepping forward. "I'm so sorry. Oh God."

The dog whimpered, tried to get up, but fell back down again. She couldn't see much blood, but she knew she had to do something. She couldn't just leave it here to die. Tentatively she reached out a hand to pat its head, and it nuzzled at her wrist, giving the pad of her thumb a lick.

The damn thing was licking her hand after she'd just hit it with her car. Stupid thing. How dumb and trusting did you have to be to do something like that? Why wasn't it angry or afraid and snapping at her?

She went back to the car and found an old beach towel in the mess that was her backseat. "Come on, then," she said, wondering how she was going to possibly move it. At her best guess, the animal weighed at least fifty or sixty pounds. She was in good shape, but that was still a hefty dog to be lifting into a car.

It took another five minutes of struggling and sweating before Oaklee had the dog half on the towel. It had yelped several times, and she was crying now, hating that she was hurting it but unable to do anything else. Why had she thought taking the backroads would be a good idea? There hadn't been another car since she stopped. There were no houses, either. She couldn't even stop and ask someone if they owned the dog.

"Lift with the knees, Oaklee," she reminded herself, squatting down and gathering the dog in her arms. She got her hands beneath shoulders and hips, beneath the towel, and hefted upward. The dog cried out and struggled briefly, then sagged in her arms. The change in momentum sent her staggering toward the car, fighting not to fall down or drop the dog, causing more injury.

With sweat, tears, and a lot of dirt, she got the animal into her backseat, shoving over a grocery bag full of garbage and a couple of jackets she'd thrown in there and hadn't taken out yet. The dog was panting more now, and its eyes were a bit wild. She stopped and patted its head awkwardly. "I'm going to take you to someone who'll make you all better," she promised. She'd never been much of an animal person, particularly dogs, but she wasn't cruel. Her heart ached knowing how much it must be hurting, and that it was all her fault.

With one last pat, she shut the door, got back in the driver's seat, and headed toward Darling.

This was turning out to be one hell of a day.

It was past nine thirty when Rory heard the tires in the driveway and the slam of a car door. He went to the window of his apartment—the living space above the veterinary clinic where he worked—and peeked outside. After-hours calls were supposed to go through the answering service. The hazard of living onsite meant that people knew he was there and sometimes stopped in at all hours.

Generally he billed them accordingly. Once word got around that an after-hours call cost mega dollars, the drop-ins stopped . . . for the most part.

But not tonight.

A woman got out of the car . . . she looked familiar, but in the semi-dark and from the angle of his small kitchen window, he couldn't quite make out her features. He could hear her loud and clear, though, as she banged on the glass door to the clinic. "Rory? You in there? I've got a dog down here." *Bang bang bang*—a flat palm on the glass. "Come on, Rory!"

Unless he was mistaken, that voice belonged to Oaklee Collier. A complete and utter pain in the ass. She'd never let him and Cam alone when they were kids. He'd been best friends with her brother, and with nearly two years of an age gap, it was enough to drive them crazy. When she was fourteen, she'd followed him around with puppy eyes.

He opened the window. "Oaklee, is that you? What the hell?"

She looked up and he caught his breath. Oaklee never looked anything but one hundred percent together. But right now he could see her tawny-blond hair was a tumbled mess, her eye makeup was streaked around her eyes à la Alice Cooper, and her outfit had once been white and was now streaked with brown and red smears.

Shit.

"I hit a dog, Rory." Her voice broke . . . another bad sign. "It's in the backseat. I need you to come take it and . . . and look after it."

He sighed. "I'll be right down. Hang on."

It didn't take more than thirty seconds for him to shove on some shoes and go down to the clinic and unlock the door, but by the time he did she was pacing in front of the entrance. "You say the dog's in your car?"

"In the backseat. I didn't know what else to do. I was out by the lake and coming into town the back way and he just . . . jumped out in front of me."

Her gaze skittered away, and she sniffed.

He went to the car and opened the back door on the passenger side. There was a dog in here, all right, though he shared the space with an astonishing amount of female clutter: shoes, a pile of clothes, what looked like a handbag though he couldn't be sure, and a few fast-food paper bags. The dog was a mutt from the looks of it, with the beard and eyebrows of a terrier and the size and coat of a lab. The poor thing looked half starved and right now was laboring to breathe. "Hey, buddy," he said softly, giving him a once-over with gentle fingers. He scooped his hands beneath the towel and lifted, cradling the animal in his arms as he stepped back and headed straight for the clinic doors.

"Hey, open this, will you?" The dog was heavy and was dead weight. Oaklee rushed to open the door, then stepped aside as Rory went through to the first exam room and put the dog down on the table.

"I looked up and he was just there," she said, her voice shaking. "I didn't know what else to do. I came the back way from the lake, you know, along Frontage Road? But there wasn't a house close or anything. He doesn't have a collar or any tags. He's going to be okay, right?"

Her voice broke on the last syllable. He knew people always felt horrible after a hit-by-car.

"Shh, and let me examine him," he said gently. "Why don't you wait in the waiting room?"

She shook her head. "I'll stay. In case you need help."

Well. He looked up at her briefly, found her mouth set in a stubborn line. Oaklee had been dramatic as a teenager, and had this sort of sorority girl appearance about her, complete with perfect smile and perky attitude. He tended to forget that she was also completely bullheaded and had a tendency to get what she wanted. He didn't want to waste time arguing.

"Fine. Put on a pair of those gloves, then." Not that he'd have much for her to do; she had no idea how to look for internal injuries or assess cuts. The most she could do was sit by the dog's head and keep him calm, and possibly help irrigate some of the lacerations so Rory could see if they needed stitching.

She was tougher than he expected, though, and followed his directions without question as he gave the pup a thorough exam. She held his paw just so when he put in an IV, and even donned an apron and helped with the

X-ray, which proved there was a broken front leg that would need to be set and cast.

They cleaned the cuts, but he noticed her paling when he took out the suture pack to stitch up the worst.

"I can do this," he said gently. "You don't have to stay."

"Yes, I do. It was my fault, and you'd normally have someone to help, wouldn't you?"

Not always, not on an after-hours call, but he didn't argue with her. If anything, he was impressed she'd lasted this long. And even more impressed she'd followed his orders without question. That wasn't the Oaklee he knew.

She looked away when he put in the sutures, but stroked the dog's head. At this point the dog was very sedated and lay quietly on the table, his tongue hanging out of his mouth. Once Rory looked up and saw a tear sneak out of the corner of her eye, and his heart softened a bit. Oaklee was known around town as a real go-getter. Seeing her a bit emotional reminded him of the cute girl she'd once been.

A cute girl with a softer heart than she let on most of the time. But Rory had seen. And he'd been the one who'd had to step in and play big brother when Cam was away playing in the junior leagues.

When he set the leg, he sent her out. He was pretty sure that as stalwart as she'd been, the process of setting the bone might be a bit too much.

By the time it was done, it was midnight and Oaklee was on a stool just outside the room, looking as if she might tip over at any minute. But she'd held up well, better than he expected. Apparently sheer force of will wasn't a thing to underestimate.

Rory sighed and peeled off his gloves. "There. He'll rest for tonight. He's going to be fine, Oaklee. A little worse for wear, but he's going to make it. Don't worry."

She smiled a little. "Okay, then." When she took off her latex gloves, the sound echoed through the silent hall. She tossed them in a garbage can, and shrugged out of the white lab coat she'd put on when she got cold. "This has been an experience, Rory. But I expect I look like a bag lady. I need a shower and my bed."

As soon as she said it, dual images popped into his brain and lodged there. There was no denying that Oaklee had always been pretty. There'd been a girlish beauty to her in her teen years, but she was more stunning as a woman, with sexy curves and a bit more knowledge behind her big blue eyes. The idea of her taking a hot shower and crawling beneath the covers of her bed did weird things to his head. He shouldn't be thinking of her this way . . .

"You don't need anything more from me, right?" Her words brought him back to the present and he frowned. Of course. She was back to her regular, practical self now, he thought. Oaklee was the type to clock out at five and head blissfully for home, no worry about taking work home with her. She probably lived in a super-stylish apartment with some sort of trendy décor. That wasn't Rory. The apartment upstairs was fairly Spartan by most standards. The fact that he'd lived there with his brother until the last month or so hadn't changed anything, except that he didn't have to go behind Aiden and pick up dirty clothes and dishes.

Blond strands of hair had slipped out of the knot at the back of her head and cascaded around the sides of her face. She did look tired . . . and her makeup was smeared from her earlier crying. The sight of the always-put-together Oaklee in such a state made him want to put his arms around her and assure her that everything was going to be okay. He'd never, ever acted on those impulses, though. Even if he'd wanted to, Rory had always known Cam would play the big brother and kick his ass for touching his baby sister. Oaklee had first caught his attention in her sophomore year . Rory remembered because Cam had caught him looking at her chest and had decked him. For just looking. Of course, Cam wasn't in Darling anymore, and Rory hadn't seen him in a couple of years. Once Cam had been drafted and made it to the NHL, he'd lived in the team city, and didn't really come back in the off-season, either. Rory's contact with him was strictly through the odd e-mail. Maybe a Facebook post, but he wasn't really into social media much and never had been.

Didn't matter, though. Oaklee was still his best friend's little sister, and that made her Off Limits.

"You go ahead," he said quietly. "I'll get this boy settled for the night."

She looked up at him with those big eyes. "You're leaving him alone?"

"He'll be KO'd with the pain meds for a good while, Oaklee. And I'm right upstairs." He looked at the clock. "Besides, I'm due back down here in about six hours anyway."

"Oh. So early?"

He nodded, wondering why she kept talking, why she didn't just go. It would definitely make it easier on him. The same urge he'd had when she was sixteen came roaring back: he'd do anything to stop her from being upset. To make her feel better. His voice was tight as he answered her question. "When you're the junior vet, you get the shit schedule. Plus I live upstairs and the rent's a steal. It's a trade-off."

"Well, okay. If you say so." She gave the dog a last, sad look and reached out to touch his silky ear—the only soft bit about him. He was terribly malnourished, and his coat had suffered, too. It was wiry and rough.

"Thanks for your help," he added.

"You're welcome. Thanks for opening up for me."

"Oh, don't worry. It'll all be on the bill."

A look of shock flattened her face. "Oh God." Then she pasted on a nervous smile. "I mean, of course. Do we have to do this now? Or can you send a bill?"

He shook his head. "We can do it later. When the office staff is in and the computers are booted up." As it was, he'd be up for a while writing up the chart for their Fido Doe.

He was sure he saw relief cross her face. "Okay, then. I guess I'll . . . I'll go."

Her gaze lifted and caught his. It was after midnight, they were both covered in blood and dirt, and he was exhausted. But in that split second, Rory was utterly aware that he was a very single man all alone with a very single woman who happened to be incredibly attractive—even at her worst.

And at her worst just happened to be when Rory found her most approachable. He imagined what might happen if he stepped forward, curled his hand through that mess of blond hair, and pulled her lips to his. As the thought raced through his mind, her lips parted, just a bit—a silent and unconscious invitation.

He swallowed tightly and clenched his hands into fists inside the lab coat pockets. This was Oaklee, for God's sake. Cam's little sister. A nosy, flirty little pain in the ass and not his type. No sir, not his type at all. Been there, done that.

"Drive safely," he said instead, and took a step backward.

"You too," she said, then her cheeks flushed with embarrassment. He only had to climb a flight of stairs. "I mean . . ."

"I know what you meant." Rory had the upper hand again, and he relaxed a little. "You can stop in anytime to settle up."

"Thanks. Bye, Rory."

"Bye. I'll lock the door behind you."

He locked the door and cut the lights in the reception area, but waited until she was in her car and driving away before he turned back toward the surgery.

CHAPTER 2

When Oaklee saw her face in the mirror the next morning, she held back a scream of horror.

Mascara and eyeliner ringed her eyes so that she looked like a raccoon. Her hair was tangled and flat on one side, and there was a brownish streak along one temple. Gross. Was that dirt? Or blood from the dog? She'd been so tired when she got home last night that she'd stripped off her skirt and top, pulled on an oversized sweatshirt, and fell into bed, leaving the shower for the morning.

She brushed her teeth, then turned on the shower.

Twenty minutes later she felt more human, though she couldn't really get the events of the previous night out of her mind. Not just the dog, but Rory.

As a teenager she'd had a horrible crush on him. He didn't have the same red hair as his brothers and sisters. His was a rich brown, like his mother's, and with just the right amount of curl without it being too long. His eyes, too, were deep blue and thickly lashed, and when he'd fixed them on her face last night before she left, her stomach had lifted with a weird, fluttery sensation. When he'd hung out with Cam, he'd been a little smaller. More . . . boyish. Now he'd filled out into manhood. He'd lifted the dog as if he weighed nothing at all, his muscles flexing as he carried the animal from car to clinic. She'd known all this, but since she didn't have a pet and they had very different jobs, they didn't cross paths often.

Until last night. And then she'd been reminded in a big way.

She slipped into a sheath dress the shade of ripe cantaloupe and reached behind her to zip the back. Today she had a meeting about the new tourism initiative, and she needed to look sharp. She had ideas for social media campaigns going right through to next summer's tourist season. She'd been on staff for over a year, but she was twenty-four. Easy to dismiss. So she tried to make up for her age—which she couldn't help—by working hard and looking professional.

Last night she'd looked anything but. As she stepped into her favorite nude heels, she thought about Rory and how gentle and competent he'd been. They way he'd touched the dog, so bloody and dirty, and spoke to him in a calm, soothing voice. And yet his tenderness hadn't kept him from doing what needed to be done, without a single flinch.

Her respect for him had gone up several notches.

Now there was just one problem. She'd have a hefty vet bill to pay and it was another week until payday. She lived alone. By the time she paid rent, insurance on her car, and the other necessary bills, she really didn't have much in savings. Like . . . a few hundred dollars. She loved her job, but it wasn't making her rich. As it was, Darling was small enough that she walked to work most days. It meant not having to find a parking spot and saving gas. Not that she'd admit that to anyone. Oaklee had an image to uphold. That image, the one that showed she had it all together, was the only thing that gave her credibility, until results—and experience—spoke for themselves.

She stopped at The Purple Pig on the way to town hall, craving one of Willow's raspberry scones and a very large coffee. She tucked the scone into her case and slid the strap over her shoulder, and sipped her coffee on the short walk from the café to the office. Anytime she considered leaving Darling, it was this main street that kept bringing her back. Lined with mom-and-pop businesses, with welcoming doors and a profusion of blooms everywhere, it was both stunningly gorgeous and warmly inviting. Darling was the perfect example of small-town America, and Oaklee's job was to help bring in both tourists and business.

She was early to the meeting, so she found a place at the conference table, took out her scone, her laptop with her presentation, and a pad and pen. Then she took a moment to send out a tweet.

@OakleeC_Darling: Eventful night. Hit a dog on Frontage Rd but he's going to be okay. No tags. Contact Darling Vet if yours. 1/2

@OakleeC_Darling: Thank God he'll be okay. Scared me big-time. Great care from Dr. Gallagher. 2/2

She sat back for a moment and pondered that last bit. Dr. Gallagher. It was hard to think of Rory in those terms. It made him sound so . . . grown up and accomplished. Eight years of school and now he knew how to set broken bones and do operations and . . . well, be a doctor. And what did she do? She played with social media for a living.

She was good at it. Oaklee knew that. But somehow, this morning, it seemed of lesser importance.

Frowning, she booted up her laptop and opened up the town's Facebook page. "This morning's meeting means having fun making plans for this." Below it she attached the two publicity photos they were incorporating in their campaign: the first a twenty-year-old shot of a flower girl and ring bearer kissing on the town's famed Kissing Bridge, and the second of a bride and groom in the exact same pose. Both pictures were of Aiden Gallagher and his new wife, Laurel. It gave an amazing bit of symmetry and inspired the town's new slogan: *Kiss for a moment, love for a lifetime.*

"Good morning, Oaklee. You're here early, I see." Brent Mitchell, the mayor, stepped into the conference room, carrying a mug of coffee and a file folder.

"I wanted to get my first morning posts done before we got into the campaign," she said with a smile.

Brent sank into his chair at the head of the table. "You always seem on top of it, that's for sure," he replied, and Oaklee felt a surge of both pride and relief.

Other staff started filtering in, so Oaklee grabbed her phone and sent out another quick tweet, making sure to tag the town account.

@OakleeC_Darling: Working on our new tourism campaign today. So excited! #loveforalifetime #kissingbridge @TownofDarling

She retweeted it from the town account and then put down her phone and focused on bringing up her slideshow presentation of possible promotions, timing, hashtags and themes. The head of publicity, Ryan Woodward, would look after the press releases and other print and media plans. The social media strategy was her baby.

And damned if she wasn't going to knock it out of the park.

Even though Oaklee knew she couldn't pay the vet bill until payday, she felt obligated to go by the clinic and see how the dog was doing. His injuries were her responsibility, and she couldn't just abandon him there and pretend he didn't exist. At the very least, she wanted confirmation that he was doing better. That he was still going to be okay.

The clinic was different in daylight. The reception area was brightly lit, a woman in scrubs sat at the front desk in front of a computer monitor, and there were two people waiting. One had a cat carrier where a pitiful meow erupted every few seconds, and the other had a fluffy white dog on a leash. The dog trotted in a semi-circle, the leash taut, and sniffed at everything.

"Hi, I'm Oaklee Collier. I wanted to see how the dog that was brought in last night was doing."

The girl behind the desk smiled. "Oh, you're the one.

Buster's fine. Or he will be. But I'll let you talk to Dr. Gallagher."

Oaklee's stomach did a little jump. She hadn't planned to see Rory at all. Not that it hadn't been a possibility. But she hadn't come seeking him out. It was about the dog. She didn't just feel guilty about the accident, but the *why* behind it. She'd never admit that she was checking her phone at the time of the accident, because she was horribly embarrassed and ashamed. She knew better.

"Buster?"

The girl grinned. "When Rory . . . I mean, Dr. Gallagher came in this morning, he walked into the kennel room and said, 'Hey, Buster, how's it going?' So 'Buster' kind of stuck."

It suited the dog. Big, not too handsome . . .

"I'll be right back." The girl stood and Oaklee made out her name on her nametag. Christy.

She was back in thirty seconds. "Dr. Gallagher's just finishing up with a patient. He'll be out soon."

Oaklee's stomach turned as she asked the next necessary question. "Um, do you have a bill for his . . . for Buster's . . . care?"

"Sure. Give me a moment to bring it up."

A printer whirred and Christy handed Oaklee a sheet of paper. So many items . . . she skimmed down the list of treatments and saw the total. She nearly passed out. Payday be damned. The only way she could pay for this would be to charge it on her credit card. Something she tried not to do unless she absolutely had to.

"Oaklee! Hi." Rory came through the door behind the desk and smiled at her. She was momentarily dazzled. Last night he'd looked sleepy and had shoved his arms into a lab coat, looking a little ragged around the edges. Today, though, he looked every inch the professional. Tan pants and a collared golf shirt beneath a starchy-looking white coat, his hair perfectly groomed, his jaw freshly shaved that morning and just showing a teeny hint of shadow. The only thing completely the same was his damnable eyelashes. Top and bottom, he had obscenely long, think lashes that could make her weak in the knees.

"Hi." She smiled, feeling off-balance both by her reaction to Rory and the reaction to the hefty bill for "Buster." "I stopped in to see how the patient's doing."

"He's getting there. Come on back for a minute and you can see him."

"Are you sure?"

"Yep." He looked over at the cat lady. "I'll be right with you, Mrs. Jones."

Christy popped up from her chair. "I'll take Mrs. Jones and Buttons back to the exam room."

Oaklee followed Rory through the door into the back of the clinic. Last night she'd been too tired and wired to notice the facilities, but now she saw that the exam rooms were on the right and the surgery, X-ray, and lab facilities were on the left. Toward the back was a huge tub, a small room that she assumed was a staff bathroom, and a tiny corner with a fridge and a few cupboards . . . a kitchen? Rory led her past it all to a separate room. When he opened the door, barking and meowing started and she was hit by the smell of several furry animals occupying a small room at the same time. Not bad, necessarily. But very . . . doggyish.

"Here he is, right on the bottom." Rory knelt in front of a large kennel. "Hey, Buster." He looked at Oaklee. "He's still resting. I'm guessing he's pretty sore. But he's been drinking water, which is good, and while his appetite isn't great at the moment, one of the girls was handfeeding him little bits earlier. He's a tough customer."

Oaklee knelt down, aware that her dress slid up her thighs as she did so. "Hey, big guy," she said quietly. The dog's eyes were wide and slightly unfocused. "He's on pain meds?"

"Yeah. And we'll try to get him out to the bathroom tonight, get him moving a bit. He'll have to get used to the cast."

Guilt piled up again. "I'm sorry, Rory. I should have been paying better attention."

"Accidents happen. Animals pop up out of the ditch all the time. And you got him help. At least you didn't leave him by the side of the road."

"And let him suffer?" She put her fingers up to the kennel, touched when Buster reached out and gave her a little lick. "I'm not that cruel."

"Some people are. So don't beat yourself up." He stood and she followed suit. "I've got to get back. He'll be here another day or so, but we can't keep him indefinitely. He'll have to either be claimed or go to the shelter by Wednesday."

"Oh."

"Yeah. I'm hoping his owner will step forward before then."

They left the kennel room and when they reached the door to the front office, Oaklee hesitated. "Rory?

I hate to ask, but is there a way I can pay his bill in installments? It's . . . well, an unexpected expense for me."

She hated admitting it. And she wasn't trying to get out of the bill, just spread it out a bit.

"I guess so," he said, but he hesitated. Of course, they were running a business. If everyone put off paying their bills, the clinic would struggle.

"Just maybe in thirds, one each payday. It'd all be paid off within six weeks."

He paused with his hand on the doorknob. "Things a little tight for you, Oaklee? You doing okay?"

His face expressed concern. In a completely brotherly way. She frowned.

"My salary covers my expenses," she said, "and I don't have any worries there. But I'm not rolling in it. That's all."

Neither of them mentioned Cam. They both knew that if she asked, Cam would make sure she wanted for nothing. And she was pretty sure that Rory knew her well enough to know she was too stubborn to take a handout. Even from a big brother.

"I'm sure it'll be fine," he assured her. "Right now I'm just hoping that his owner comes looking."

"I'll ask around and put it up on social media."

Rory nodded. "That'd be great. I think the animal shelter has a lost dog account on . . . I don't know. Maybe Facebook. You could try them first. Do you have a picture of him? That helps. Sometimes people recognize a neighbor's dog or something."

She went back and took out her phone and snapped a quick pic. "Will you guys do that, too?"

"Um, I don't know. I don't think Victoria's made social media a priority."

"So you don't have a Facebook page or twitter account? What about Instagram?"

"I don't think so. If we do, someone else manages it." He shrugged and sent her a lopsided smile. "I've never much been into that stuff, to be honest. Too much of a time suck."

Oaklee's brain kicked into drive again as the seeds of a plan began to sprout. "I know you have to go. I'll be in touch about Buster, okay?"

"Okay. Thanks for stopping in."

"You bet."

He opened the door for her, but instead of following her through, he disappeared back into an exam room and a waiting Buttons the Cat. Oaklee smiled at Christy. "I can . . . put a few hundred against the bill today. Is that okay?"

"Certainly. Let me bring up the bill again, and we'll get this started."

Oaklee sighed and reached for her wallet and credit card. But an idea was forming in her mind. There might just be a way for her to do an exchange with the Darling Veterinary Clinic. Because despite Rory's degrees and expertise, there was something she knew how to do that he obviously didn't.

Convincing him couldn't be too hard, could it?

She got home and changed out of her dress, leaving it in a heap on the bedroom floor as she searched for clean jeans and a T-shirt. After a quick supper that consisted of a frozen entrée, she threw the container in the garbage and piled her glass and utensils in the sink of still-dirty dishes from yesterday. Instead of tidying, she booted up her laptop and sat on a bar stool at her kitchen counter. She brought up the clinic's website. It was okay, but bare and without any bells and whistles. There was a homepage with their location and hours of business, and a brief "our staff" page, but that was about it. Maybe they felt they didn't need a stronger web presence, being the only clinic in Darling. But Oaklee saw opportunity. Where was the outreach? The community spirit? Pictures? She sighed. Everyone loved cute cat pictures. Or ones of happy dogs smiling around floppy tongues. Hell, even pictures of Rory would go a long way to making the clinic inviting.

With the town strategy well in hand, Oaklee was looking for a new challenge. Doing up a proposal for the Darling Veterinary Clinic would fit the bill perfectly.

She'd just started a tentative plan when her phone rang. It was Rory's sister, Claire, who also interned at the town office in the summer. At twenty-two, she had one more year of school and she was closest to Oaklee in age at work. They'd become better friends this summer, particularly as they often found themselves working side-by-side.

"You wanna hang out?" Claire asked. "I'm going crazy here at home."

"It's a Monday night," Oaklee said, laughing a bit. "The weekend just ended."

"Yeah, and you went to Becky's shower and I stayed home and did laundry and hung out with Ethan's kids."

"I think I would have traded you." Oaklee already knew that Claire had felt slighted, not being asked to the shower when nearly everyone else in the office had. It sucked being the youngest one, on top of being an intern.

"So . . . let's go to the Suds and Spuds. I seriously just want some chili fries and a beer."

Oaklee's lemon chicken entrée hadn't exactly filled the hunger hole, and the suggestion of the Spuds' chili cheese fries had her stomach rumbling. She checked the time. It was only seven thirty. Surely she could pop out for an hour or so.

"I'll meet you there in twenty? I'm just finishing something up."

"Sounds good."

They hung up and Oaklee typed in a few more lines, completing her thought. With a deposit made on the bill, all she had to do was sell Rory and his boss on this proposal. Then maybe she could convince them to let her work off the balance in exchange for a consultant fee.

CHAPTER 3

The Suds and Spuds was not a high-class establishment by any standards. The inside of the pub was plain and functional: heavy wood tables and chairs, plain painted walls with some beer signs and boards to take away the bareness, and the staff wore plain jeans, comfortable shoes, and simple T-shirts sporting a logo of a foamy beer mug and a smiling potato. In fact, Darling was in need of a trendier bar in the style of something a little more "après-ski" or post-golf game. The Purple Pig wasn't licensed, and Papa Luigi's served beer and wine but nothing else. Still, the Spud served the best fries in Vermont, in Oaklee's opinion. Plain, with gravy, chili cheese, bacon and cheddar, and her personal favorite, pulled pork. What it lacked in ambiance and variety, it made up for in taste.

Claire was already waiting inside when Oaklee arrived, and right away Oaklee noticed a look of consternation on the younger girl's face.

"What's wrong?"

Claire rolled her eyes. "I ordered a beer. Unfortunately, my big brother also happens to be here. I'm legal. I don't see what the big deal is." She flounced her strawberry blond hair, which made her look younger than she was. Oaklee chuckled at Claire's cute pout. Claire was smart and always showed up to work looking professional. She didn't gossip and she did her job with a smile. In a lot of ways, she reminded Oaklee of herself, just a year ago when she'd started working for the town full time. But Oaklee also knew very well how dealing with an older brother could be infuriating.

Oaklee scanned the small space. Sure enough, over in the corner, was Rory. He was sitting with a woman she didn't recognize, and the woman seemed to be hanging on every word out of his mouth. As if he sensed he was being watched, he glanced over and caught her staring. A slow smile tipped his lips and he inclined his chin ever so slightly in greeting.

Only two hours ago he'd been kneeling in front of Buster's kennel, every inch the caring professional. It was a Monday night, for Pete's sake. Who had a date on a Monday? Ugh. From serious doctor to flirting Lothario in no time flat. He turned back to his date and treated her to a brilliant smile. Oaklee grit her teeth. She was not jealous. That was ludicrous.

Claire lifted her mug and took a sip. "Sometimes I think Darling is a little too small for six Gallaghers. We trip over each other."

Oaklee laughed, determined not to pay any more attention to Rory. "Where's Cait?" Cait was Claire's twin sister.

"At home trying to convince Mom and Dad that she should switch her field of study." She laughed. "Me having a beer is small potatoes. Don't mind the pun."

Oaklee grinned. "Have you ordered anything else?"

"No. I was waiting for you."

Oaklee tried her hardest to avoid looking over at Rory as Claire ordered her chili fries and Oaklee opted for loaded skins for something different, as well as a mug of tap beer. Ignoring him was hard, though, since there weren't many people in the place and he had the obnoxious gall to laugh as if he were having the time of his life.

"So. New girlfriend for your brother?"

Claire raised an eyebrow. "Rory doesn't do girlfriends. He does dates. How he gets away with it, I don't know. But he hasn't had a girlfriend since he was in vet school."

Hmm. Curious.

"Maybe he's been busy with the job and everything."

Again with the eyebrow. "The number of dates he's been on, he'd have time for a girlfriend if he really wanted one. I'm not saying he's a player . . . but he's sure not looking for anything serious. It's kind of funny that he's so laid back in his personal relationships, really, because his apartment is like . . . weirdly clean. Seriously. He's some sort of neat freak."

Oaklee looked over at Rory. He seemed so easy going. "Maybe it's just a bachelor's apartment. Not big on décor."

Oaklee's beer arrived and she took a long drink, then let out a satisfied sigh.

"It's not that," Claire persisted. "There's like nothing

out of place. Not a glass left on a table or a sock on the floor. It kinda freaks me out." She grinned. "Aiden said he used to leave things lying around just to piss Rory off."

She shook her head a bit as she laughed, and then lifted her glass again. It was nearly empty. Oaklee hoped their food arrived soon.

Wouldn't Rory have a field day in her apartment? She was in no way, shape, or form, a neat freak. Oh, once a week she'd muck out the apartment, out of necessity. Clothes had to be laundered. Clean dishes to eat off of. But she'd never understood the logic in making a bed when you were just going to climb back into it again.

She snuck a glance at Rory again. His date was reaching over and selecting one of his fries, her raspberry-red nails gleaming as her dark hair curled over her shoulder. Ugh. So obvious. And he was grinning right along, leaning forward, as if everything she said was so very interesting.

"Oaklee. Dude. Sit back a bit."

Claire's voice brought her back to the present and she realized the waitress was waiting to put down her platter of potato skins. "Oh, sorry," she said, moving aside to give room for the hot plate. A bowl of sour cream came on the side of the skins that were loaded with cheese, crumbled bacon, and green onion.

Rory's date laughed, a tinkling little sound and Oaklee looked up at the waitress. "May I have another beer, please?"

Claire ordered a second one as well. "So what's got you uptight tonight?" she asked innocently.

The same thing that's got you in a knot. Rory. She didn't say the words, nor would she. There was no reason why seeing him out on a date should irritate her at all. She'd known him for years. She'd got over her teenage crush long ago. If anything, she should be mad at herself. He'd looked into her eyes last night and she'd gone all gooey inside. Thought about kissing him, for Pete's sake. He was just being Rory. She was the one being ridiculous.

She smiled and let out a big breath. "Oh, I just need to wind down. I'll be fine." She dug into the skins and changed the topic to the new marketing strategy. Claire had done great work helping with the new town rack cards that were going to be placed all over Vermont in tourist centers.

They were halfway through their food when Claire posed an interesting question. "So, do you think there really is anything to the Kissing Bridge thing? I mean, no one's really ever come up with a consistent story about why it's supposed to be good luck." She shrugged. "It's worked for Aiden, I guess. But Ethan . . ."

Ethan was the oldest of the Gallagher brothers. He'd lost his wife to cancer a few years back, and was now a single dad of two boys. Lately he'd been seen out and about with Willow Dunaway, the owner of The Purple Pig.

"What about Ethan?"

"He and Lisa kissed on that bridge. And look what happened to them."

It had been a sad day for Darling when Lisa had passed. Oaklee had come home from school and went to the funeral with her mom and dad. Truthfully, the stark, grief-stricken look on Ethan's face had always stuck with her.

Cam hadn't been able to come home, but Oaklee also remembered seeing Rory that day. He'd also come home from school for a few days, and he'd been dressed in a dark suit with a tightly knotted tie that had bobbed at his throat as he swallowed, fighting back tears.

She was surprised she remembered all that. But then, she'd always been pretty aware of Rory.

"Oaklee, I swear to God you're somewhere else tonight. I was saying, do you think an idea for the future would be to find Kissing Bridge success stories?"

"Like Aiden and Laurel's?"

"Yeah. I mean, that's what the slogan is built around. Love for a lifetime and all that crap?"

"Careful." Oaklee laughed. "You almost sounded cynical there. And you're too young for that."

Claire scowled. "That and everything else."

Oaklee took pity on her. "I was where you are, Claire. Hell, I'm still there. We're smart but we're young. Why do you think I dress as I do and put my hair up?"

"Me, too," Claire admitted.

"We still have to prove ourselves," Oaklee said. "But it's not a bad thing. At least not all the time."

"Do you think it's harder because we're pretty?"

It was an innocent, honest question, but it took Oaklee by surprise and she burst out laughing. Claire had said it not out of ego but plain curiosity, and that made it even funnier to Oaklee. She put down her mug and laughed until she let out a sigh. Oh, that had felt good.

Claire was watching her with amusement. "Okay, I know that made it sound like I was full of myself . . ."

"Just a bit. Though I know you well enough now to just say thank you for thinking I'm pretty."

"Are you kidding? And guess what? My brother can't stop looking at you since you started laughing. And not in the 'she's annoying' way, either."

Oaklee refused to look, but something warm crawled up through her chest and out her limbs at the idea of Rory staring at her.

"You should date Rory."

Oaklee choked on her mouthful of beer and reached for a napkin to catch the dribble that threatened to run down her chin. "What on earth . . . why?"

"He dates these really nice girls. Like . . . sweet and perfect. He needs someone different."

"Once I get over the fact that you don't think I'm sweet and perfect, I'll ask you what you mean."

It was Claire's turn to laugh. Whether it was simple relaxation or aided by the alcohol, Oaklee wasn't sure, but she was suddenly having a good time. She hoped Rory was looking at her. And to be sure he got his money's worth, she flipped her hair back over her shoulder and smiled at Claire, knowing he'd see her profile.

"I mean, you're quick and smart and you definitely wouldn't put up with any of his bullshit."

"Yeah well, he's my brother's best friend. Or used to be. And he's never seen me that way. So, no. Besides, he's a vet. And I'm not an animal person. I'm pretty sure we wouldn't be compatible."

"Holy shit. You've actually thought about this, haven't you?" Claire stabbed her fork into a particularly chili-y section of her fries and scooped it up, careful not to let it drip as she moved it to her mouth.

"I had a crush on him when he and Cam were still hanging out," she admitted. "But I was what, fifteen? Sixteen? We've grown and changed a lot since then. And he was never interested."

"Are you sure? Because he keeps glancing over here."

Oaklee's cheeks heated. "He's probably counting how many beers you've had."

"Shut up, Ms. Buzzkill."

Oaklee laughed again and dunked a chunk of cheesy potato skin in her sour cream. She was going to have to get up and go for a run tomorrow morning to counter all the carbs and fat she was ingesting tonight.

She was just wiping her mouth with her napkin when someone cleared their throat behind her.

She swiveled around and looked up at Rory, smiling down at her and Claire, his date at his side and slightly behind.

"Just wanted to say hi. And to tell Claire that two beers is enough on a school night."

"Piss off," Claire said succinctly, scowling at Rory. Then she smiled brilliantly. "Hello. I'm Claire, one of Rory's little sisters. Perfectly legal and capable of counting to two on my own."

The woman smiled back. "Patricia. You can call me Patty."

Of course we can, Oaklee thought.

When it didn't look like Rory was going to introduce her, she decided to do the honors herself. "Hi," she said, holding out her hand. "I'm Oaklee Collier. Rory's friends with my brother."

Patty looked suitably impressed. "Collier . . . as in Cam Collier? The hockey player?"

"That's the one."

Patty looked at Rory. "You didn't tell me *that*."

"It didn't come up." He looked at Oaklee as if he could crown her and not in the good way.

"That must be so cool."

Oaklee smiled at Rory, perhaps a little too sweetly. Seemed his date was more interested in Cam than in Rory. By the strained smile on his lips, she figured she'd just inadvertently caused a major cock block.

"Well, we should be going," Rory said, taking Patty's elbow. "Don't be out too late, sis."

"You either, Rory. Mom will be waiting up to tuck you in."

As they disappeared toward the door, Oaklee heard Patty ask, "You live with your mother? I thought you had your own place?"

The door shut and the two of them dissolved into laughter. But Oaklee's was a little bit different. For Claire, she'd just got back at her nuisance of a brother. But Oaklee was left with a rather unfortunate truth. She still had a thing for Rory. Maybe she always would. Whether it was based on nostalgia or something more, there was a soft spot for him just the same.

She wondered how many dates he'd taken to the Kissing Bridge over the years. There wasn't anything more romantic in Darling, and surely a kiss in the moonlight got him that much closer to scoring.

And then she wondered what it would be like to kiss him on the bridge. Or anywhere else. And she wondered if he would score with Patty tonight, and wondered why on earth it should even matter.

Rory drove Patty home. She lived with two roommates in a little apartment in Stowe where she waitressed in the off season and was a ski instructor in the winter. She'd picked his profile on a dating site, and he'd liked what he saw in return.

But that was as far as it would go. Rory was getting really, really good at first dates. Sometimes there were second and third dates. But then that was it. He always made it clear he wasn't looking for anything serious. And in his experience, most women were. He was quickly coming to see that women looked at each date as a potential Prince Charming.

She leaned across the seat as he parked in front of her building, and gave him a soft kiss on the lips. "Thanks for the date," she said quietly, running her tongue over her lower lip.

For a moment he considered kissing her again, but that wouldn't be fair.

"There's not going to be a second one, is there?" She asked it casually, without any trace of annoyance or disappointment. Thank God.

"I had a really good time," he said honestly. "But . . ."

"It's the blonde." Patty smiled at him, her cute face illuminated by the dashboard.

"Sorry?"

"The blonde at the table with your sister. With the pretty name."

"Oaklee?" His lips dropped open in surprise. "Of course it isn't."

Patty put her hand on his forearm. "Rory, I had your full attention until she walked in tonight. And then you couldn't take your eyes off her. Who is she? An ex?"

He sighed. "It's not like that. I'm good friends with Cam, and she used to follow us around all the time. Total pain in my ass." Funny how he continually kept thinking of her in that particular term since yesterday.

"Teenage girls grow up to be pretty women, you know."

"I know."

Then he looked at Patty, saw her eyebrow raised, and let out a laugh. "This is a very strange way to end a date."

"Hey, I got a beer and the best fries in Vermont, and nice company. It was a good night. I think you're probably a good guy, but you're not my guy."

For a moment he kind of wished he were. She was truly a great person. Fun, friendly, pretty, easy to talk to . . . "Which says way more about me than you," he replied, reaching out and squeezing her hand. "You're beautiful, and sweet. I hope you find someone great."

"Thanks. Now I'd better go in. Good luck, Rory. Think about Oaklee. She was looking at you, too. Might be worth testing the waters there."

"Other than the fact Cam would kill me, she's not my type."

"Keep telling yourself that," she said with a laugh. "Thanks for the date."

She didn't even wait for him to get out and walk her to the door. She simply slid out the passenger side and gave a little wave before heading to the apartment building. Rory waited, though, until she was safely inside.

He looked at the clock on the display. It wasn't even nine o'clock yet. Was he losing his touch? What kind of guy ended a date with a single, chaste kiss before nine o'clock?

It was a stunning drive back to Darling. The sun was setting and the shades of green on the grass and trees held a gilded edge. He turned off the air conditioning and rolled down the window instead, letting the fragrant summer air in to ruffle his hair. When he got to town limits, he looked at the welcome sign and felt a senti-mentality that was both comforting and constricting. He loved this town. Loved being close to his family. Loved being able to practice as a vet. But he also knew that privacy was sometimes hard to come by. He knew very well that his "bachelor" nights with Aiden had been talked about around town, though most of the time they'd ended up going home alone. He wasn't into play-ing with someone's feelings. And he wasn't into building up false hopes, either. He knew how shitty it felt when someone pulled the plug on a relationship.

No one, not even the family, knew the extent of his broken heart. They knew he'd met someone in vet school. Knew they'd dated a while and then broke up, and that was all he'd wanted them to know.

But he'd been in love with Ginelle, heart and soul. And more than that, she'd had a kid. A fun, laughing, adorable boy. Rory had been more than willing to step in as a father figure. He'd wanted to propose after graduation, and make them his family. When she had ended the relationship, his heart had been broken twice. He'd loved her, and he'd loved her son. It wasn't some-thing a man got over that easily.

He thought about Oaklee as he headed home toward the clinic. Was Patty right? Had he really stared at her all evening? He frowned, thinking about Cam. What would his old buddy say if he knew Rory was thinking of kissing his sister? After all, Rory had been gone for a long time, and when he came back, Oaklee was all grown up. It hadn't been until the last few days, though, that his radar had started pinging. Suddenly she was everywhere, and he was noticing.

The clinic was dark when he drove into the lot, and he went inside, disabled the alarm system, and checked on the animals before heading up to bed. Buster was improving by leaps and bounds, aided by regular food and water. No one had come forward to claim him; he couldn't stay at the clinic indefinitely. Rory either had to find a foster for him or contact the shelter.

Maybe he needed to focus on that rather than thinking about Oaklee all the time. After all, he liked to keep things casual and easy in his personal life. And starting something with Oaklee would be neither.

She was too important. The very thought left him unsettled.

CHAPTER 4

@OakleeC_Darling: RT @TownofDarling Come on out to
the Kissing Bridge today at 4 p.m. for the big unveiling!
Free BBQ. Keepsake photos!

Oaklee smiled at the tweet. The event had been Claire's
idea, the night before last at the Spud, after Rory and
his date departed. First thing yesterday morning, they'd
gone to the head of publicity, who'd looked at the budget,
given them a number, and said if they could pull it off,
to do it. Oaklee had arranged for the new photos and
promotion graphic to be blown up and backed on foam
core, promising a shout-out to the copy center for the
rush job. Two easels had been secured to hold it, and
she found a gorgeous green velvet cloth to cover it until
the unveiling. Claire had come up with the idea of taking
keepsake photos for the public, and had approached a
friend of hers who was a photography student to see if
he'd donate his time. The town had its own huge grills

for hosting casual events, so Claire had taken the slim budget and had hit a big-box store for hot dogs, hamburgers, buns, sodas, and bags of potato chips.

In less than twenty-four hours they'd put together all the details. Now Oaklee just had to pick up the poster and help set up at the site, as well as promote the heck out of it. There was a portable sign set up at the entrance to the park, the radio station had been notified and promised to give it a mention during their morning show, and Claire's brother, Aiden, offered his truck to transport stuff to the site and to help with the food.

Such an event called for her to look her summery best, so she put on a floral print dress that hugged her curves, secured her hair in a topknot, and grabbed one of her favorite pairs of shoes from her closet—china blue peep-toe pumps that exactly matched the blue of her print. She shoved her makeup bag into her work case so she could freshen up before the event, and felt ready to conquer the world.

As she went out the door, she glanced back at the inside of her apartment. She really needed to clean this place one of these days. She didn't mind mess, but at some point the apartment needed a reset. It was Wednesday . . . she made a mental note to give it a good going-over on the weekend.

By the time four o'clock rolled around, she was totally hyped. Aiden had not only helped transport supplies, he was also manning the grill, grinning at the ladies, and serving up hot dogs and burgers to a growing crowd. Despite being newly married, he got approving glances from the female contingent, particularly since he was still in his cop uniform. His brother, Ethan, was nearby with his boys, handing out sodas, though one of Ethan's arms was covered with a cast. He'd become quite a town hero earlier in the month, when he'd been injured during a fire call at the food bank. Oaklee stopped for a few minutes to catch up with Emily, the assistant manager at The Purple Pig, and nibbled on a carob chip cookie. Claire's photographer friend was helping couples pose on the bridge, making them laugh and kiss and catching the moment. At the last minute, Oaklee had drafted a release for couples to sign if they consented to having their photo shared on the Darling Facebook page and website. Content was king, and having a wall of love stories was pure gold.

She'd just performed the unveiling when she saw *him*. And Buster. And her heart did this warning little thump that set her on edge. She should not be reacting this way to Rory. Not now. He definitely wasn't interested in her. And she wasn't interested in any guy who was the type to go on a few dates and move on. She'd been down the road of men with commitment issues and didn't want to go through that again. Rory was a serial dater and everyone knew it.

But he *was* gorgeous. And the dog at his side . . . they moved slowly, in deference to Buster's cast on his leg. Buster looked like a changed dog, all cleaned up and fed. His ears perked up a bit and Rory leaned over and patted his head.

Then he looked up and saw Oaklee and her traitorous heart did that thumpy thing again.

Business. She had to keep this businesslike. The last few days she hadn't been able to approach him about her idea for the clinic, but now that the rushed community event was winding down, nothing was stopping her.

She looked away and made a show of wandering through the crowd, offering hellos, helping wherever it was needed. She snapped a few candids and posted them on the town Instagram profile, and stopped briefly to chat to a reporter from the *Darling Register*, a local paper that came out once a month. All the while she was aware of Rory, never too far away, and his stupid chick-magnet wounded dog. Like he needed help getting attention in the first place.

They finally crossed paths at around five thirty. She put on a smile and decided that since she was still officially at work, she should act like it, and not get all fluttery over stupid Rory Gallagher.

"Nice event you've got going on here," he offered. He touched Buster's head and then his bum, and the dog sat. "He doesn't do commands much," he explained easily. "I don't think he's ever been trained to."

"Oh? I take it no one has stepped forward to claim him, huh?"

Rory shook his head. "Not yet. I don't expect them to, either. He's got some raw spots around his neck. I'd say he was chained outside a lot. Scrawny, too, and full of fleas."

Oaklee took a step back. Gross.

Rory laughed. "Not anymore. We got him all cleaned up, didn't we, boy?"

Buster stood and wagged his tail, but Rory got him to sit again.

"So what now?" Oaklee asked, looking around. She

half wished that something would require her attention. She was far too aware of Rory, and his perfect hair and perfect teeth and perfect body . . . argh. What was she, sixteen again? And why was it that after months of living in the same town, their paths had never crossed as much as they had this past week? And all because of the dumb mutt sitting at his feet.

"I can't keep him upstairs at my place. We discovered he's not overly fond of cats, and sometimes I end up having to nurse some animals at home. What he really needs is a home where he's the only animal and can learn some manners first."

"So the shelter?" Her heart dropped. She knew what going to the animal shelter meant. Dogs and cats couldn't be kept there indefinitely. It would be a shame to go to all the trouble of saving his life only to have him lose it because he was unwanted.

"Unless I can find a foster for him."

"Oh."

Rory looked at her meaningfully.

"Wait . . . me? No way, Rory."

"But you rescued him."

"No, I nearly killed him. Big difference. Huge."

"Well, you didn't leave him to die. Look at him, Oaklee. Look at that face."

She did. It was hairy and whiskery and Buster's tongue hung out as he panted. His big brown eyes looked up at her and he had the oddest eyebrows that arced up and out.

"Rory, I live alone in a single-bedroom apartment. What would I do with a dog this big? And I go to work all day . . ."

"So do lots of pet owners. And you don't have a commute, so that cuts back on your time away."

"But what if I have to be somewhere? A dog ties you. Right? I mean, they have to go out to do their business all the time. Not like they have a litter box. I don't want to be tied down."

She said the words and then bit down on her tongue. Huh. She'd meant everything she just said, especially the part about not wanting to be tied down. Maybe she was the one with commitment issues. She liked having the freedom to come and go. To not be responsible to and for anyone.

"It'd be good for you. I think pets are good for everyone. Sometimes people get so caught up in their work lives that they forget to take a break. Pets make you do that."

"So I'll get a goldfish."

"Goldfish can't love you back."

"Do I look like I'm looking for love?"

Their gazes clashed. Chatter filled the air all around them, but all Oaklee could hear in her head was that last sentence out of her mouth and how it said so much more than she'd intended.

"Maybe," Rory said softly.

She stiffened. "I'm not. I'm perfectly content the way I am."

He slumped his shoulders. "All right, then. I won't twist your arm." He looked down at the dog. "Sorry, Buster. The lady isn't interested. Looks like it's the shelter for you. Maybe they'll have a big cage there so you're not too cramped."

Oaklee's heart seized even as she recognized the

deliberate manipulation. "For God's sake, Rory. That's playing dirty. Besides, I live in an apartment. I'm pretty sure we're not allowed to have dogs."

"You're in one of the four-plexes, right? Kincaid's developments by the golf course? Don't worry about that. One of my clients lives in those and she has a dog. Besides, Tommy Kincaid's wife brings her cats to me. I'm pretty sure we could get him to come around."

Oaklee got the sense that she was losing the upper hand—something that rarely happened, if ever. "Come on, Rory. Surely you have another foster you could talk to. You don't have to guilt trip me into it."

"Why? Because you're the one who hit him?"

She let out a frustrated breath. "Oh. My. God. Could you be any more obvious? Just stop. I don't want to be tied down to a dog, okay?"

His lips formed a thin line. "Do you want to be tied down to anything, Oaklee? Other than your precious social media? The whole time today you've been glued to your phone." He frowned. "I watched. You were either taking pictures or using your opposable thumbs. Maybe a dog would give you some balance."

Now her temper was getting fired up. "It's my job, dumbass, and I'm very good at it. And your clinic could use a little more web presence. Seriously, all you've got is a contact page and a little bit about the business. What about community outreach? Pet pictures? Education, like dental month or adopt-a-pet stuff or how to care for your exotic parrot or whatever it is you should talk about to your clients?"

Now he was standing stiffly, too. "We never have any trouble booking appointments. We're busy all the time."

"Maybe it's not about being busy; you're the only game in town. Maybe it's value for money. Maybe it's a personal touch or a deeper sort of professionalism." She huffed out a breath. "You could use someone with my skills to bring you into the current decade instead of being such a . . . such a . . . troglodyte."

She was acutely aware of Buster sitting at Rory's feet, watching the both of them with a blank stare.

"A what?"

Her cheeks heated. "Look it up."

He blew out a dismissive breath. "No need to flaunt your five-dollar words at me, Miss Collier. I could counter with a few."

But Oaklee pressed on. "Know what? You might think I'm glued to my phone and that my job is silly, but guess what? Over beers the other night, your very smart baby sister came up with this idea. We had a shoe-string budget. Know how we afforded to put this on with such short notice? We reciprocated with free promotion for businesses. The sign, the photographer, the food . . . we slammed this together in twenty-four hours because smart people saw the value in getting their name out there. Aiden's serving up burgers in his uniform because it's goodwill for the department. Ethan's handing out soda despite his injury. Hell, even Willow sent over seven dozen homemade cookies on very little notice. And we were able to do it all because everyone knows that the town publicity department will make sure they get a mention. That's more than just using my 'opposable thumbs.'"

Silence dropped between them. Oaklee took a step back and inhaled sharply; the speech had quickened her breath and her heart rate. Rory's gaze heated as he stared at her, and she felt it right to her core.

"Damn, but you're beautiful when you get riled up," he said, his voice low and husky.

"Don't. Don't do that." Add confusion to the crazy feelings rushing through her right now. It had felt *good* to argue with him. Invigorating. Stimulating. Like verbal foreplay . . .

"It's the truth."

"I'm not interested," she replied sharply. *Liar,* her brain accused. She'd had a thing for Rory since she'd hit puberty. It was a blatant lie to say she wasn't at least curious. Particularly now that he seemed to be paying attention. She realized that he'd said he'd been watching her. She wasn't sure how she felt about that . . . but the truth was, she'd been seeking him out, too.

He paused for a moment, then smiled, trying a charm offensive. "Then perhaps I can interest you in a real gentleman. Come on, Oaklee," he pleaded. "Look at him. It's not like he is going to outrun you with this cast on. He's really a good boy."

She tried a last-ditch excuse. "Dogs are expensive. And there's . . . poop."

He laughed. "I can get you a great deal on dog food, and if you foster him we'll throw in a big bag to get you started. And we have pooper-scooper bags that are lavender scented."

She was going to lose this one, she could feel it. "Fostering isn't forever, right?"

"No, we'll keep looking for a forever home for him."

"And you'll have to be the one to talk to my landlord."

His grin widened.

"And," she emphasized, "if I take him in, you'll let me amp up the clinic web and social media presence."

His grin slipped. "I don't have a lot of say in that. It's Victoria's practice." Victoria Stewart was the senior vet at the hospital, and the owner. Oaklee knew her from around town and liked her, but she was a bit old school.

Sensing she had the upper hand, she threw in one last condition. "I won't charge a consulting fee, but my time goes toward Buster's vet bill."

Rory scowled. "That's a hard bargain."

"Take it or leave it."

Buster barked and Oaklee jumped, suddenly realizing how intense she and Rory had gotten in the last several minutes. The activity around them had ceased to exist. And here she was, supposed to be doing her job.

Rory held tight to the leash, though Buster was pulling valiantly against the restraint, desperate to run after a duo of dachshunds.

"Consider it done," he said, with a brief nod. "I'll bring Buster over tomorrow after work and you can get him settled in."

"Tomorrow? Are you crazy?"

"He can't stay at the clinic any longer. We need the bed."

"He needs a better HMO," Oaklee replied, irritated. "I've got to go. I'm supposed to be working."

"Fine. I'll see you tomorrow."

"Fine."

She stomped away, though felt a little bit bad that she hadn't at least given Buster a pat. Maybe Rory was right. With Buster's gimped-up leg, he probably wasn't going to be any trouble. She'd keep him for a few weeks, and work like hell to find him a new home. Maybe someone at the office would be willing to adopt him.

When she looked for Rory again, it took a bit for her to find him. He was over by the bridge, Buster sitting beside him, looking every inch the loyal companion. A boy of six or seven was patting him, and Rory was talking to the mom.

She wasn't jealous. She wasn't. He could talk to whomever he damned well pleased.

Except deep down she knew she was. And she had no idea what to do about it.

Rory pulled up to the four-plex and cut the engine. Buster was in the hatch, whining. Car rides were apparently an unfamiliar or at least unpleasant thing. Rory had been careful to take the turns gently on the way over, so that the poor dog wouldn't get sick.

Oaklee's apartment was on the end, so at least she didn't have neighbors on one side of her walls. Buster wasn't a big barker, but it was possible he'd be more vocal as he got stronger and healthier. Tommy had been fine with the dog staying there, it turned out. He had a soft spot for wounded animals and when Rory said he thought Oaklee had been lonely and could use the company, the deal was done.

Truth was, Rory *did* think she was lonely. Sure, she went to work and seemed to love her job, but there was something else about her. Something he couldn't quite put his finger on, but it lurked behind her eyes. It was almost as if her bubbly, efficient manner was more of a persona than a personality and that behind it was some sort of deficiency in her life. He knew firsthand that a pet could fill a large hole in a person's life. After his breakup, he'd fostered a diabetic cat. Chuckles had only lived six more months, but when Rory had gone to bed at night, the big bundle of black fur had curled in close to his side and purred. That old cat had got him through some of the worst nights of his life.

He got out of the car and went to the back to open the hatch. Buster was curled up on the blanket, looking a bit worse for wear. His eyes were dazed and he was panting heavily, a sure sign of anxiety. "Hey, buddy," Rory said softly. "Sorry about the car ride. Let's get you out into some fresh air."

He lifted the dog out of the hatch—no jumping allowed—and clipped on the leash. Buster shook, the wiggle progressing from his shoulders down to the tip of his tail. Okay. So car rides were not a favorite. Something to tell Oaklee.

He held the leash in one hand and grabbed a large shopping bag with the other. "Ready to go see your new girlfriend?" he asked, giving the dog a reassuring rub. Buster limped slowly up the walk to Oaklee's front door and Rory rang the bell.

There was no answer.

Dammit. If she reneged on their deal . . . it had taken some decent smooth talk to Victoria to convince her to expand the web site. It had helped a little that Rory thought Oaklee might be right—as long as he wasn't the one who had to do the posting and sharing.

He rang the bell again.

A crash and muffled voice came from inside, then the front door opened. "It's five o'clock. What the hell?"

"Nice to see you, too. I did say I'd be over after work."

"I got home ten minutes ago. I've barely had time to change."

"My shift ended at four."

She sighed. "Well, you're here now." She stood to the side.

Rory stepped inside and froze. Holy shit. "God, Oaklee. Did someone break in and ransack the place?"

There were clothes lying everywhere, mixed in with magazines and unopened mail. A stack of DVDs had toppled over, leaving the cases scattered on the carpet by her TV. Two pairs of shoes were in the middle of the floor, and one brown leather boot, and an empty bowl and wine glass sat on an end table.

"I haven't had time to clean this week."

"This week? How about this millennium?"

"Would you like to criticize anything else? Because you could take Buster and go right back the way you came."

She was understandably irritated, but Jumpin' Judas. Oaklee was always so *together*. He had never imagined that she was a total slob. Worse, too, because he knew he was a neat freak and a bit extreme about it. Not OCD, and not a germophobe, but he did like things clean and orderly. This was . . . bedlam.

Maybe he should have guessed, after seeing the inside of her car that first night.

Buster strained on the leash, sniffing at something underneath a chair . . . Rory was horrified to think what it might be.

"Sorry," he offered weakly. "It's just . . . well, you know how people have to childproof their houses?

Sometimes people need to dogproof. Dogs are like toddlers. They're apt to put anything into their mouths."

"You gave me twenty-four hours. I worked until seven last night and was back at work before eight this morning. I'm sorry if my personal space isn't up to your standards."

Oh, he'd really made her mad. She took that snooty tone when she was miffed. Like that word yesterday—troglodyte. He'd gone home and looked it up. Not that he'd admit it to her.

It made him feel marginally better that despite her expansive vocabulary, she seemed unable to keep a clean house.

"I can help you," he offered. "I'm pretty handy with a vacuum and dust cloth."

She stared at him. "Seriously. You're seriously offering to help me clean my house?"

He couldn't *not* offer. It was driving him that crazy.

"Sure." He lifted the shopping bag. "I brought some bowls for Buster. Why don't I fill them up and tie him outside? He'll be fine. Today I learned he loves sunbathing." He smiled winningly.

"You're crazy. You want to play maid service? Go ahead. I need food. You want some?"

Food in exchange for cleaning? Fair deal. Rory could cook but not well; his specialty was tacos or spaghetti with canned sauce. "I could eat," he ventured. "Let me get Buster settled."

He'd brought a lead with him, so he anchored it around a six-by-six post and clipped it to Buster's collar. Then he took out the bowls, filled one with food, and went back inside to fill the other with water. Oaklee had put something in the oven; he heard the fan running and his stomach rumbled. After leaving Buster with the basic amenities, he went back inside with the food and blanket from the hatch, and a Kong toy to hopefully keep Buster chewing something other than Oaklee's stuff.

"Where do you want me to start?"

Oaklee reappeared in sweat pants and a ratty T-shirt that said "Bubba's Burgers" on it, a laundry basket on her hip. "Outerwear on the hook by the door. Other clothes in the basket. I'm not sure what's clean and what's not."

Clearly.

Oaklee picked up the magazines and piled them on the coffee table, then stacked the DVDs again beside the TV while Rory grabbed shorts, shirts, skirts, socks and threw them all in the basket. With a sufficient amount of horror he realized she probably didn't even sort her laundry into darks, colors, and whites but threw it all in together. Oaklee picked up the shoes—the other boot was uncovered, hidden beneath a pink cardigan sweater. When Rory went to pick it up, a pair of underwear dropped to the floor. A powder-blue, lacy, cover-next-to-nothing thong.

Oaklee didn't notice. He snagged a piece of the lace with one finger, dropped it into the basket, and reminded himself he was not to think about Oaklee wearing such a thing. Nope, not think about it at all. And especially not think about her wearing it and nothing else.

Damn.

Now things were really uncomfortable. Physically.

A clatter of dishes in the kitchen brought him back to his senses . . . somewhat. He shook his head and grabbed the rest of the dirty clothes, then put the basket on the now-clear sofa. Oaklee was in the tiny kitchen, running soapy water in the sink for dishes. The smell from the oven was distinctly tomato-y and spicy. "Frozen pizza?" he asked, his heart sinking.

"I'm not much of a cook."

He couldn't say anything since he wasn't, either. But he'd hoped . . .

"Whatever fills the hole, right?" he asked. "Where's your vacuum?"

"In my bedroom. I'll get it in a minute . . ."

But he was already on his way down the hall.

He should have known better.

Why on earth did she have a closet if she never used it?

"Don't go in there . . . oh dammit, you already did. Jeez, Rory."

"I don't know what to say."

"I'm a horrible housekeeper. Truly. I keep telling myself I'm going to do better and I just never do. There. My secret is out."

"And the bathroom?"

"I don't want to give you a heart attack."

He turned and looked at her. She was blushing profusely, clearly embarrassed at having him discover her lack of domestic skills. "I just don't get it. You seriously always look super organized and . . . unwrinkled."

She bit down on her lip. "Okay, so here's my confession. My mom always tried to keep things neat, but my dad . . . he's a bit of a hoarder. I'd come home from school and he'd have something all torn apart on the kitchen table. Small engine parts, car parts . . . you name it. After a while I think my mom gave up because she couldn't keep up. I never actually, well, learned how to clean."

He remembered going to the Collier's and how it had always looked . . . well, neglected was the best way to put it, and very different from the Gallagher house. But there had always been snacks in the cupboard, and as a teenage boy, he'd ignored the clutter and chaos and focused on what was important: food and hanging out with his best friend, either playing video games or shooting pucks around in the driveway.

"It's not that difficult," he offered helpfully. "You wipe stuff off, vacuum the floors, put things away."

"Easy in theory. I don't know what to say. Obviously I'm mortified that you've seen the chaos that is my inner sanctum."

That particular sentence made him laugh; he couldn't help it. Oaklee moved forward and unearthed a cheap vacuum and they went back into the hall. She shut the bedroom door with a firm click. Whatever scintillating thoughts he'd had, handling her underwear, were now banished completely by the state of her bedroom. It was definitely not a scene for seduction.

"You could hire a cleaning service," he offered. "They could come in once a week. Give you a hand."

She went back to the kitchen and he heard the squeak of the oven door opening. "There are two problems with that," she called to him as he found an outlet and plugged in the vacuum. "First of all, some stranger would then know my dirty little secret. And second . . . I can't really afford it."

He paused at that. She'd mentioned dog food being expensive, too. And had asked to work off her vet bill. "Things are really tight for you, aren't they?"

She came back around the corner, bearing two plates with pizza. "I suppose I have no pride left now, do I? I'm not making big money at the town office, you know. In addition to the regular expenses, I'm paying off my student loans."

Rory considered. He, too, had a loan, but he also got a great break on his rent, his utilities were included, and his salary was still pretty decent. "Does Cam know? I mean, he'd pay off your loans in a heartbeat. You know he would." He took the plate from her hand.

She met his gaze, her eyes wide and earnest. "I won't cash in on my brother's success. Or ask for a handout."

"But you know he'd be happy to do it. You're his sister."

"And I can stand on my own two feet." She frowned, then led the way to the sofa—apparently the substitute for a proper table and chairs. "Honestly, if I didn't like this job so much, or Darling, I could make nearly twice as much in the private sector."

They sat together, and Rory mulled that over for a minute. "I know what you mean," he said, taking a bite of pizza. The crust was the texture of wet cardboard. "I came back to Darling because my family's here. Because I worked for Victoria in the summers and I knew I had a job waiting. And yeah, living above the clinic is fine, but if I moved to the city I'd be making a lot more."

"So are we stupid, do you think? Or smart for putting sentimentality ahead of money?"

He laughed. "This pizza is horrible. Right now I vote for stupid. Let's toss this and I'll order something from Papa Luigi's."

She looked over at him, her eyes soft with humor, and he felt something click into place. Something more than the fun of arguing with her, or the attraction that simmered from time to time. It was friendship. Grown-up friendship, adult to adult, and not to someone he'd always considered an annoying little sister. The attraction he could dismiss because she was beautiful and he wasn't blind. But this . . . Despite her deplorable lack of domestic skills, he liked her. A lot.

And that wasn't so easy to dismiss.

CHAPTER 5

Oaklee had never been so embarrassed in her life.

There was a reason why she never entertained. Housekeeping wasn't a priority, but it didn't mean she was oblivious to the state of her apartment. Tonight she'd planned to have something to eat and do a blitz through the main living areas before Rory arrived. Instead she'd barely had her shoes off and he'd shown up with Buster on a leash, and her at a complete disadvantage.

She'd just run the vacuum over the rug when the pizza from Papa Luigi's arrived, and she had to admit that it smelled much better than the cheap frozen one she'd thrown in the oven. Rory paid for it before she could find her wallet, and they ate it sitting on the tall stools in front of her kitchen counter. He'd ordered an Everything pizza, and she picked off the black olives. He took them from her plate and popped them in his mouth, then grabbed himself another piece.

When they were full, Rory pushed his plate forward a little and patted his belly. "That's better."

"Much," she agreed, swiping up some sauce with a piece of crust. "Thanks."

"No problem. Least I can do, considering you're taking Buster in. Speaking of, we should bring him in here soon. Let him get used to you and the place."

It was just a dog, she reminded herself, but the thought of him coming in here now and her being responsible and stuff . . . it made nerves bubble around in her stomach. She didn't know anything about keeping a dog.

"I guess," she answered.

"You don't sound sure."

"I didn't want to do this in the first place, remember?"

Rory looked at her for a long moment. "It's just until we can find him a forever home."

"Right." She squared her shoulders. "Okay. Let's bring him in."

Rory went outside and came back a moment later with Buster on the leash. "My advice is to keep him on the leash and attached to you for a bit, to let him get acclimatized and not overwhelmed. It helps with housetraining a lot, too. Fewer accidents."

Her mouth dropped open. "Housetraining? He's not trained? No way, Rory. No way in hell."

Rory merely laughed. "He is, but now he's in a new environment with new things and new smells. Trust me, this helps." He handed her the leash; the loop hung loosely in her hand. Buster looked up at her expectantly.

She looked at Rory. "Does his leg hurt him? To put weight on it?"

"He's okay for short walks to use the bathroom. From

your door to the sidewalk, that kind of thing. No jumping on or off anything, though. You're all on one level here, so that's great. You'll have to help him with the two steps out front, though."

She walked over to the sofa. Buster followed politely, then sat at her feet. He panted; she could smell his doggy breath and wrinkled her nose. "Pew."

Rory laughed. "It's summer and he's hot. Plus, he's probably a little anxious. He'll stop panting once he cools off. Good boy, Buster," Rory said, reaching into his pocket and taking out a tiny treat. He fed it to the dog. "Instead of sitting down, why don't you take him around the apartment? Just the areas where he's going to be allowed. I'd suggest keeping your bathroom and bedroom door closed. That way his environment won't be so big and overwhelming."

She went to the kitchen and, with the leash looped around her wrist, put the plates and forks in the dishwasher. Her apartment wasn't very big; she led him down the short hall to where the other rooms were, back to the living room, and let him sniff the corners and nooks and crannies, hoping he didn't lift his leg. He didn't. Maybe this wouldn't be so bad.

They were making their way to the sofa again when Buster pulled against the leash and made like he was going to jump up on the furniture.

"No, Buster. Stay down." Rory's voice was firm, and he held out his hand to stop Buster's progress. The dog stopped, and Rory looked up at Oaklee. "When you feel his attention being diverted, just give a quick little snap on the leash."

"Won't that hurt him?"

Rory smiled. "No. It just reminds him that he needs to be paying attention to you."

"Oh."

"I brought a blanket for him to sleep on. And there's a bag of food—he'll need a cup and a half twice a day. In the grocery bag is a container of treats. Only a few of these each day. He needs to put on some weight, but he's not getting a lot of exercise at the moment so we don't want to go overboard. There's a box of poop bags, and a chew toy so he can gnaw on that and not on any of your stuff. At least he's not a puppy. They like to get their puppy teeth into everything."

"A cup and a half twice a day. Poop bags . . . Okay." She was already feeling over her head. "What about when I leave, Rory? I have to go to work. How often does he need to go out? I can't keep him attached to me at the office."

What had she been thinking, agreeing to this?

"My recommendation? Put a few things on the sofa so he doesn't jump up. Put water in his bowl but maybe don't fill it to the top while you're at work, and leave him here in the living room with his blanket-bed and his toy. I'm betting he'll just sleep. He's not much of a barker, but he'll let you know when he needs to go out, other than before bed and first thing in the morning."

She swallowed against a tightness in her throat. She'd never been responsible for another living creature before. She'd always had to look after herself and no one else. Even with Jeff . . . they'd been two very independent people, with their own friends and pursuits. She'd liked that about them. Apparently he hadn't, because he'd stood her up at their wedding and left a note saying they had nothing in common anymore.

Oaklee looked down at Buster. She didn't do codependence. Or any sort of dependence. Shit.

"Oaklee, it's going to be fine," he said gently. "He's a good dog."

"Easy for you to say," she grumbled, uneasy. "You're around dogs all the time. You probably had one growing up."

He grinned, his face lighting up. "Yeah, we did. First it was a Border Collie that got into everything if we didn't keep him busy. Then Mom came home with this mutt one day and Dad nearly had a fit. Mom named her Pebbles. Dad just called her 'That Dog.' And now they have Waffle."

She snickered. "Waffle?"

He chuckled. "They got him when Ethan's oldest was almost three. When he said 'Waffle,' everyone started laughing. But one of the twins had made Connor toaster waffles and he hopped down from his chair, took it over to the dog, and held it up to his coat. 'Waffle,' he said, really proud of himself. So it stuck."

It was an adorable story, and the affection Rory had for his family was obvious in the warmth of his voice. Oaklee got along with her folks okay, but they weren't overly close, and Cam was gone all the time. She envied Rory his tight-knit family.

"You going to be okay here?" he asked, and she realized it was going on eight and Rory probably wanted to get home and do . . . whatever he normally did in the evenings. Maybe he had another date, and the earlier warmth evaporated. Maybe he was going to see Patty What's-Her-Name again.

"I'll be fine. He's a dog. How much trouble can he be?"

"Well, call me if there's an issue. You got my cell number?"

"No."

"Give me your phone and I'll put it in."

She got her phone and unlocked the screen. He added his number and handed it back to her.

"Let me know right away if he starts chewing at the cast. He hasn't so far, so I didn't make him wear a cone. But he'll have to if he starts chewing it."

"Okay."

"And I'll check in over the weekend to see how he's doing."

"Great."

"Okay. I should get going."

He was nearly to the door when Oaklee remembered their original bargain. "Hey, did you talk to Victoria about the website and stuff?"

He stopped with his hand on the doorknob. "I did. We didn't really discuss it beyond saying it should probably be done, though."

"That was one of the conditions, Rory. Don't make me doubt your word."

He looked at her strangely for a second, then his forehead smoothed out and he smiled. "I promise. I'll ask for something more concrete tomorrow."

"You tell her I can set it all up and that she doesn't have to learn a thing if she doesn't want to. I'm sure there's a staff member who's familiar with this kind of thing. Or heck, you could hire your sister. Or a high school student."

"Got it."

She walked over to the door, Buster following slowly behind. She was well aware that tonight Rory had probably brought over close to a hundred dollars' worth of stuff by the time the bags, food, bowls, and leash were tallied. Would that be going on her bill as well? He'd mentioned a bag of food, but not the other.

Rory knelt down in front of the dog and rubbed his ears. "You be a good boy now, Buster. Don't be causing trouble."

He stood and looked at Oaklee. "Don't you be causing trouble, either."

"Me? Believe me, I'm going to be doing my best to make sure there is no trouble whatsoever."

He hesitated, and Oaklee wanted to look away from his gaze but couldn't. He hadn't always been this good-looking. Close, but cute teenage boys weren't the same as full-grown, sexy, capable men. His compassionate side was pretty darn attractive, too. But not once, in all the years she'd known him, had he ever let on for one moment that he saw her as anything other than a kid sister or a pain in the ass. Except maybe the night she'd taken Buster to the clinic, but they'd both been exhausted. She wasn't quite sure anymore what had happened there.

But now . . . now he lifted his hand and put it gently along the side of her face. Buster sat obediently by her foot, and she held perfectly still, shocked at the gentle touch, her heart racing.

"Thank you, Oaklee. I think this is going to be really

good for both of you." He smiled a little, the warmth reaching his eyes, and she was increasingly aware that only a few inches separated them. "Imagine. Your accident the other night might have actually ended up saving his life."

"Let's not get carried away," she said, but her voice came out all breathy and soft. Dammit. His hand was still on her cheek and she wanted to lean into it and close her eyes, just for a moment. Her stomach trembled from anticipation and fear as they drifted a little closer. A kiss was no big deal. But a kiss from Rory . . . he wasn't like other guys. He was her teenage fantasy.

So close now . . . her eyes drifted closed, waiting for that first touch of his mouth on hers.

Instead his lips touched her forehead. She froze in place, both from surprise and dismay. A kiss on the forehead was what you gave a sister or a friend. She'd been moving in and he'd just friend zoned her big-time.

"Bye," he said softly, and her eyes slowly opened as he slipped out the door and shut it with a click behind him.

Heat rushed to her face as she stood there staring at the closed door. There was the faint sound of his car starting and driving away. Oaklee looked down at Buster, who was also staring at the closed door, as if waiting for Rory to come back.

"Looks like it's just you and me," she said quietly. "What do you want to do tonight?" She spoke to him like he was a pal over for a relaxing evening. "Watch a movie? Cute cat videos on YouTube?" She sighed.

Buster did move slowly with his cast on, so she kept him on the leash and went to the fridge to grab the bottle of white wine she'd opened earlier in the week. She poured herself a glass and then went to the sofa, Buster's nails clicking on the floor beside her. When she sat down, he eyeballed the cushions hopefully, but she shook her head. "No, Buster. You lie down here." She pointed to the floor.

He put one paw on the sofa cushion. But she didn't want doggy smell and hair on her furniture, so she frowned and used a stronger voice. "No. Down, Buster. Lie down."

He gave a whine and dropped at her feet, arranging his front paws so he was comfortable before heaving a sigh and dropping his chin to the floor. She felt guilty being so stern, but it had worked, so there was that. Maybe this would go smoother than she hoped.

The wine was tart and crisp and Oaklee relaxed into the cushions. Truth be told, she liked having the place cleaned up a bit. There was something soothing about it. At the same time, she always felt a little more alone anytime everything was put away. It seemed to highlight that she was by herself, that no one else would be coming through the door to drop their jacket or shoes before sneaking a kiss. Dishes washed or in the dishwasher meant no one coming in late to dirty more and leave them on the table after a long day.

In a weird, twisted way, leaving her stuff all over the apartment gave the illusion that she didn't live such a solitary existence. She liked her independence, and she never wanted to be the little woman at home. But she might like to be somebody's woman.

They managed to watch TV for an hour or so, and then Oaklee woke Buster to take him outside for a pee. It was getting dark now, and the leash jangled against his collar as she wrapped her arms around his middle and helped him down the front steps. At the bottom she straightened and pulled down the hem of her T-shirt, then took him on a slow, short walk down the driveway. He lifted his leg and peed on a shrub, and she praised him before starting back up the driveway. Halfway there he stopped and did his number two business, and with a sour face she pulled a bag off the roll in the leash handle and scooped it. Ugh. Once she'd tied a knot in the end, and only gagged once, she wondered where to put it. There was no way this was going in her inside garbage can. She dropped it at the corner of the front step to wait until tomorrow. She'd have to get an outdoor can.

Then arms under his middle again . . . heaving him up the stairs, thank goodness there were only two . . . back inside the door, pulling her T-shirt down again.

"What do you say?" she asked him. "Time for bed?" It was early, but she was tired after putting in an already long week plus the events of the evening.

He looked at her hopefully.

She unclipped the leash and put the blanket Rory had left in a corner, where he could lie down and get comfortable. "Let's go to bed," she said, and went over and patted the blanket.

He went over and gave a wag of his tail, then looked up at her.

"Okay. A bit of a reprieve while I do *my* business."

She brushed her teeth and got ready for bed, all under Buster's watchful eye. Then she led him back out to the blanket, holding his collar, and patted the soft surface again. "Buster, lie down. Go to bed."

He stood on the blanket, staring at her blankly. She stared back. Finally, he turned in an awkward circle—twice—before dropping onto the blanket with a huff.

She really hoped he'd be okay for the night. There was water in his bowl and he'd gone to the bathroom . . . how much more could a dog need? As insurance, she took out his chewy toy and put it on the blanket beside him.

"Good night," she said. It sounded awkward and strange.

She got in bed but lay there with her eyes wide open, listening for any rustling. When none came, she closed her eyes and breathed deeply, willing sleep to come. She was nearly there when her eyes flew open again. There was the click, click, click of doggy toenails on the floor, coming closer to her room. A whine, right by her doorknob. And a scratch at the door.

"Go lie down," she called to him.

Silence for . . . ten seconds. Then more whining, and another scratch.

"Buster. Go to your blanket."

Whine, whine.

She took a deep breath and reminded herself, quite grumpily, that this was the dog's first night in a strange place. When the whining persisted, she got out of bed, opened the door, and encountered the saddest-looking face she'd ever seen. She wasn't an animal person, but she wasn't heartless. He looked positively bereft.

"Okay. We'll put your blanket on my floor." She grabbed the clothes littering the floor and threw them all onto an already-overflowing bedside chair. A few seconds later and she had Buster's blanket installed at the foot of her bed. "Okay, now lie down, Buster."

It took several tries to get him to lie down, but he finally did and she shut off the light and got back in bed.

There were several doggy sighs.

She let out a breath of her own and closed her eyes. She kept seeing Rory's face in the moments before he'd kissed her forehead. Had it really been platonic? Because his face hadn't looked friendly. It had looked . . . hungry. Or was that wishful thinking? Maybe if she'd just . . .

Whine, whine.

"Buster, please, for the love of God." She sat up. "Lie down and go to sleep."

He got up from the blanket and came to the side of the bed, resting his chin on the mattress.

It was dark in the room but light enough she could make out his face. How could she say no to that? He was . . . lonely. And not that Oaklee would admit it to another soul, but she was, too. For all her go, go, go, she didn't have many close friends. She had work friends, but even those people were mostly older than her and in a different stage of their lives. She hung out with Claire, but they weren't what she'd consider best friends. Even in university, she'd start to get close to someone only to have them move on when whatever shared interest had brought them together ceased to be a thing anymore. Like when she'd volunteered with a *Technology in the Classroom* program. Once the twelve weeks were over, people went their own way. Right now her closest friend was Emily, who put in so many hours at The Purple Pig that they barely ever got to see each other. They'd only managed to hang out once or twice during the whole summer.

"Are you lonely, Buster? Is that it? Do you just need to know someone's there?"

He whined.

She got out of bed, got the blanket, and put it on top of her comforter on one corner of her bed. Then she grabbed him around the middle, bent her knees, and lifted. With a grunt she put him down on the bed and patted the blanket. "Okay. You can sleep with me. But don't tell Rory. I'd never hear the end of it."

It didn't even take a "lie down" command. Buster flopped onto the blanket and rolled over on his side, instantly content. With a shake of her head, Oaklee got under the covers and got comfortable, fluffing the pillow before rolling to her left side, facing outward.

Buster's tail thumped once . . . twice. He sighed. So did Oaklee.

And then she finally went to sleep.

CHAPTER 6

She woke the next morning with something heavy pressed against her back and her tank top sticking to her skin . . . and for a moment she wondered if the air conditioning had gone on the blink in the night.

Then her head cleared and she realized that Buster hadn't exactly stayed on his blanket in the night. Not only hadn't he stayed, but he had abandoned it completely and was now rolled over on his side with his spine flush with hers.

Her first thought was that her bed was going to smell like dog.

Her second was that it was kind of nice to wake up and not be alone in the bed. She sighed. How pathetic did that make her, anyway? She preferred sleeping with an ugly stray dog with a busted leg over sleeping alone?

She gingerly rolled to her back and turned her head. The stupid thing was sprawled out in a most undignified manner, legs splayed, one ear flopped over. She nudged him with her arm. "Buster. Hey, Buster."

He groaned and rolled over, giving her a full-on nose-full of dog breath.

"God. Gross!" She rolled away and out of bed, sputtering. "That's rancid, dog."

He rolled to his belly and looked up at her. She sighed, then sat on the edge of the bed. "Did you have a good sleep, huh?" She rubbed his ears. "Me, too. Our secret."

She figured she could sneak outside in boxers and a tank, so she hefted Buster off the bed—one of these times she was certain she was going to put out her back—and headed for the front door. Within seconds he was clipped on the leash and she lugged him down the steps. One long, long pee on the shrub later, and she padded back to the steps, scuffing the bottom of her feet on the steps to scrape off any pebbles.

She fed him, topped up his water, ate a container of yogurt leaning against the sink, and when she was sure he was okay, jumped in the shower.

He was sitting on the sofa when she came back out, fully dressed and ready for work.

"Buster, no. Down." She had to help him off the sofa because of his leg, which left a smattering of yellowy dog hair on her raspberry blouse and navy skirt. She put the laundry basket on one cushion, and then, in a hurry, threw two handbags on the second cushion, hoping to deter him from getting up again. The blanket! She retrieved it from the bedroom and put it back in the corner, getting more hair on her skirt, then went back and shut the bedroom door. He didn't need access to that today.

Then she stood at the doorway, tension settling

between her shoulders. She didn't feel right leaving him here today. What would he get into? What if he made a mess? But she had to go to work . . . oh, damn that Rory. All the warm and fuzzy feeling she'd had upon waking this morning were long gone. This was just one big old complication.

Work. She had to go to work. She'd deal with everything else later.

She went out and locked the door, hoping for the best.

Oaklee returned home at four fifteen; she'd cut her day short by half an hour by working through lunch. Her paranoia about what Buster might be doing in her absence turned out to be less imagination and more premonition. When she opened the door, the smell hit her first, nearly knocking her backward.

"Oh God," she moaned, stepping inside carefully. It wasn't hard to discover the source; it looked as though Buster had known exactly where the door was. The pile of offending poo was on top of her shoe mat. More specifically . . . on top of one of her favorite wedges.

Which would now be thrown out. Dammit.

"Buster?"

She skirted the mess for the moment and went to look for him. He was sound asleep in the corner, curled up on his blanket. She nudged him and he opened one eye, as if to say, "How dare you interrupt my nap?" He closed his eye again.

Her laundry basket was upended and the clothes strewn all over the floor. Had he taken each item out individually? And her handbags . . . also on the floor. The red leather one had the strap chewed off.

Her head started to pound.

Well, first things first. She'd go get a bag from the kitchen for the garbage, then take the mat outside and wash it off. And open the windows. Air conditioning be damned . . . right now she wanted the crap smell out of her apartment.

She went into the kitchen and nearly slipped on the kibble on the floor.

He'd eaten through the bag of dog food. There was a gaping hole in the middle of the bag, and food everywhere. How much had he eaten? Enough to be sick? She prayed there wasn't a hidden pile of vomit somewhere, just waiting for her to discover by accident. She shuddered at the thought.

She grabbed a bag and pulled her collar up over her nose as she scooped the mess, including the poor shoe that was beyond saving. Once the bag was knotted, she tossed it out the front door and then took the rest of the shoes off the mat and took the mat outside, too. Somewhere inside was a bucket she could use to put soapy water in. In her search, she discovered that he'd also peed on one of her bar stools.

Another bag and paper towel, and now her temper threatened to blow. Why on earth had she let Rory talk her into this?

Buster made his way over from his bed, looking up at her with contrite eyes. "Don't look at me like that," she growled. "I might have got suckered by another pair of pretty eyes, but I'm immune to yours, you horrible creature."

"Is that any way to talk to a poor, wounded dog?"

She looked up at the doorway. Rory stood there, in

faded jeans and a T-shirt, hands in his pockets. He sniffed the air. "Had an accident today, huh?"

His casual observation tipped the scale from annoyance to meltdown. "Accident? *Accident?*" She got up and shoved the wet paper towel in another bag and viciously knotted it. "He crapped on one of my favorite shoes, and peed on my stool, chewed through his bag of food, and now there's kibble all over the kitchen, ate one of my handbag straps, and pulled my laundry basket with my newly-clean clothes off the sofa and now they're all over the goddamn floor!"

His eyes cooled. "Apparently he's not as housetrained as I thought. Or—"

"Or? How can there possibly be an 'or'?" She got up, hating that he'd caught her on her knees. Instead she refilled the bucket, grabbed a rag, and squatted down this time to wipe off the leg of the chair and the front of the island. Buster was so happy to see Rory that he'd gone right to his side and sat there like an angel, tail swishing against the floor.

"It might have been anxiety. From being left alone all day."

"Well, what am I supposed to do? Quit my job?"

"Of course not."

She finished with the cleanup, got rid of the bucket, and moved to the living room. The handbag had been a special purchase, and he heart sank when she realized it was ruined. "Do you realize that this is a Kate Spade bag? Do you know how much it cost?"

"Maybe you can get a new strap."

"Sure. I'll just go into the Kate Spade store and ask if they have any Kate Spade replacement straps for a bag that was out two years ago. It doesn't work that way. Duh." She wanted to cry. She hardly ever bought designer labels. She'd bought the bag the day she'd landed the job at town hall. It had sentimental value, too.

She threw the bag on the sofa and picked up the laundry basket. Some of the clothes seemed okay, but others were damp, hopefully with drool and not . . . something else. She was going to have to wash them again just to be sure.

"I'll take him out for . . ."

She waved him off. "Yeah. For whatever he didn't do in here."

When they were gone she sank down onto the sofa and put her head in her hands. Was she a horrible person for being so upset over this? It wasn't like keeping a spotless apartment was a top priority. Still, it was a bit overwhelming to go from cozy sleeping companion to the spawn of Satan in an eight-hour period.

They came back inside and she got up from the sofa, finished picking up the clothes, and tried to get her temper under control. Rory opened a few windows to let out the stink.

"Maybe a doggy day care would be an idea for during the day?" Rory suggested.

"You do remember me saying that there are budgetary constraints, right?" She didn't know how much something like that would cost, but she expected that at five days a week, it would add up.

"Right." He looked slightly embarrassed. "Sorry. Hmm. Maybe a dog walker? That'd be a lot cheaper. They could come in once during the day, take him out for a pee?"

She paused. A dog walker might work. Or something. "But what if that's not enough? What if as soon as I go out the door, he's like this? I know my stuff isn't expensive, but it is my stuff. And I don't want my home smelling like poop every day."

Buster came over to her and put his chin on her knee. Despite her irritation, she melted just a little. What if Rory was right? What if it was something like . . . well, separation anxiety? What if he was lonely? Lonely she could relate to . . . more than anyone might imagine.

"Don't suck up to me," she said sternly, but her heart wasn't in it. She was just weary. She'd wanted to come home and have a relaxing night and now she was going to be doing laundry again and lamenting the untimely demise of a three-hundred-dollar handbag.

Rory had gone to the kitchen and was picking up kibble. "You should put this in a closet or a tub or something," he suggested. "So he won't chew through the bag."

Thanks, Einstein, she thought, but instead replied, "Put it in the front closet for now. I'll get a tub tomorrow or something. If I dare leave him to go shopping."

Rory came over and sat down beside her on the sofa. "I know this was a little like trial by fire," he said, sounding sincerely sorry. "I really didn't think he'd be this much trouble."

She nearly confessed that he'd been adorable and slept with her last night, but she wasn't sure Rory would approve—he seemed more into structure and manners than spoiling. Besides, then she'd reveal that she'd actually been that soft-hearted, and she didn't want to give Rory any ammunition.

"I'm overwhelmed is all," she admitted. Buster dropped down on the floor by her feet, utterly contented. "You know we never had pets growing up. I live alone. I'm not used to having to share my space. Even with a dog. I thought the laundry hamper would keep him off the sofa, you know?"

Rory smiled at her, his eyes warming as he met her gaze. "Maybe tomorrow you can keep it empty and put it upside down instead."

She felt silly. Why hadn't she thought of that? And putting the food away? And using something other than expensive handbags on the other cushion?

Rory put his arm around her and jostled her a bit, a friendly gesture that didn't really help. She closed her eyes. "Remember when I was a teenager and you used to call me a drama queen and a diva?"

His arm stayed around her, his strong fingers warm on her tricep. He chuckled a little. "Sure."

"I'm not sure I outgrew that," she admitted. "I really might be just that self-centered and self-absorbed."

He turned a bit on the sofa, and put a finger under her chin, forcing her to look at him. "Why on earth would you say that?"

She swallowed tightly. "Because I don't like to share. Because I live alone and do exactly what I want. Because I . . . I like doing my own thing and not having to answer to someone else, even if it's just a dog. I'm selfish, Rory."

"No, you're not. Look at me."

He cupped her chin so she couldn't look away.

"You do lots for this town and the people in it, and I know for a fact that most of it isn't on the clock. And for your friends, too."

"What friends?" She frowned, pulling her chin away from his grasp. "I have acquaintances, Rory. I'm not really that close to anyone."

"That sounds lonely."

"It is."

The admission was out before she could think better of it. Her cheeks heated. "Wow. I didn't mean to admit that."

"It's okay. I understand."

She laughed. "Right. Mr. Social Butterfly." Then she remembered that she had the same nickname—Ms. instead of Mr.—and it was only true about the frequency of her social life and not the quality.

Was it the same for Rory? That was hard to believe.

She sighed and leaned back against the cushions. "I'm sorry. I shouldn't assume."

"It's okay. And I have my family, and with there being six of us kids, it's never quiet. Still, other than my brothers, I've only ever been close with Cam, and we don't talk a lot these days."

"He should call you more."

Rory smiled. "It's okay. Life took him in another direction, and it's pretty awesome. I don't begrudge him one bit of his success. He's worked hard for it."

Oaklee's foot inadvertently nudged Buster, and he popped up, disconcerted at being jarred from his nap. He pushed himself between Oaklee's and Rory's knees, tail wagging, looking for attention. Rory chuckled. "I think Buster's a social dog. He seems much happier when he has company."

"If you're suggesting I get him a companion . . ."

Rory burst out laughing, Buster gave a low woof, and

even Oaklee smiled. She reached out to give the dog a pat at the same time as Rory, and their fingers touched through the wiry fur.

A zing went through her fingertips, straight to the pit of her stomach, and her breath caught. She felt about thirteen years old, sitting on the bus with a crush, and their hands brushing accidentally on purpose.

Rory wasn't laughing anymore.

He was looking at her, his fingers still resting on Buster's shoulder. She knew what she wanted and knew it would be a horrible mistake. She wanted Rory to kiss her. Even though they were supposed to be just friends. Even though she didn't want to start anything romantic, which would naturally come to an end and ruin any friendship between them, not to mention the perfect girlish fantasy she'd harbored all these years. She didn't want to risk messing it up completely.

But it wasn't so easy to remind her teenage heart of that. That girl still longed to know what his lips felt like, tasted like. Some crushes never really die. Maybe the trick would be to find out and just move on.

"Oaklee," he said softly, but it wasn't a caution. It was something else. Something like wonder. Or recognition.

She lifted her hand and did the one thing she'd always wanted to do, particularly when he'd been in high school and kept his hair a little too long. She slid her fingers into the dark waves, just above his ear.

It was soft, just as she knew it would be, and she bit down on her lip for a second, luxuriating in the feel of it slipping over her skin.

He leaned forward and she only had a moment to see his eyes close before his mouth touched hers.

She was kissing Rory Gallagher. At some point she'd freak out over that, but right now she was far too entranced with the feel of his lips, soft and supple, moving over hers. Buster nudged her leg with his head but she ignored him, desperate to hold on to this moment for as long as she could.

And Rory definitely knew what he was doing. His kiss was firm but gentle, compelling but not forced, beguiling. Oaklee melted into him, her fingers sliding from his hair down to the nape of his neck while his arm came around her, pulling her closer.

It was everything she'd ever imagined. More. So much more. It wasn't just a simple kiss; it inspired a longing so intense and so great she wondered how far he'd be willing to go before jamming on the brakes. He nibbled on her lower lip and it was as if he'd plucked a string, the sensation vibrating straight to her core. She couldn't stop it yet. Not yet.

She edged closer to him, lifting her arm to slide it around his back. At the same time, his hand grazed over her ribs, and his thumb slid along the outside of her breast.

Oaklee pressed into his hand, craving his touch.

It only lasted a moment, though, and Rory pulled back, breaking the kiss, his chest rising and falling with increased effort.

"I can't," he said, meeting her gaze. The intensity in his eyes sent a different message, but he moved back on the sofa a bit, putting extra space between them. "Oaklee, this . . . I just can't."

"Is it because of Cam? Because I'm a big girl. My brother has nothing to do with this."

She wanted to erase the distance between them and experience more than a single touch through two layers of fabric.

"Yes. No, I mean, it's more that we have history. As friends. As a little sister . . ."

"Oh, eww. You did not just say that." Talk about a mood killer.

He laughed a little, running his hand through his hair. "Not like that. I just mean that for a lot of years, that's how I saw you. Clearly you are not my little sister and never have been."

"What are you trying to say, Rory?" Oaklee could still taste him on her lips. Maybe there wasn't such a problem for her because she'd never seen him as a big brother. He'd always been her big brother's really hot best friend.

"I'm saying . . ." He sighed. "Dammit. Look, we have enough history that a hookup would be just wrong. And to be honest, I'm not up for anything more serious than that. I care about you too much, Oaklee, to use you for a bit of fun."

"Is that what you do with the other girls?" He dated all the time. She'd seen him around town with various women, though barely any of them were local. "Hook up and have a bit of fun?" She raised an eyebrow.

"Sometimes. Not always. I'm always up front that I'm not looking for a long-term relationship. We go on a few dates and that's it. I never promise more than I'm willing to give."

"Wow, lucky girls then. And what about your latest . . . Patty, was it? Was she fun?"

Rory's stare was penetrating. "Jealous?"

"You were out with her earlier this week. And kissing me two minutes ago. It's a legit question."

He moved closer to her again, and took her face in both his hands. Her heart leapt and her body tensed, unsure of what was coming, hoping and dreading it all at once. Rory wasn't necessarily wrong in his logic. It was just so inconvenient!

"I might not do relationships, but I only see one woman at a time. Patty and I had one date and there's not going to be another."

"There's not?"

"No."

"Oh."

He placed a soft, but too-brief kiss on her lips. "And now I'm going to go. We can't do this, and with the way you're looking at me right now . . . my willpower isn't that strong."

He got up from the sofa and gave Buster a pat on the way to the door. "Be a good dog, dude. No more messes like today, okay?"

She watched, stunned that he was making such an abrupt departure. He had his hand on the doorknob when he turned back. "Oh, Oaklee?"

"Hmm?" She looked up hopefully.

"Try a radio or the TV."

"Sorry?" She was still reeling from the kiss and the pronouncement about his willpower and what the really meant. His last words weren't making sense.

"For Buster, tomorrow while you're at work. Try turning on some music or the TV. The voices and sound might keep him company and ease any anxiety."

She was about to say thank you, but he was already out the door, shutting it with a click behind him.

Oaklee fell back against the cushions and put her fingers against her lips. What the hell? Her life was generally boring and, well, predictable. In the last two days she'd slept with a dog, cleaned up the disaster that was Buster's way of acting out, and had been thoroughly kissed by Rory Gallagher.

The last was the most surprising of anything. He'd never let on that he was attracted to her. Maybe it was a recent thing. Maybe it had been strictly in the moment. She wasn't complaining either way. He kissed like an angel. Or the devil. Right now it felt like the same thing.

And the way he hightailed it out of here . . . well, she was pretty sure he hadn't found it unenjoyable. Which meant he'd probably enjoyed it a little too much.

As had she.

Except she wasn't sure that there was such a thing. Had she really thought that they'd kiss and it would be out of her system? That once she knew what it was like she'd be satisfied?

She wasn't. Not even close.

CHAPTER 7

It was times like this that Rory really missed having his brother as a roommate. He'd gratefully take a few things lying around the apartment just to have some company to take away the emptiness. He turned on the TV so there was at least a bit of background noise, and grabbed a beer from the fridge.

Aiden was too busy playing newlywed to be around much, and Rory didn't feel like going to his parents' place all the time. Now he'd do anything to have a decent distraction. Kissing Oaklee had been foolish. Maybe it would have been okay, except he'd enjoyed it far too much.

He'd said he'd always seen her as a little sister, but that wasn't exactly true. Maybe at first, but not by the time she was fifteen or sixteen. It was Rory and Cam's graduating year. Cam was only home on vacations, since he was going to school and playing hockey in Minnesota while being billeted with a team family. Cam wasn't there every day but Oaklee was, a sophomore with a blond ponytail and long legs and perky breasts. He'd noticed, all right. But Cam had instructed him to look out for his baby sister, and so it had been strictly hands off. A guy didn't move in on his BFFs little sister. Not without permission.

Until now. They'd kissed. He'd touched. He couldn't rid himself of the feeling that he should call Cam and confess.

They were both adults now, though. And one thing had been crystal clear this evening. He'd wanted it all. He hadn't wanted to stop with a kiss, or a simple touch; he'd wanted to pick her up and carry her into her disaster of a bedroom and get tangled up in the sheets with her, mess be damned.

Which would only end badly. He didn't do relationships, or commitments, and a one-night stand with Oaklee would never be a good idea. It would be awkward at best. It would ruin any friendship they'd built as adults. And he knew damned well that she'd had a crush on him back in the day and she deserved better.

Yeah, that was the part that really stopped him up. Oaklee deserved better. She definitely deserved more than he'd be able to give her. Ever.

He sat down at the small kitchen table and opened his laptop. So the date with Patty hadn't worked out; he could try again. The best way to forget about Oaklee would be to see someone else, right? He clicked on the dating site icon, and started to peruse the profiles. Some he passed by without a second glance; others he stopped for a few seconds before dismissing them. The sophisticated-looking brunette had funny lips, the black-haired woman with the pixie cut was in her mid-thirties and a single mom—no thanks. Been there, done that, had the broken heart to show for it. There was a redhead with nice eyes, but his family was already full of redheads and she was nineteen. What the hell did a nineteen-year-old need to be on a dating site for? He frowned as the truth sank in. He didn't want to go out with anyone else. He'd rather sit here and stew and sip on his beer and think of Oaklee than take someone else out on a date.

And that wasn't good. At all.

He opened up his Facebook profile and sighed. His last posting had been from Aiden's wedding, and he'd snagged a pic of himself with the bride and groom, the town's famed Kissing Bridge in the background. The word that Oaklee had called him—a troglodyte—popped back into his head. He'd had to look it up and had figured out that she'd basically called him a caveman. Old-fashioned. Ignorant. But he wasn't as out of touch as she thought. Just because he chose not to be glued to his phone or posting pictures of what he ate for dinner didn't mean he was stupid. He'd had a profile forever, and a friends list that included people from high school right up through his vet degree. He just didn't like the constant barrage of information and pointless videos and "post this on your status" things. He had better things to do with his time.

Still, he searched for her name and she popped up right away. Her friends list? Three hundred and twenty-three. And she'd posted something this morning—a pic from her phone.

"Fostering this guy until we can find him a home.

HMU if you're interested in taking in a sixty-pound ball of fur and drool."

It might have sounded mean, except the picture was so darned cute Rory smiled. Buster had the neatest eyebrows, and it looked like he was smiling for the camera, silly mutt.

Before he could think better of it, he hit the button to send a friend request, then sat back in his chair.

She accepted it immediately. My God, did she live on her phone or what?

A tone sounded and a message box popped up. "OMG. You're on FB?"

He shook his head and typed back, "I have been for years. DUH. I'm selective."

A quick response: "I'm flattered."

"Shut up. Nice pic of Buster. Have you forgiven him yet?"

Little dots hovered in the chat window, showing she was typing, and then he got the response. "For now. He's being cute so it's hard to stay mad."

Rory hesitated for a minute, then took a drink, frowned, and started typing. "What about me? Am I forgiven?"

A longer pause, and he wondered if she simply wasn't going to answer at all. Finally, when he'd all but given up, the ding sounded. "Forgive you for what? The kiss? Or leaving?"

He put down the beer bottle. Huh. It was easier to type things in a silly message box than it was to say them face-to-face, when he got distracted by the way she looked at him and smelled and smiled . . . or got mad.

"Whichever you're mad at me for," he answered, feeling a teensy bit clever.

"You're forgiven," she responded. "For what . . . I'll leave that for you to guess."

Damn. They were flirting. There was no question about it. And if she were mad about the kiss, she probably wouldn't have messaged him in the first place.

Which meant . . . she hadn't wanted him to leave.

Oh, God. This was going to get messy.

He changed the subject. "So. This Twitter thing. And the office. What will that involve?"

She typed back. "You could have asked me this earlier."

He hesitated, then typed, "I forgot." It was easier to say than the real reason: she'd distracted him.

There was a bit of a pause and he wondered if she'd come back with another innuendo. Maybe something like, *If you hadn't been so busy kissing me* or *If you'd stuck around a little longer we might have got to it.* Instead she came back with a very on-point message. "I'll do an official assessment and maybe we can meet on . . . Monday or something. Or should I meet with Victoria?"

While that might have been best—to keep some space between them—he'd spoken to Victoria who had said she didn't mind but that she didn't have time and she'd leave it up to Rory. Translation: another item on the junior guy's plate.

"With me. Apparently I'm taking point on this. Victoria's orders."

Damn. That made it sound as if he didn't want to do it. Which he didn't . . . but he did, too. He just knew it wasn't wise.

"Come by around seven. Bring food."

He laughed then. So the pizza hadn't been just convenient; she really couldn't cook. He seemed to remember the Collier place being messy, what he would have called "lived in," but that Mrs. Collier could at least make a meal for four, or five if Rory stayed.

Those had been good times.

"Anything in particular?" he asked.

"FOOD." She put it in all caps and he chuckled again.

They signed off after that, but as the night wore on, Rory found himself thinking about her more and more. There was definitely attraction between them. The kiss tonight had proved that without a doubt. But how far could it go? He wasn't looking for anything serious. The last thing he needed was to pin his hopes—and his heart—on someone who would disappoint him again. Oaklee wouldn't mean to, but even though he liked being with her, they weren't compatible. He brought wounded animals home in the night. She wasn't, by her own confession, a pet person. He was a neat freak, and she was . . . well, he didn't know what the hell she was. Not neat, for sure. He was laid-back in jeans and T-shirts and she was high heels and Kate Whatever-Her-Name-Was handbags.

So far the only two things he could figure they had in common was their shared love for Cam and an affinity for Papa Luigi's Everything Pizza.

He couldn't kiss her again. That much was crystal clear.

Oaklee took Rory's advice and left the local radio station on when she left for work. To hedge her bets, she also decided to go home on her lunch hour and let Buster out to do his business. When she arrived, she found Buster on the floor, lying on top of her favorite throw blanket, which was crumpled up in a messy heap. But no pee or poop accidents, and nothing like the mayhem of the day before. Damn that Rory for being right.

"Come on, Buster. Let's go outside for a few minutes."

She hooked him onto his leash and took him for the short walk down the driveway and back up again. It was sunny and warm, so she tied him outside briefly while she went in to wash her hands and then grabbed the sandwich she'd brought home from The Purple Pig. Today's special was turkey, Havarti, and cranberry on some sort of seeded bread. She sat outside on the front step, soaking in the sun and eating her lunch, occasionally throwing a little bit of turkey or a corner of the bread to Buster, who was begging with his big brown eyes and waggle-licious eyebrows.

It was so relaxing and perfect she nearly didn't want to go back to work. But she had to, so she helped him back up the two steps to the front door, made sure his water bowl was full, the radio was on, and headed back to the office.

Dinnertime was better, too. Even though Buster only ate his kibble, Oaklee found she didn't feel like takeout or something frozen. Her cooking skills were limited, but she managed to heat up a bowl of tomato soup and make a grilled cheese sandwich for herself, then ate sitting on the sofa, with Buster pleading with her for scraps again. This time she wasn't sharing, so she told him to lie down. Later, when he made a move to lick off her plate, she got up and took the dishes to the kitchen and washed them up.

During the evening, she put a movie on in the background and sat on the sofa, working on her laptop. She examined the vet clinic site, and made notes as to what she'd expand, what needed to be included, and recommended social media accounts. The whole time she worked, Buster curled up on the floor, snoring contentedly.

Not that she'd admit it to Rory, but it was kind of nice having another . . . well, not person, but company, she supposed, in the apartment. The company was appreciated even more on the weekend, when she didn't have the routine of work to get her out of the house. Instead she took Buster to the backyard and tied him in the shade, while she sat nearby and worked on the clinic's proposal on her laptop.

On Monday, Rory sent her a message asking if she'd like to meet for supper somewhere instead of her apartment.

She sat at her desk and stewed about it for nearly an hour. Why the change in plans? Was this . . . a date? After his quick departure the last time they'd met, his request was surprising. Granted, they'd flirted a bit by private message, but she'd definitely got the impression that he considered kissing her a big mistake.

Then again, he was just asking her to supper at the Sugarbush, the local diner. Not exactly datelike atmosphere. It was probably completely innocent.

Finally, she sent back a reply. "What about Buster?"

Another hour passed, and he returned with "I think

he'll be fine for an hour or so. Craving a pulled pork sandwich."

Which he could get to go, she thought, frowning. Still, he seemed stuck on it, and she knew the tables were big enough to use her laptop, so she said yes and they agreed to meet at six instead of seven. It gave her enough time to go home, let Buster out, and feed him his supper.

It was nearly five when she arrived home to a series of barks and tail wags that made her laugh. Buster wiggled so much that he left a swath of hair across her pants. She threw them in the laundry hamper and changed into a pair of denim capris, a cute shirt, and a pair of red wedges that were more comfortable than her work shoes. After patting Buster on the head, she grabbed her laptop bag and decided to walk to Main Street, since she had some time and she could use the fresh air.

The Sugarbush wasn't slammed with customers on a Monday night, though maybe half the tables were occupied. When Oaklee arrived she saw Rory already there, a glass of soda and an open menu in front of him. She paused for a moment. He was so damned good-looking it was unfair. No wonder he never had a problem finding dates. But there was more, too, things she hadn't really realized when they were younger, things that she'd only noticed since watching him with Buster. He had patience, and gentleness, and compassion. Maybe those things were aimed more at the dog and cat population than at humans, but they were still pretty amazing qualities, and ones she wasn't really used to in the men she knew.

He looked up and saw her standing there and a smile lit his face. The impact of it hit her right in the solar plexus. It was different from anything she'd felt before. She'd never really felt like the center of attention with Jeff. Instead, he'd been full of plans. Preoccupied and not really in the moment.

But when she was with Rory, it seemed like the moment was all that existed. And that his attention was completely on her.

Perhaps the diner was a smart choice after all. Being alone together in her apartment might lead to a repeat of what happened last time. She wondered if that was his reason for changing locations. There was a world of difference between not wanting to be alone with someone and being afraid of what might happen if you were.

Oh, Lord. She couldn't be thinking that way when they had legitimate business to discuss. Sure, she'd been thinking about kissing him again, but her reaction just now felt like a warning. With Rory it wouldn't just be kissing. Not for her. It went deeper than chemistry, and into territory she was pretty sure she wasn't ready to explore.

She adjusted her laptop bag and made her way over to the table. "You're here early."

He grinned up at her. "I finished at five thirty. If I'd stayed around, I'd still be there. There's always something to be done and the longer I hang around, the bigger the chance I get roped into some odd job." He gestured to the chair to his right. "Why don't you sit here instead of across from me? That way we'll both be able to see your laptop screen."

"Sure." She pulled out a chair and sat, then unzipped the laptop bag. "You haven't ordered yet?"

"Naw. I was waiting for you. We should probably eat first, and then have a look at what you've worked up for the clinic. There'll be more room on the table, then."

She zipped the case closed again. "If that's what you want."

There was that grin again, the one that lit up a room and made him impossible to say no to. The dimple in his cheek put in an appearance. "I'm starving," he admitted. "I had a peanut butter sandwich in the clinic kitchen for lunch. It was crazy today. Appointments plus all the drop-in things people hold off on over the weekend."

A waitress came over and took Oaklee's drink order and then they spent a few minutes going over the menu, which featured the standard diner fare like burgers and shakes, plus a good dose of home-cooking. "I'm surprised you're trying to decide. I thought you wanted pulled pork," she said, looking over at him.

"I did. I still might. But I like to keep my options open."

Hmm. She stared at the print in the menu and wondered if that was how he managed his revolving door of relationships, too.

Though perhaps that wasn't fair. It wasn't like she was rushing toward serious with anyone and the idea of a commitment scared her to death.

If you couldn't trust someone to keep their word after five years together . . .

He snapped the menu closed. "Changed my mind. Meatloaf. Because mashed potatoes."

Oaklee shook her head. "Boring."

"What are you having?"

"Probably a Cobb salad."

"And you call me boring." He nudged her elbow. "So how's Buster? Ruin any more shoes?"

"I've started going home on my lunch hour to let him out. And the radio trick worked, or at least I think it did. I'm not willing to take the chance on turning it off and then coming home to something that looks like it happened in *The Exorcist*."

He laughed, the sound a warm rumble from deep in his chest. It made her laugh, too, and so they were both smiling when the waitress came back with her soda and took their orders.

"Seriously, though, it's been better. No messes, or at least not many. He likes to find blankets and towels and he'll ball them up and lie on them. And he begs. Stares at me like he's starving and I have the last food on the planet, and won't I give him some?"

"Big fat no to people food," Rory cautioned. "Particularly anything that's . . . well, that's processed. Carrots are okay, and apples. As long as they don't make him, you know." He stuck out his tongue and made a raspberry sound.

Oaklee choked on her drink. "Honestly. Twenty-six-year-old men should not be making that sound."

"Thanks for pointing out my age. My inner child is fourteen. Ask my mother."

"Your inner child is incorrigible and always was."

He merely shrugged, flashed her that lightning grin again, and she felt herself sliding deeper and deeper into a comfort zone with him. Worse, it felt a little like old times, only they were slightly more mature. At least they had grown-up responsibilities these days.

"I did feed Buster a bit of my sandwich the other day. I couldn't help it." She smiled back at him, her lips twisting with impishness. "No *thbbbt*." She made the sound back at him, and he laughed right out loud.

"And we drove to a pet store on the weekend and I got him some treats and a couple of toys. One Kong just wasn't going to cut it. The girl at the store sold me a stuffed duck that she says is indestructible. So far it's passing the test."

His smile had softened, and his eyes were warm as he looked at her. "Look at you. Settling into being a pet owner."

Her brows pulled together. "This is temporary, Rory. I'm only fostering him until a family comes along."

She was relieved when he didn't contradict her. Sure, Buster was less trouble now, but that was a far cry from committing to . . . goodness. However many years he would be alive. Rory had said he was only two or three years old, hadn't he? She was looking at the possibility of a decade-long commitment if she agreed to keep him permanently.

A lot could happen in ten years. She might not even still be in Darling. Doubtful, but true.

Their food arrived and for several minutes they ate and made small talk about other things. Oaklee didn't eat much beef, but Rory's meatloaf smelled delicious and he had a whole mountain of mashed potatoes. By contrast, her salad was colorful and fresh and . . . She sighed. Boring. She really should try to learn to cook. She thought of Willow over at The Purple Pig, always making stuff that was so good and, well, healthy. This past spring Oaklee's favorite had been a curried squash soup. She couldn't make something like that. Food came from a can or the freezer.

"You want some?" Rory asked.

"What?"

"You're staring at my meatloaf. I asked if you wanted some."

She shook her head. "Sorry. I was just thinking how I wished I knew how to cook."

"Me, too. I make tacos. Really good tacos. And if there's leftover meat, I make nachos. And fried eggs. That's about it. Aiden's not much of a cook, either. Ethan though . . . he's learned out of necessity. He tries to cook good stuff for the boys. We've always just gone to Mom's when we wanted something good."

"I heard Ethan's been seeing Willow Dunaway," Oaklee mentioned. "I'm glad. It was so sad when his wife died."

"I'm not sure what's happening with Willow," Rory said, scooping up some potato on his fork. "Ethan's very private. And cautious. It makes sense. At least with Aiden off the market and Ethan dating, it takes some of the pressure off me to procreate."

Oaklee laughed. "There was pressure?"

"Are you kidding? You should try being Hannah. Because she's the oldest girl, she gets it the worst. Sometimes I think she stays single just to spite Mom and Dad."

"Cam, too," Oaklee admitted. "He never mentions a girl. And we never see him paired up with anyone in the news or anything." She laughed a little. "I actually had one reporter come up to me a few years ago and ask if he was gay."

"Cam?" Rory snorted. "No way. In high school we . . ." He coughed. "Well, never mind. Anyway, maybe he's just really private."

"Maybe."

"So is there pressure on you?" Rory asked. "Being the only girl and all."

Oaklee shrugged. "Not so much yet. I don't visit my parents as much as I should, considering we all live here together. I don't know . . . I guess I just do my own thing. And I'm only twenty-four. I'm not in a huge rush for kids."

Not in any rush, but that didn't mean she hadn't thought about it. She and Jeff had had this great ten-year plan that had included work and a house and some travel before settling down with a family. What a crock.

"Me, either," Rory admitted, though something flitted across his face that made her wonder. Pain, perhaps? Something that stung him the way that Jeff's betrayal had stung her? He picked up his glass and took a drink. "I'm just enjoying where I am right now. New job, no commitments."

"Lots of time for playing the field," she replied, and for some reason, it annoyed her. There was dating and then there was just . . . too casual. Like deliberately avoiding anything resembling something meaningful.

She was well aware of the irony.

"I guess," he said, and that look was back again, but he replaced it with a smile so quickly that she wondered if she'd actually imagined it.

The waitress collected their plates and they ordered coffee, and then Oaklee cleared a space and took out her laptop. "Okay, so let's get down to business. You said Victoria's left this up to you?"

"Sadly. I don't spend a lot of time online."

"As is shown by your abandoned profile."

"Ouch."

She laughed, typed in her password, and clicked through to the document with her proposal on it.

"Okay, so here's the thing. If you're not a social media kind of person, you might want to pass this task off to someone else in your office. Maybe one of the front-end staff, who are on their computers more frequently, anyway."

"You don't think I can do it?"

"I'm sure you can. It's more a matter of if you want to and who's better positioned time-wise to do it. How computer savvy are you?"

He shrugged. "How do you mean? I can navigate around no problem. I game a bit. Surf. And I use the programs at the office for patient files and stuff."

"Do you know how to edit the website files? Use any code?"

He treated her to a blank look.

"Get into the website?"

"Victoria said it's Wordpress. That's all I know. I can navigate it, but I've never had to update a site or anything."

"I can teach you. You don't even need to know any html. It's all plug-ins and drag-and-drop. Once the pages are set up, it's easy to edit the content. If you can type, and form a coherent sentence, you can do it." She smiled at him. "Can you form a coherent sentence, Rory?"

He lifted an eyebrow. "It's been known to happen."

"Good."

She walked him through what changes she'd make to the existing pages, then outlined what she'd recommend adding, including a testimonials page and a blog where one of the vets could regularly highlight an issue or topic. "Then we can set it up so that whenever you or Victoria post something new, it'll cross-post directly to your Facebook page and Twitter account. I'd say Twitter is optional. You'll probably find most of your clients on Facebook, and you could do Instagram as an option as well, particularly if you wanted to highlight events or pets looking to be adopted or whatever."

"And you can set all this up?"

"All you have to do is make me an administrator on your Facebook page, and I'd need to be given a user name and password for the site in order to access the dashboard. Otherwise, I'm good to go. I'm not great at graphic design, but I can do some simple stuff to make it a little more visually appealing."

"How much time are we looking at?" he asked.

"I can work on it in the evenings this week, and it'll be up by the end of the weekend, I'd say."

"That soon?"

She smiled. "Yeah. I mean, if you wanted a whole redesign, it would take longer. But I don't think you need to do that. It just needs some tweaks to make it more dynamic and then someone to add weekly or monthly content. If you write me a column about something that's really timely, I'll add it to the blog page. You only need three or four hundred words."

Their coffee had arrived and they hadn't even noticed. Oaklee sat back and added some milk and sugar to hers, and took a warm sip. Damn. She liked it hot. But this would do.

Rory sipped at his thoughtfully. "I've been meaning to do something about car safety, and harnesses, and that sort of thing. The other day I stopped at a light and there was a dog in the front seat with his head out the window and the driver was texting. If anything were to happen because she wasn't paying attention, the dog would probably be killed by the airbag. I have no idea why people feel the need to pick up their phones when they're in the damn car." He made a sound of disgust.

Oaklee tried to swallow her coffee and choked on it, reaching for her napkin as she coughed and her eyes watered.

"God, are you okay?"

She nodded, blinking furiously as she tried to get rid of the tickle. "Went down the wrong hole."

He chuckled, reached over and rubbed her back, his palm warm through her shirt. "You know that's not really possible, right?"

"Whatever." She coughed twice more, then reached for her water glass. She hoped her face wasn't bright red. What would Rory say if he knew she'd been checking her phone when she hit Buster?

At least she could say she'd learned her lesson. Her phone now stayed in her purse at all times when she was driving. And she was very lucky that Buster had pulled through as well as he had.

"That would be a great topic," she replied weakly, hiding behind her water glass. "If you send it to me, I'll copy and paste it into the page. I'll give it a proofread, too, if you like."

"That'd be great."

"So we're good?"

"Consider yourself hired. And I'll talk to one of the girls about maybe taking on updating the social media. I'm really not online all that much. It's not my thing. Besides, I don't want to add IT to my job description."

"Oh, I think you're probably more savvy than you let on," Oaklee said, exiting out of the program and shutting down.

"What makes you say that?"

She gave him a sideways glance. "For you to have so many dates? You're on a site, aren't you?"

She looked over. His lips had fallen open and his cheeks were ruddy. She laughed a little, but it felt forced. "It's okay, Rory. Nearly everyone is these days."

"Are you?"

She looked away. "No."

"Why not?"

She shrugged, made a show of putting the laptop back in the bag. "I'm not really interested in dating much." And that was where they differed. Rory was a master at casual dating. She'd never learned how.

Rory made a humming sound. "Really? You're twenty-four. Single. Pretty. You've got a job. What are you waiting for?"

She looked over at him, flattered that he'd called her

pretty, and unsure of what she wanted to say, feeling like this was a moment where a little truth might actually be a good thing.

"I'm not waiting for anything. I'm just . . . not ready for really getting out there."

"Because of you and Jeff? Whatever happened there? Cam said you were dating all through college. Then he said that you'd broken it off or something. But that was a couple of years ago now. Don't you think it's time to move on?"

Wasn't he one to talk? "I could ask you the same, but your 'moving on' is legendary," she replied, draining the last of her nearly cold coffee. It seemed to her that she'd heard about him dating someone in vet school, too, but clearly that hadn't worked out.

"Ouch."

She didn't want to smile, but she couldn't help the slight curve of her lips. "Maybe we should just call a truce about our love lives. Or a moratorium on discussing it."

"Maybe. But I don't think that's going to be completely possible."

"Why not?" She faced him and lifted her eyebrows as she asked the question.

His gaze held hers. "Because of last week. Because of . . . you know."

Yeah, she knew. And she appreciated him not spelling it out in a semi-busy restaurant. Things did have a way of getting around in Darling.

"That doesn't have to happen again. You can be my client, and Buster can be yours, and that's it. And probably for the best."

"You're right." He nodded a bit, but his damnable

eyes kept her hooked. Why was it she needed eyeliner and mascara, but Rory could lower his eyes a bit and his lashes were thick and gorgeous and just totally unfair?

"Good."

"Except . . ."

That one word made her pause, made her stomach start doing that swirly thing that spoke of nerves and anticipation. Damn him. One of them being foolish was bad enough. She was depending on him to be reasonable. Logical, even.

"I know it shouldn't have happened. It complicates things. But I can't stop thinking about it."

She swallowed tightly, agreement sitting on her tongue, waiting to be spoken, while her brain urged caution and common sense since his had apparently deserted him. Why would he admit such a thing, when it was sure to add fuel to the fire?

"Well, try. We're too different, Rory. It would never work and it would just become a big ugly mess. I know I give you a bit of a hard time, but I do value our friendship. And yours and Cam's. Even if he isn't around much."

Huh. As if thinking of Cam would stand in her way. Sure, his opinion mattered, but she knew the bro code was *sacred*.

"And I'm not a long-term guy."

"And I'm not looking for romance."

"So that's it, then. Well, let me get the bill for tonight. Dinner's on me."

"I want to pay my share."

"Not this time, Oaklee. Just . . . let me do this. As a thank you for taking Buster in."

"You already gave me food." Confused, she looked up at him as he rose from his chair.

A wrinkle appeared between his eyebrows, just above his nose. "So? It's a salad. And this is way better for Buster than being at the shelter."

Dogs at the shelter definitely didn't get lifted onto a nice fluffy bed at night, she conceded. Though she still wasn't about to tell Rory that she was letting him sleep with her.

Rory paid for dinner and they left the diner, stepping outside into the warm, late-summer evening. It was nearly Labor Day and summer activities would soon wind down. Kids would be back in school. The office staff would be at a full complement now as the last of the vacation days were taken. Oaklee liked autumn, but she was sad to see the summer go.

"Thanks for dinner. I'll be in touch about the site."

Rory put his hands in his pockets. "Sounds good."

Oaklee started to walk away, when Rory called out. "You walked?"

She turned around, smiled, and shrugged. "It's a nice day."

For a moment she thought he was going to ask if he could walk her home. There was a momentary hesitation, a look of indecision. Then he smiled and lifted a hand. "Enjoy," he said. "Give Buster a pat for me."

"I will."

She kept her smile on until she was turned back around, then closed her eyes for a step or two as she exhaled. That was crystal clear, then.

She should be relieved. After all, he was respecting her wishes. Instead she felt like she was one of his one-time dates, blown off after a single evening. After knowing each other for over a decade, she'd hoped she'd meant more to him than that. That maybe he'd disagree with her assertions of keeping things platonic and be willing to take a risk.

As she made her way home, she realized that she'd set him up for a test . . . and she was the one who'd failed. She was the one afraid of risk and stepping out of her comfort zone. The only thing Rory was guilty of was honesty—he'd said he hadn't been able to stop thinking about it—and then backing off when she asked him to. He'd been . . . a gentleman.

Which only made her like him more.

Dammit all.

CHAPTER 8

Labor Day came and went. Rory was on call most of the long weekend, but took time to hang out with the family a little more. Aiden and Laurel were looking radiant, excited about Laurel's pregnancy, and there was definitely something brewing between Ethan and Willow. For the first time, Rory had felt very much the odd man out with his brothers, and he found himself thinking back a few years and how he'd imagined himself with a family of his own.

And he didn't even bother logging on to the dating site. Maybe he was done with that now. Done with filling his time with amusing company but nothing more.

By the middle of September he decided to seek out his brother for a little guidance. It wasn't something he usually did, mostly because as guys they didn't over-share in the feelings department. They tended to have a few beers, watch a game or something, and let the silence work out any problems. Rory managed to catch Aiden at a time when he was both off shift and Laurel was off doing something with her mom. He made tacos, Aiden brought over a six pack of beer, and they sank into their favorite chairs in the living room, just like old times.

After the tacos were gone and they were each on their second beer, Aiden looked over at Rory. "So. Are you going to tell me what's eating you?"

The ball game played in the background. Rory thought for a minute, then said, "How did you know you were ready to get serious about Laurel?"

Aiden's eyebrows went up. "Dude. Really? Is there actually one girl right now who is threatening your bachelor status?"

Rory scowled. "Dude," he replied, adding extra emphasis to the word. "I'm being serious here. I know you're not used to that, but . . ."

"But you're coming to your big brother. Aw, that's sweet."

Rory gave him a one-finger salute and said, "Never mind."

Aiden laughed, which only made Rory more frustrated. But then . . . he should have expected some teasing. That, too, was what family did.

"Okay, in all seriousness," Aiden said quietly, looking over at Rory. "Is there a girl who's got you tied up in knots?"

"Yeah. I guess you could say that."

"Who?"

"You have to promise to keep this in confidence, okay? I don't like talking about my love life, but I need some perspective."

"Okay. So I repeat. Who?"

"Oaklee Collier."

"Shit, Rory! I figured this was one of your online dating chicks from wherever. Not Oaklee. Jesus. She's a ball-breaker."

"You think?" Rory frowned. Oaklee was efficient. She wasn't . . . easy. She was stubborn for sure. But a ball-breaker?

"A couple of the guys down at the department have asked her out. She is cold, man. Cold. No mercy. Just flat-out said, 'I don't think so' and boom. Shut down."

Rory stared at his brother. "So she didn't say yes to a couple of your 'I'm so special I'm a cop' buddies. That doesn't make her a ball-breaker. That means she's discerning." He took a drink of his beer.

Aiden's grin nearly split his face. "You think? How far'd *you* get?"

The tone implied that Rory had got the same treatment, and it irritated him enough that he spoke without really thinking. "Second base."

Aiden whistled. "Impressive, bro. Impressive."

Rory pointed at the living room door. "If you're going to make fun of me, Aiden, or take cracks at Oaklee, just go. I didn't give you shit over Laurel, did I? And who helped you with planning that surprise wedding, anyway? And making sure you got there on time?"

"All right, all right." Aiden held up his free hand in a sign of submission. "So you're sweet on Oaklee. What's the problem? She's pretty. She's got a decent job, and while she's scary efficient, she's probably nice enough. Or is she not interested?"

Rory sighed. "I think she is. She seemed to, uh, enjoy

it. And we did some flirting online. But then she started doing some website stuff for the clinic and she's been professional all the way. I mean, one hundred percent professional. Like nothing ever happened."

"And you want to pursue it? Her?"

"I don't know." He flopped his head back against the headrest of the chair. "When we met to go over the clinic stuff, I told myself I couldn't kiss her again. She's different, you know? I've known her a long time. Hell, she had a crush on me in high school. She's Cam's baby sister. The thing is, I want casual and easy. No commitments. I'm not sure that's possible with Oaklee, because we've known each other so long. So instead of offering to walk her home, we just came up with all the reasons to back off, and went our separate ways."

"So you kissed her, and flirted, and then acted as if nothing had happened? Completely platonic?"

"Yeah."

"Oh, bro. Women love it when you give them mixed signals." Sarcasm dripped from his voice.

"Shut up, Aiden." But he knew his brother was right.

"So what's the problem now, then?"

Rory turned his head and met his brother's gaze. "I can't stop thinking about her."

Aiden's teasing grin softened. "Good."

"Good?"

"Yeah. Good. Because you've been playing the field for a long time now, and I've never seen you go on more than two or three dates with anyone. You turn on the charm and dazzle them a bit, and then let them down easy before any real feelings get involved."

"You did the same."

"Sometimes. But it wasn't out of fear. And I think yours is. I think whoever broke your heart when you were away at school really did a number on you. And the whole family's been waiting for you to finally open up about it. If getting your ass in a knot over Oaklee is what it takes, then it's about time."

Rory wasn't sure what to say. He'd been so certain that he'd kept his pain to himself. He had been all-in when it came to Ginelle. Totally in love. Visualizing their future. He swallowed tightly, because it still hurt. He'd been prepared to step into being a father to Kyle, too, with all sorts of love to give. He'd been sure. Ready. And he'd been wrong.

How could he ever trust his own judgment again?

He got up from his chair and went to the bedroom, and then came back and tossed a small box in Aiden's lap.

"What's this?"

"Open it."

Aiden opened it with a tiny creak and a click. The lump in Rory's throat grew larger as he looked at the engagement ring he'd given Ginelle on the night he'd proposed.

"What the hell?"

"Her name was Ginelle. She was in my class and I was going to ask her to marry me in our third year. The plan was to wait until graduation and then do it. Get married and I'd . . ."

He stopped for a moment, instead of trying to push forward and have his voice break. "She had—has—a kid. Kyle. I wanted to adopt him."

Aiden's mouth dropped open. "I can't believe you never told me this before."

"It hurt too much. I didn't want to answer questions. I still don't. Looking back now, I think I'm glad she broke it off when she did. It would have been worse now, if she hadn't really loved me the way I loved her. She said I was too perfect. Too convenient." He laughed, a bitter, pained sound. "I was like, 'Excuse me for being too awesome.' What a load of shit."

"I'm sorry, Rory."

Rory hadn't wanted pity, either. Luckily Aiden wasn't the "oh, you poor bastard" type. He didn't waste time on feeling sorry for himself or other people. He just tried to get it done. It was a good part of what made him a great cop.

"Imagine what it would be like, right now, if Laurel said she didn't want to be married to you. That the family you pictured wasn't going to be a reality. That you couldn't have her and the baby she's carrying."

"It would kill me."

"Right. So since then . . . I smile. I date. I don't do love or commitments. Not because I don't think they exist, because I know they do. But because I'm not willing to put myself out there and let someone stomp on my heart like that ever again."

And Oaklee could. She was the first person since Ginelle who even came close to having that sort of power. Maybe simply because he knew her. She probably didn't know how much Cam loved his little sister, but he talked about her all the time. He was proud as shit that she'd gone to college and was working in a job she loved. He thought—rightly so—that she was beautiful and that no guy would ever be good enough for her. And he knew so many of Rory's secrets that Rory was sure he'd never get the green light to be involved with her.

Not that it was Cam's call. But the opinion held weight.

"So you want me to tell you how to proceed."

"It would be helpful." Rory gave a half grin in Aiden's direction.

Aiden took a few moments to deliberate. "Well," he said, brandishing his beer bottle, "it seems to me you have three choices here. One, you can say forget it, forget her, and move on to a new flavor of the month courtesy of 99flavors.com or whatever dating site you use. I know you do, don't deny it."

"I wish. The problem is I can't seem to forget her."

"Then two, you can have a raging affair and get her out of your system once and for all."

Rory got stuck for a moment, imagining that pleasurable event, but then he shook his head. "I can't treat her that way. Not Oaklee. Not any woman, okay? I'm always up front about what I want and what I'm capable of giving. Some are okay with it, some aren't."

"Honorable, I'm sure." Aiden's smile disappeared. "Then I'm afraid, buddy, you're stuck on number three."

"What's number three?"

Aiden sighed. "Honesty. Tell her the truth. Tell her you're struggling. Then you can work through it without wondering what the other person's thinking. Really, things with Laurel were tense until we started talking about what was really important."

Rory closed his eyes. "That's not helpful. I mean, I pretty much told her I hadn't been able to forget about her and she shut me down." He laughed a little and shook his head. "Damn, you know what happened? We traded places. I totally picked meeting in a neutral place to avoid temptation, and it backfired."

"I know it's hard. But if you care about her at all, even as a friend, she deserves honesty. And so do you. If you care about her, tell her. And if it doesn't work out, it doesn't work out. But you can't keep running away your whole damned life. Is there any rule that says you have to go from zero to sixty in five seconds flat? You guys could take your time, you know. Go slow."

There was a huge problem with that. Rory knew that "taking it slow" wasn't the same thing as "falling slow." Words didn't need to be spoken, a relationship didn't need to go all the way for deeper feelings to be involved. For people to get hurt.

For him to get hurt.

"Helpful?"

"Not really."

Aiden chuckled. "That's because she matters, bro. None of the other ones have. Good luck."

Rory and Aiden watched the rest of the game, but Rory felt just as unsettled as he had before. None of Aiden's recommendations felt right. He couldn't seem to get her off his mind, he couldn't in all conscience engage in a shallow affair, and the idea of opening up to her was just . . . no.

The sad thing was he suspected his brother was right.

And that left him screwed. And not in the good way.

Oaklee figured when she didn't hear from Rory for the whole of the week following their dinner, that whatever had flickered between them had died. At least on his part, and she wasn't about to go chasing. It was probably for the best, anyway. She wasn't interested in being another on his list of conquests.

Rory had e-mailed through his blog post and she'd posted it on a "From the Doc's Desk" page. She'd also added a "Happy Tails" page with client testimonials and pics of happy, healthy pets sent through from the office staff. The Facebook page was revamped and one of the vet techs was going to look after keeping it updated. And they'd added a Twitter account, too, as a trial. The first post had been about Buster and his quest for a forever home, complete with a picture. She'd taken a recent one with her phone, because several weeks of care and good food had fattened him up and he looked much healthier. Almost handsome, to her mind.

Buster's bill was officially cleared from the books. And yet . . . not so much as a word from Rory other than the work correspondence, which had been completely impersonal. She'd attended a few Labor Day weekend events around town, but most of the social media announcements about community functions had been set up as scheduled posts. She'd even gone home to her folks' place for a meal, but it had felt strange leaving Buster at home and she wasn't sure how he'd act at someone else's house. The memory of his first day at her apartment was still a little too fresh in her mind.

Now September was waning; she'd traded her summer dresses for trousers and light sweaters, and her strappy sandals for closed-toe pumps. She looked down at Buster. He was settling in much better now, though he'd had a few minor accidents this week and one incident involving an empty potato chip bag in the garbage, which apparently had contained a few crumbs in the bottom. She'd found the kitchen garbage strewn on the floor, the chip bag split open and licked clean.

Right now he was snoring at her feet while she sat on the sofa in sweats and a hoodie, flipping through a magazine. In a few days she'd take Buster back to see Rory to have his cast off. She knew she could really leverage her social media to find him a permanent home, but she wasn't going to push it until she was sure his injuries were fully healed. They were her fault, after all, and her responsibility. He could stay here until he was a hundred percent healthy.

The crazy rush of wedding and baby showers had ceased as well, and Oaklee found herself at loose ends. Claire had gone back to school for her final year, and more than ever, Oaklee was aware that for someone known as a social butterfly, she really was lacking in the friends department. Part of that was due to a desire to keep her distance and avoid talking about Jeff. He was gone, his parents had moved closer to the city, and the last thing she wanted was for the story of their breakup to get around Darling. Instead, all those high school friends were now mere acquaintances she spoke to in passing at the drugstore or at town events.

Forget letting romance into her life; she'd turned her back on her friends, too. Except Emily. Em was the one person who knew the whole sordid mess and was sworn to secrecy.

She called Emily, wondering if they could get together and finally catch up, but Emily was still at work— again. Apparently Willow hadn't been feeling all that well the last few days, and Em was putting in even more hours to cover. Oaklee frowned. There was dedication to a job—she certainly had that—but there was overkill, too. They made plans to meet up the next Monday for sushi, and Oaklee vowed to hold Em to the agreement.

She flipped through another magazine and then glanced at the phone sitting on the end table. Nothing good would come of calling Rory, would it? Clearly he'd taken her at her word. He was probably out with one of his dating site matches. The thought bothered her more than she wanted to admit.

She turned on the TV, scrolled through the listings, and turned it off again. Stared at the pile of DVDs. Looked over at her bookcase; the spines were lined up neatly since she didn't dare leave anything lying around anymore. If nothing else, having Buster had prompted her to be a little more diligent with her housekeeping.

She picked up the phone again, scrolled through her feeds, and wondered, not for the first time, if her after-office hours checking meant that she was actually avoiding having a real life with real relationships. She had to do something. Get out of here before she went crazy.

She updated her Twitter feed once, and then shut her phone off, put it on the table beside the sofa, and gave Buster a pat. Maybe what she really needed was to unplug for a bit. Clear her head.

"I'll be back in an hour or so, buddy. If you're good I'll bring you a treat." She grabbed her keys and wallet, tucked them into her jacket pocket, and headed out into the cool fall evening.

There was still lots of light left for a walk, and instead of turning up toward Main Street, she went right and followed the walking path along Fisher Creek. The path meandered from two blocks east of the golf course, straight past the Kissing Bridge and on toward where the town limits met the highway. The leaves had only just started to turn, the maples hinting at a ruddy hue while the leaves of the birches shifted to a yellow-y green in anticipation of full autumn.

The town had just cut the grass, and the rich, summery scent rose up from the ground, blending with the spicy scent of the asters, mums, and dahlias still blooming in the flower beds. Oaklee wished she could have brought Buster along, but she was still leery of taking him on longer walks, unsure if his leg was strong enough and not wanting him to reinjure it. Instead she breathed deeply and thought of detouring at the bridge to Main for a takeout cup of tea before The Purple Pig closed at eight.

She was nearly to the bridge when she saw Rory walking, hands in his jeans pockets, wearing a Tufts sweatshirt. Her traitorous heart leapt at the sight of him. Hadn't she resisted texting him earlier? Decided to get out in the fresh air on her own? And here he was, striding along the path, reminding her of Darcy striding out of the mists in *Pride and Prejudice*. He was just missing the messy hair and coat flapping about his Hessians.

She considered turning the other way—after all, he hadn't called her in weeks. Then he looked up, saw her standing there, probably fifty feet away, and a smile broke out over his face, popping his damnable dimple. She wasn't sixteen anymore. That dimple wasn't part of a teenage fantasy. She was twenty-four and it was a grown woman's longing that responded to its appearance.

All Oaklee could do was smile back at him.

They met next to a big oak tree, the wide branches spread over their heads and a smattering of little acorns at their feet.

"Hey," he said softly, his eyes warm on hers. "Nice night for a walk."

"Isn't it just?" It occurred to her that the clinic wasn't that close to Main Street, so he'd have to be here on purpose. "What brings you to our bustling downtown?"

He held her gaze for a few moments. "I saw your tweet," he admitted.

She thought back to what she'd sent before leaving her phone at home. *Beautiful evening for a walk along @TownofDarling's Fisher Creek.*

"You did?"

He nodded. "I was at the soccer field watching Ethan's boys play. Thought maybe I'd run into you."

A bubble of consternation formed in her chest. She wasn't quite sure what to make of him. On one hand it sounded as if he'd sought her out, but it was couched in a family activity and that he was here anyway. Argh.

"I was at loose ends. I just wish I could have brought Buster. I think he's dying for a good walk."

"Once he gets his cast off, we'll know better. He's young and much healthier now than when you brought him in. I bet he's healed up just fine."

She smiled. "He eats like a horse."

"Well, once he's a-okay, you can really start looking for a permanent home for him." Rory smiled, as if the suggestion was nothing at all. She didn't really want him to know how fond she'd become of Buster. She was probably going to miss him when he wasn't there anymore.

Rory swept his hand to the side. "Want to keep walking?"

"Sure."

They ambled along, and Rory started a conversation about work and the website, which led to talking about her work, and somehow they ended up near the end of the Green. Laurel's Ladybug Garden Center, now closed for the evening, was in view. "I can't believe we walked all the way up here," Oaklee said, giving her head a small shake. "Time flies, I guess."

"You're much better company than my brothers," Rory replied, and they turned around to make their way back.

"I am?"

"Yeah. They're either giving me grief about something, or talking about wives and kids." He looked over at her and shrugged. "Did you know Laurel and Aiden are expecting a baby?"

She grinned widely. "Oh, that's lovely. I was in on the whole wedding thing, remember? Laurel thought it was all part of the town promotion, and I got to see her pick the wedding dress and everything. After the way her first marriage ended . . . well, she deserves to be happy." She stopped and looked over at Rory. "They are happy about it, right?"

Rory laughed. "Over the moon. Anyway, since they broke the news, Aiden's been getting really papa bear about it all. Tonight's conversation was a welcome change."

Right. Because he was so not into marriage and family. She looked straight ahead and injected a nonchalant tone into her voice. "And am I better company than your string of dates?"

"Yes."

The immediate, complete answer took her by surprise, and she stopped in the middle of the path. "Do you really mean that?"

"Yes, I do." His eyes searched hers. "I'm more comfortable with you."

"You've known me a long time." She started walking again, but looked over at him. "You don't have to try to impress me. I already know who you are."

"Hmm. You might not know me as well as you think you do. But you're right. We have history. Shared friends, experiences, memories."

"That's me. Just another Darling buddy."

Except she really couldn't get that kiss out of her brain, or how it felt to be sandwiched between his hard body and the soft sofa cushions.

"I like you, Oaklee. More than I should. I've stayed away because of it."

Oh, crap. All he had to do was say something like that and it felt like a fire being lit inside her body, a rush of heat and awareness that she was unable to guard against.

"You've stayed away?"

"Come here," he said, and pulled her off the path to a nearby bench. They sat down. "I think we need to talk about this," he said.

"About . . ."

"About what happened at your place. About what hasn't happened since. Oaklee, I'm not in the market for

a relationship. And you're . . . well, you're too important
to me to indulge in a fling. So that left me with only one
option. Keep my distance."

"You wanted to . . . but you left so quickly that night.
And when we met at the Sugarbush . . . I said it would
be foolish to start anything. And you totally agreed. I
mean, you just walked away."

He sighed, ran his hand through his hair. "I was trying to respect your decision. Hell, I picked the Sugarbush so we'd have a neutral location and I wouldn't be
tempted. I was going to walk you home and didn't trust
myself to leave it at your front door, and you'd said we
needed to try to forget about that night on your sofa.
Damn, Oaklee. I had to get out or we would have done
something really stupid."

It took a lot of effort to keep her mouth from dropping open. He'd wanted to stay, then? Her hands itched
to touch him. That night they could have *flinged* all
over the place. She'd certainly wanted to. The worst part
of this whole situation was that her head was telling her
to be sensible and her libido was telling her to go for it
and see what happened.

"I'm not looking for anything serious either, Rory,"
she admitted. "I have major trust issues. So you don't
have to worry about me going and getting over-attached."

Rory was quiet for a minute, as if absorbing what
she'd said. Her cheeks were hot; this was not small talk
in any way, shape, or form. They were talking about mutual attraction. Sexual attraction.

Terms and conditions, if it came right down to it.
Maybe it was between the lines, and slightly cryptic, but
he'd basically just said he hadn't wanted to treat her

carelessly and she'd replied that she was open to the idea since she had no intention of falling in love.

None.

Maybe someday she'd be ready for it. Maybe someday she'd be able to trust someone as much as she'd trusted Jeff, but it wasn't going to be today.

"What are you saying? Are you saying you didn't mean what you said? About letting it go and forgetting about it? Because I keep feeling like I'm getting mixed signals from you and I don't have any idea what you want."

She thought very carefully before answering, and then simply said, "We're consenting adults, Rory."

"But you had a thing for me in high school. I know you did. I don't know if we can be casual about this."

"Because of Cam."

"No, not because of Cam." His eyes met hers, dropped to her lips, and moved back up again to capture her gaze. "Because of you. And me. And how it can get messy. I don't want to ruin a friendship because I . . . we . . . shit. This is just hormones. Or something."

She laughed a little, but it sounded breathy, full of anticipation and possibility. There was no denying that she'd had a thing for Rory years ago. Or that she still found him impossibly hot now, years later. Plus that kiss . . . there had been chemistry for sure, and the charged atmosphere between them now confirmed it was real. The big question was, how far were they both willing to go? And how much would they regret?

"Maybe it is just hormones. Maybe it's good we're talking about what happened. I was there, too, you know." She smiled at him, her lips a saucy little curve. "I know what was real."

He chuckled, low and sexy. "Clearly, chemistry is not the issue. We've got that."

She wanted to say they could have had it long ago, but didn't. The truth was, she'd given up on Rory ever noticing her once he graduated and went away to school. She'd gone into her junior year in high school a bit lost without him, and Jeff had arrived on the scene right after Christmas. They'd spent five years together before it all blew up.

She'd been young and naïve and innocent back then. She wasn't now. And if she and Rory embarked on some sort of affair, they'd be meeting as equals, and not as a love-struck little girl making big eyes at her crush. The idea was both exciting and terrifying.

"Basically," she said, putting on her all-business voice, "we have to decide if we're going to do this or not. If we want to." There was no question in her mind—she did. "Look, we both know the score going in. Neither of us wants anything serious. But we do seem to want each other." Something felt off when she said it, just a niggle of conscience that said she shouldn't take sex so lightly. That it was supposed to be meaningful on an emotional level, and not recreation. But where had that got her for the past two years? Celibate and . . . emotionally frozen, too. Utterly stuck in place when it came to men.

"Why does this feel like a negotiation?" He leaned back against the bench for a moment and closed his eyes. "Damn. I was just going to meet you for a walk, you know? Stop avoiding you so much. Talk about Buster. And we're discussing terms for hooking up. Either I'm crazy or we're both crazy."

She shook her head. "Maybe we are negotiating, Rory. But it's to protect each other because we care. Isn't it a good thing that we consider our friendship, too? Nothing wrong with a few ground rules."

"So we both agree we're not looking for any sort of commitment."

"Agreed."

He frowned. "Maybe we can each come up with one more? Too many conditions and . . ."

"And the spontaneity is gone?"

"Yeah."

"Okay. You go first. What's your one condition?"

He met her gaze once more. "We keep this between us. Private. My family's so nosy, and this town is small and gossipy. This is just between you and me."

"Done." While it felt a little like sneaking around, or that there was something to be ashamed of, being public would just open them up to awkward questions and rumors. She was fine with keeping things quiet.

"Yours?" he asked.

"There's no one else."

"I beg your pardon?"

She squared her shoulders. "If we're sleeping together, you're not sleeping with anyone else."

This time his mouth did drop open. "You think I'd do that?"

She blinked, but didn't avoid his gaze. "I just want to be clear. I know you play the field, Rory. I'm not judging you for it. I'm just asking that for as long as we're . . . whatever, you're not doing it with someone else."

"Not a problem. I'm a one-at-a-time kind of guy, Oaklee. Despite what you or anyone else might think."

He was offended. It added a layer of tension to the discussion, and Oaklee wondered if they could really go through with it. His annoyance was also strangely reassuring. As he'd said before, he was up-front about what he was capable of . . . and what he wasn't. Apparently he was capable of fidelity, which was good, because it was non-negotiable for her.

She wondered why he was so determined to stay single. And then she thought of Jeff and figured Rory had a right to his own secrets.

"When?" he asked quietly. "I mean . . ."

And then he started laughing. First a low, husky chuckle that built in his chest and rumbled up and out. His shoulders shook a little and he shook his head. "Oh my God, Oaklee. What are we doing?" His eyes twinkled at her. "We just talked about this like one of your damned business meetings."

"It kind of killed it for you, didn't it?" she asked softly, but she relaxed back against the bench.

"Yeah. I mean, this was what I was afraid of. Everything getting weird. Ever since you showed up at the clinic with Buster, it's just been different. You're different. Maybe I am. I go back and forth and change my mind ten times a day. Maybe we both have too much baggage to even consider this. Maybe we should just let it alone."

"Or maybe," she said gently, "we had to lay out some basic rules so that we each know where we stand about stuff. Maybe the trick now is to just step back and let whatever happen, happen. Let it unfold naturally. Without a plan."

His smile was so sweet she nearly melted. "You do

know me, right?" he asked. "I don't do anything without a plan."

"No life-by-the-seat-of-the-pants?"

"Never. I don't like surprises."

"Interesting. You know, I used to be a planner. And then I found that when my plans blew up, I had no idea what to do next. So I learned to roll with it. Work on the fly." She lowered her lids a little. "Live in the moment."

His tongue ran over his bottom lip. She wondered if he realized it.

"And see," he said quietly, "I like to know exactly where I stand, and where I'm going. Then I don't get blindsided."

"Right."

They were silent for a few moments. Dark had fallen now; she'd left Buster far longer than the single hour she'd promised. Foot traffic on the path had dwindled, and the cheers from the athletic field were silent. Instead there was a single call from a mourning dove, somewhere in the trees along the creek. The Kissing Bridge was an arced shadow in the distance.

"What if you were blindsided by something good? Wouldn't it be a shame to miss out on it because it wasn't in your plans?"

She stood and held out her hand. "Walk me home, Rory. And then we'll just see."

CHAPTER 9

She was surprised when he put his hand in hers and let her lead him off the bench. They walked along in the dark, an evening chill settling over Oaklee's shoulders, but Rory left his hand in hers. It was a sweet sensation, one that spoke of affection and gave their previous conversation a depth that she wasn't sure she was comfortable with.

This was Rory. *Rory*. The guy who'd watched over her in his senior year while her big brother was absent. Maybe he didn't think she knew, but she did. When she'd been at a party in her sophomore year, she'd had too much beer and had been hanging all over Michael Schultz and his big football arms. And Michael hadn't minded. They'd started necking in a corner, indulged in a little feeling up, and he'd gone off to get her another drink before they found an "empty room." He'd never come back. In the morning she'd been rather glad, because finding a bedroom with Michael would have been a huge mistake. It wasn't until her friend, Sherry, had told her about seeing Rory in Michael's face that she'd put two and two together.

And when Michael had started to bad-mouth her in the cafeteria, Rory had stood up and stared him down. She'd never had trouble after that. More than that, though, was how he'd cared for her after she'd run out of the cafeteria. He'd hugged her and held her in his arms and asked if she was okay.

She'd been more careful at parties, after that. And then the next year there'd been Jeff, and they'd been inseparable.

Now she and Rory were walking to her home, hand in hand, and despite her words to the contrary, she still had enough of that idealistic girl inside to realize that she was considering getting intimate with the man who'd once been her adolescent knight in shining armor.

"It's getting colder at night," Rory said, his arm warm against hers.

"No frost yet, though. Maybe the next full moon."

"Maybe."

"Rory . . ."

They stopped, near the end of the trail, about thirty feet from where it met the street leading to the golf course. Her house wasn't much farther, but she'd heard the yearning in her voice, and apparently he had, too. It was as natural as anything for him to tug on her hand, pull her close, and kiss her.

And oh, he knew how to kiss. Knew just how she liked it, soft and teasing and so damned romantic it hurt her heart. He kissed as if he paid attention to every sensation, every taste, nuance of her lips. He kissed as if he were giving instead of taking. And it made her knees weak.

"Mmm," she murmured, closing her eyes and savoring the taste of him on her lips. "Damn, Rory, you're good at that."

She could hear the smile in his voice. "So are you, Oaklee."

"Walk me the rest of the way?"

"Are you sure?"

She opened her eyes and saw his blue ones staring straight into hers. "I'm sure."

They didn't speak again until they reached her apartment. Barking punctuated their arrival as she put her key in the lock, and then Buster bounced up and down as they went inside. "I'll take him out," Rory offered quietly. "He's not going to settle until he goes."

"Okay."

He was only gone a few minutes. She filled Buster's bowl and then took out two glasses and a bottle of whiskey. She didn't drink it often, but she thought Rory was probably the type to appreciate a drink. When they came back in, Rory shivered with the chill and she held out the glass. "To put some fire in your belly," she offered.

They touched rims and she lifted her glass and sipped, while Rory drank half of his in one gulp.

He looked around the apartment. "It looks good in here," he commented. "Lived in, but good."

She took it as it was intended—a compliment. "Buster-proofing has made me a better housekeeper," she replied. Buster had gone over to his blanket again and plopped down. "If I leave stuff out, he's into it."

She didn't bother saying that Buster filled the lonely

spots in the apartment better than any clutter. The dog wouldn't be staying, so she couldn't allow herself to get too accustomed to it.

"So." He put the glass down on the counter. "Can I kiss you, Oaklee?"

Her throat tightened at the sweetness of the question. "I wish you would," she answered, finishing off her drink and putting her glass down, too.

He stepped forward and slid one arm around the hollow of her back, drawing her a little closer. Then, without any further preamble, he put his lips on hers.

Her whole body sighed with pleasure. His lips were soft, warm, sharp with whiskey and so very persuasive. She stepped backward until her hips hit the counter, then she twined her arms up and over his shoulder, melting into him. The kiss grew in intensity, with delicious nips and licks until every inch of her felt charged with a sexual current. Still, he hadn't touched her anywhere besides her back, where he held her close. She was full of want and need and it was all from simple kissing.

Except there was nothing simple about it. Her head clouded with everything about him; his taste, his scent, the feel of his body pressed so firmly against hers. The boy she'd wanted so fiercely and the man he'd become. She moved her arms away from his neck and instead found the hem of his sweatshirt and slid her hands beneath the fabric to touch the warm, smooth skin of his stomach and ribs.

"Mmm," he hummed into her mouth, and she moved her fingers over his ribs, back to his shoulder blades, around front again to slide up to his chest. He broke the kiss for a brief moment to pull the sweatshirt off, and she tried not to lose her mind as she saw him without his shirt. Where had all those muscles come from? He had very little chest hair, and she let her hands touch every inch of his chest and shoulders, her thumb flicking over one of his pebbled nipples.

"Your turn," he murmured, reaching for her hoodie. She didn't stop him, but welcomed his participation as he pulled the soft fleece over her head and she stood there in her pink lacy bra.

"God, Oaklee. Aren't you pretty."

Her cheeks heated. She kept expecting something a little more . . . base. Raunchy, even. And he kept saying these sweet little things that made her melty.

"Touch me, Rory." Her voice came out low and husky, but she couldn't help it. It had been so long since she'd felt this aroused. Over two years now. There'd been no one since Jeff. She hadn't really wanted there to be. And despite their assurances to keep things "casual," she knew part of the reason why she could go through with this now was because Rory would always make sure she was safe. It was who he was. Who he'd always been.

"You don't need to tell me twice," he replied, his voice equally low, rich with intent. He dropped her shirt on the floor and then cupped her breast in his hand as he kissed her again, this time trailing kisses over the crest of her cheeks, the corners of her eyes, her temple, down to her ear. Her scalp tingled with taut sensations as he pulled an earlobe into his mouth, her nipple hardened against his palm. He reached behind her and unhooked her bra.

They were skin to skin now, and it was a shockingly intimate feeling. The zipper of his jeans pressed against her sweatpants, and she shifted her hips a little, wondering how much she could get away with before things got absolutely crazy. Rory ground against her once, twice, then spanned her ribs with his hands and lifted her onto the counter. She barely had time to breathe before his mouth was on her breasts.

She briefly wondered if a person could die of pleasure.

Her head hung back so that her ponytail grazed the length of her spine, and she moaned as Rory took his time, thoroughly tasting and kissing. The sound, though, got Buster's attention, and he trotted over to the counter and started to whine at their feet.

Oaklee laughed, her head and shoulders rolling forward, breaking the moment. "Oh my God. We have an audience."

"Maybe we should move this somewhere else."

"He'll scratch on the door."

"Ignore him. I will, if you will." He slid his hand down between her legs. "I don't want to stop yet, Oaklee."

"Me, either."

He leaned in, pressed his mouth to her parted lips. His tongue danced with hers until she lost all coherent thought. Then he put his hands on her hips, slid her off the counter, and took her hand. "Bedroom, yes?"

"Oh, yes." And they left Buster behind. The last Oaklee saw of him, he was staring at the bedroom door with a confused expression just before they closed it.

The bedroom was dark, and Oaklee didn't bother turning on a light. There was enough pale light through the blinds from the streetlights for them to see each other in gray shadow. It added to the intimacy, the subtle mystery. She hooked her thumbs on the waistband of her sweats and pushed them down, stepping out of them. For a brief moment she wished she had on sexier underwear, instead of the pink cotton bikini panties she wore.

But Rory clearly didn't mind. "Oaklee," he said again, and a shiver rolled over her body.

This wasn't casual. Not anymore. Not standing in front of him nearly naked, knowing what was to come. She'd only ever had one lover in her life. Rory was going to make two.

It doesn't have to be a huge deal, she reminded herself, panic rising in her chest. Neither of them wanted commitment. They wanted to scratch an itch. Satisfy a burning need. It didn't have to be bigger than that if she didn't want it to be.

And she didn't. The whole idea was paralyzing.

He came to stand before her. "Second thoughts?" he asked softly, running a hand over her shoulder.

"Maybe? It's . . . well, hell, Rory." She met his gaze. "This is you, you know?"

"I know. We can stop anytime."

"Maybe kiss me again?" She wasn't ready to let him walk away. She wanted this. So, so badly.

He cupped her face in his hands and kissed her, long and thorough. Kissed her until her head was clouded, until all her thoughts disintegrated and there was only him and the sensations of her body. He moved his hand to her breast, and she didn't stop him. Slid his hand lower, over her bottom . . . she didn't stop him. And when he dipped his hand inside the front of her underwear, she pressed herself into him, desperate for his touch.

"Okay," he murmured against her lips. "Okay."

He found her core with his fingers and she wasn't sure

how long she could remain upright. Awkward and uncaring about being graceful, they made their way to the bed and she lay down on top of the fluffy comforter. She could see Rory's eyes blazing at her in the semi-darkness, and she lifted her hips. He slid her underwear off and joined her on the bed, still wearing his jeans.

He touched her everywhere, lighting her skin on fire, creating a desperate need that fought for release. Hands and mouth worked together to bring her to a fiery peak, until the sensations overwhelmed and she pulsed against him, crying out in the darkness. And still he was beside her, and she was acutely aware that while she'd been thoroughly satisfied, he had not.

"Rory," she whispered, feeling awe and relief and an amazing bonelessness from the force of her orgasm. "You haven't . . . you . . ."

"Shh," he said, shifting to lie beside her, resting on one elbow. "Not tonight."

"But . . ."

"But you're not ready for that. We said we'd see what happens. Tonight, this happened."

She wanted him. She did. But he was right, too. There'd been a moment when she'd hesitated, and he'd seen it. And just as she'd thought earlier, Rory had taken care of her . . . first. Before himself.

He smoothed a piece of hair off her face.

"I just . . . feel like it was very one-sided," she admitted, looking up at him.

A smile curved his lips, and his dimple flashed. "Oh, honey. If you think I didn't enjoy myself, think again."

Her cheeks heated, and she was increasingly aware that she was lying there naked. Once again, she was struck by the strange reality that she was naked with Rory Gallagher. A man she'd known since he'd been a boy. There was a certain gravity to the situation because of it.

He leaned over and kissed her, softly, gently, lovingly. She relaxed into the mattress and enjoyed the sensation. She felt . . . cherished. As if she were the only woman in the world. God, if this was how Rory was with the ladies, no wonder he was so successful. They hadn't even had sex and she was convinced he was pretty damned amazing.

The thought succeeded in cooling her jets just a bit. Rory, by his own admission, had had lots of practice. Maybe he made every woman he was with feel this special. And suddenly she doubted whether she was really that special at all.

"You okay?" he asked, pulling back a bit.

"Just cold," she replied.

He reached down for a blanket at the bottom of the bed, then hesitated. "Oaklee, have you been leaving your bedroom door open during the day? There's Buster hair on the corner of the bed."

She crossed her arms over her chest, feeling suddenly exposed now that the heat of the moment had cooled. "No. He . . . well, he sleeps with me at night."

"Oaklee."

There was chastisement in his tone, but she didn't care. "I don't like sleeping alone, okay? And neither does he. I lift him up. There's no jumping up and down. If he's not up here he whines and paces, so we both sleep better if he has his corner."

Rory came back up and sat on the edge of the bed. "You love him."

"I care for him. That's it. I'm not interested in a long-term commitment, Rory. Even with a dog." Maybe even particularly with a dog. What would happen if she really fell for the mutt? Clearly his life span was much shorter than hers. She'd lose him at some point. Why put herself through that?

"Right." He nodded, as if he understood. But he didn't. She knew he didn't. Suddenly they seemed very far apart, when only minutes earlier they'd been extremely close. Extremely.

"I should probably go," he said quietly. "I have an early day tomorrow, and so do you."

She nodded. "I do." And yet she wasn't comfortable with how things were ending tonight. It didn't do justice to what had happened between them. She sat up a bit and curved a hand around the side of his neck. "Rory, I'm glad we went for a walk, and talked, and that we . . . well, I don't regret this. It was amazing." She smiled a little. "For me."

His posture relaxed a bit. "For me, too, honey. I don't want things to get weird . . ."

"They won't. One day at a time, that's all. And I'll see you in a few days to get Buster's cast off."

"What time's your appointment?"

"Four-thirty. Right after work."

He nodded. "Let's do something afterward."

"Will you make me tacos?"

He chuckled. "If you want."

"I want. I'll bring dessert."

The way she was feeling right now, she figured she knew exactly what would be for dessert. She would try not to think of Rory's "experience." Especially considering she was relatively inexperienced when it came to partners. How could she be when she'd only had one? She knew she was an anomaly by today's standards.

"You got that weird look again just now," Rory observed. "Are you sure you're okay?"

"I'm sure," she said, taking a deep, restorative breath and smiling. "Positive. Hang on. I'll put on a robe and see you out."

He shook his head. "No, it's okay. Stay right there, on the bed. That's how I want to remember you tonight."

Oh, gracious.

She reclined against the pillows as he stood. He dropped a brief kiss on her lips and then went to the bedroom door, but before he opened it he turned and looked back at her, as if memorizing every square inch of her body.

"Damn, Oaklee. Just damn."

And with a flash of his sexy smile, he was gone.

CHAPTER 10

For two nights now, Rory dreamed of her.

In his dreams there was no hesitation. No moment where she got that vulnerable, scared look on her face. In both dreams, she'd come to him willingly. She'd sometimes taken the lead, and their pleasure had been mutual and complete.

And each morning he'd awakened with a rock-hard erection. She wasn't even here and she was causing havoc in his life.

He rolled to his side and sighed. Maybe it would have been better if they'd just gone for it, instead of leaving him feeling unfulfilled. She'd certainly become pliant enough in his arms. Beneath his mouth. God, she'd been sweet, like honey on a warm biscuit. It wouldn't have taken much convincing and he would have been inside her, where he so desperately had wanted to be.

And yet he'd held back, because she was Oaklee. Because he cared. And so he'd put his own pleasure aside and saw to hers instead. And now all he could think about was the sight and sound of her falling apart in his arms.

Wouldn't Aiden have a field day with this? This was where honesty led, and it was both wonderful and horrible.

Today she was bringing Buster in. And he was making her tacos and they were having a date. Or hanging out. Or . . .

He rolled out of bed and headed for a cold shower. There was no way he could go through the day in this state.

Work was going to be busy, as it was Rory's surgery day. They'd booked a few spays and neuters, and then he removed a tumor from a cat's abdomen—that prognosis wasn't a good one and he hated telling the owners—followed by a lipoma removal from a dog's armpit and a dentistry while the dog was anesthetized. By the time four o'clock rolled around, he needed a brain break. He grabbed himself a soda from the small fridge and a granola bar from a box in the cupboard.

"Rory? Oaklee's here with Buster. I put them in room two after we did the X-ray."

"So early?" He checked his watch. It was four-fifteen. He had Buster and two quick appointments before he could clock out for the day, as well as checking on his surgical patients again.

"He's turned into a real handsome dog, don't you think?" Christy smiled at him. "And he adores her. He doesn't take his eyes off her. It's so cute."

I know the feeling, Rory thought, draining his soda and throwing the granola bar wrapper in the garbage.

He gave his arms and shoulders a quick shake to loosen some of the tension of the day and then headed into the exam room.

It was the first time he'd seen her since he'd left her naked on her bed. When he walked into the room their eyes met instantly, and he saw a blush rise to her cheeks. At the same time, heat rushed through his body. There was nothing else to do but acknowledge it, he figured. He went to her and gave her a brief kiss, then pulled back and smiled.

"I wasn't expecting that," she said, her blush deepening.

"I didn't expect to do it, either," he admitted. "But I saw you there, and after the other night . . . it's weird. Not a bad weird. I just don't want to pretend that nothing happened."

"Me, either." She smiled back at him. "Okay. Ice broken."

"Right. So let's have a closer look at Buster. Hey, boy."

He lifted the dog up onto the exam table, and used his hands to reassure the dog as he felt all over the much healthier body. "Everything else has healed nicely," he said, "though I kind of knew that already." He grabbed the film from today's X-ray and put it on the screen, flipping on the backlight. "Hey, this looks like it's healed well. Good job, buddy." He gave Buster a pat.

"So the cast can come off?"

"Yep. He'll favor it for a few days. It'll feel strange without the cast, and his leg will be a bit weak, but within a week I bet he'll be running around good as new."

She smiled brightly. "Oh, I'm glad. Yay, Buster!" She

rubbed the dog's head, and he responded with a happy pant.

Whether she acknowledged it or not, he knew she cared for Buster a lot. Otherwise she never would have let him sleep on her bed. And Rory followed her now on Twitter and Facebook. She'd posted occasionally about looking for a home for him, but she certainly hadn't been aggressive about it.

"Do you mind waiting in the waiting room while we take off the cast? One of the staff will give me a hand, and there's not a lot of room in here." Plus he didn't need the distraction.

"Oh. Oh, sure. I can do that."

"I'll bring him back out when we're done."

"Okay."

He met her gaze. "Do you want to hang around until I finish for the day? I have a few minor appointments that got jammed in at the last minute. We can take Buster upstairs and he can visit, if you want. Or you can run him home and come back. It's up to you. Right now I'm not caring for anyone in my apartment. It's a kitty-free zone."

"I'll think about it," she said. Her gaze turned troubled. "This isn't going to hurt him, is it?"

Oh, she was way more of a softie than she knew. "No, Oaklee, it won't. But he has to be still and it can be a bit stressful. It doesn't take long, particularly when we can be really efficient about it."

"Right. You don't need me in the room." She smiled. "I'll wait out front. Hang in there, buddy."

To his surprise, she leaned over and kissed Buster's head. His tail thumped against the stainless steel table.

It was only minutes and it was all done. The leg looked good, though thin, and Rory lifted him off the table and walked him out to the waiting room. Buster hobbled along, but his hobbles got faster as he saw Oaklee waiting for him. It seemed the affection was mutual.

"Aw, look at you!" She got up from her chair and came forward, kneeling in front of Buster. He wiggled and walked right into her embrace, giving her face a lick. "Gross, Buster. Blech."

But she didn't look upset. Rory's heart warmed. This was a woman with a professed noninterest in pets. Now look at her. He'd expected this to happen, or at least hoped. In his opinion, everyone's life could be a bit richer with a pet. Or as a lot of his clients called them, "furbabies."

"Almost as good as new," Rory said. "And I bet he'd like a walk in the grass, if you get my drift. Nerves."

"Oh. Sure." She smiled brilliantly. "Thank you, Rory. I'll take him out for a short walk, and then maybe we'll come back?" She lowered her voice. "I think I'll keep him with me. I don't want to leave him alone tonight, after having his cast off. I'm afraid he'll jump and hurt it again or something."

"That's fine. I shouldn't be more than thirty minutes."

"Perfect."

He was actually closer to forty-five minutes by the time he finished with clients and checked on his patients, and he found Oaklee and Buster sitting outside. Oaklee was sitting on the concrete curb, and Buster was beside her, nudging her hand every now and again for a pat. He could hear her talking, her voice low, and he smiled.

She'd mentioned once that she didn't have a lot of friends. That she was lonely. Dogs made great confidantes.

"Hey, you two. How's he making out?"

She looked up and smiled at him. "Good. He's limping a bit, but nothing major, I don't think." She held a daisy in her hand. "We picked a flower. Pretty exciting times out here." And then she lifted her arm and offered the daisy to him. "Here. For you."

No woman had ever given him a flower before. A lot of guys he knew would have laughed at such a gesture, but Rory was touched. He took it between his fingers.

"There are outside stairs to the apartment. Let's take those instead of going through the clinic."

"Okay. What about Buster and the steps?"

"I'll carry him," Rory said.

They walked around back, past the cars of the last of Victoria's clients, and the other vehicles to the side that belonged to the support staff. "How come you're finished and no one else is?" Oaklee asked.

"Because I started at seven-thirty this morning, doing surgeries. The staff that opened with me left at three-thirty. We close at six, so Victoria started taking her appointments at nine."

"Oh."

They reached the steps and Rory squatted down, gathered Buster in his arms, and lifted him up. He'd definitely put on weight since that first night. "Wow, dude. You're feeling much more solid."

At the top of the steps he put Buster down on the landing and reached inside his pocket for a set of keys. He led Buster inside and kept him on the leash. A few minutes to get over the excitement of a new place was usually a good idea.

"You were so not kidding when you said you were a neat freak. Holy crapsticks, Rory. I think underneath that mop of hair you're a balding guy with an earring."

"Huh?" He wrinkled his brow.

She laughed. "Mr. Clean. You know."

Rory rolled his eyes. "Now you understand the culture shock when I went into your apartment."

"Ouch. I know I'm a slob."

"It was a lot different the last time I was there." He'd almost said "better," but he didn't want to be insulting. "Even the bedroom was a lot tidier."

She reached for Buster's leash, and met his gaze. "So know what? I discovered that the clutter made the place seem more . . . I don't know, lived in. Not so lonely. With Buster, I have to keep things out of his circle of destruction. And, well, he kind of fills up the empty spaces where I used to keep 'stuff.' "

"I knew he'd be good for you."

"Don't gloat. I'm fine on my own, too. Been managing for quite some time. Now my hovel is just a little tidier."

"Well, come on in and have a seat. Do you want something to drink? I have beer, or a few sodas in the fridge."

"Water's fine. Do you want me to help with anything?"

He shook his head. "You're my guest, remember? Besides, my tacos are a well-kept secret. Can't have my special ingredients being leaked to the public."

She laughed a little. "Next thing you know, Willow'll be serving them at the café."

"I doubt it. They're not exactly health food."

"My favorite kind."

He grinned in appreciation and put some ice in a glass for her water. "Do you want to watch TV or something?"

"Why don't we just put on some music? All that's on right now is the news, and believe me, I got my fill reading my feeds today."

Right. Because like a lot of people, Oaklee relied on the Internet for her daily information. He couldn't say anything. He watched sports and a few shows, but did his fair share of surfing, as well. Hell, even his veterinary magazines and newsletters came via e-mail.

He put on his music app and ran it through a Bluetooth speaker, filling the kitchen with the sounds of a random playlist of current hits. Buster found the big dog bed that Rory kept upstairs for "guests," and plopped down with a contented sigh. Rory took out the ground beef and put it in a fry pan, and then turned and saw Oaklee watching him with a smile on her face.

"What?"

"You," she said softly. "In your own environment. It's kind of weird and neat at the same time."

"I'm afraid to ask what that means."

"I'll tell you sometime. Not right now. I'm still figuring it out."

He raised an eyebrow and reached for a wooden spoon. "Believe me, I am not hard to figure out."

She got up from the table and went to his side. "Oh, I think you're more difficult than you want people to believe. You want people to see the surface Rory. That way they don't have a clue what's going on underneath."

She'd hit so close to home that he stopped stirring. Was he really that transparent? Did other people see through that, too? Or only the ones that he let get a bit close? Like Aiden. Like his mom, who rarely said anything that could be construed as prying, but had this way of looking at him as if she knew what was going on in his mind.

Oaklee backed away then, though, and didn't push, which confused him a bit. Instead she went for a walk around the apartment. He added spices to the meat as she ventured into the living room, pausing to examine the books on his bookcase, the DVDs and video games lined up beneath them. He was aware of her moving down the hall and sticking her head in the bathroom, then standing in the doorway of his bedroom. His body heated. His bed was in there. A nice, comfortable, queen-sized bed that she would look amazing on, or in, or . . . yeah. Whatever happened now was up to her. She had to decide. There was no way on earth he was going to pressure her into the next step.

She came back to the kitchen, placed her hand between his shoulder blades. It was a simple touch, but it was intimate in its deliberateness. He turned down the burner to let the mixture simmer, and turned to face her. He leaned back against the kitchen counter and looped his hands around the small of her back, while she put hers around his neck so they stood in a loose embrace.

"Hi," she said softly, and he smiled.

"Hi."

"That smells good."

"Thank you."

They kept smiling at each other. It was goofy and felt

really, really good. She still wore a pair of simple heels, and the added height put her nearly at eye-level with him. For a long moment, they just stared into each other's eyes. This was different than the girls he'd dated since Ginelle. He was more comfortable. It was probably because he and Oaklee were friends, first.

"Your apartment is very Rory the Veterinarian."

"Thanks?" He wasn't sure if it was a compliment or not.

"It's efficient. Nice. Outwardly pleasing. There's also not much of you in it."

He dropped his hands. "I don't know what you mean."

"I mean Rory the man, and what's important to him. You've got one family picture from Aiden's wedding in the summer, and it's sitting on a shelf in the living room. But no other pictures. No decorations that reflect your taste or even your favorite colors. All your walls are white."

Her observation made him uncomfortable. Granted, the walls were a plain eggshell color and he really wasn't much for picking out things to hang on them. As far as taste, well, he was a bachelor in his mid-twenties. His taste generally ran to the necessities.

"What, you want to pretty up my apartment like you fancied up the clinic website?"

She frowned at him and shook her head. "No. That would just be more Rory the Vet. I'm more curious about Rory the man."

He slipped away from her touch and her piercing gaze and busied himself getting items out of the fridge. "There's not much to know about him. What you see is what you get."

She laughed. "I get you fighting it, Rory. I do the same thing. Doesn't stop me from being curious."

He put salsa and sour cream on the counter. Grabbed a tomato from the crisper and a block of cheese. "I'm a pretty private guy, Oaklee."

"Okay."

She went to the fridge and refilled her water glass from the dispenser, then returned to his side. "So do you want me to chop something or what?"

"That's it? No prying?"

"No prying." She looked up at him. "I'm your friend, Rory. Before any of the other stuff. I know you had my back at times when we were kids, even when I was probably embarrassing myself by my awkward and obvious attempts at flirting." She flashed a grin at him, and he couldn't help but smile back. It was true. Teenage girls were rarely subtle. And yes, at times he'd felt pretty awkward about it, considering his relationship with Cam, and the age difference at the time. There was no question he'd seen her as a little kid. Mostly.

But yeah, there'd always been an element of friendship. Of caring about each other.

"You used to put on fresh lip gloss every time I showed up at your house," he said, handing her a cutting board and a knife for the tomato.

"I know. Sad, really." She laughed. "There was this one time that I bought my first padded push-up bra. I didn't have a lot to push up, but the bra made me look like I did. I couldn't wait for you to come over so I could put it on and get you to notice my boobs."

He nearly dropped the box of taco shells. "Oh my God. For real?"

She laughed. "Yes. And do you know what Cam said?"

"I haven't a clue."

"You hadn't shown up yet, and I came out of my room, and he asked me if I had tube socks shoved in my bra and to go change before Mom saw me in that ridiculous thing."

Rory laughed. It sounded exactly like Cam, right down to the inflection.

"I was so humiliated that I didn't even come out of my room when you came over."

He felt bad for the young girl version of Oaklee, so he decided to let her off the hook just a little. "Well, I'll tell you a little secret," he said, taking a cheese grater out of a drawer. "I can't say if it was the push-up bra or not, but one time in your sophomore year, when Cam was home? He caught me staring at your chest. And boy, did he give me hell for it."

She stopped chopping. "Wait. You noticed?"

He shrugged. "Oaklee, you were a cute kid. And by the time puberty really kicked in . . . yeah, hell, I noticed. So did Cam. And since he wasn't here, he made me promise to look out for you while he was gone. He made me swear by our friendship."

"My brother?" She put the knife down now.

"Yeah, your brother. He loves you a lot."

"I never knew that."

"You were never supposed to. And then I went off to school, and you started dating that Jeff guy, who seemed like a decent shit."

"He was. For the most part."

He continued grating the cheese, noticing that she didn't elaborate, either. He knew she and Jeff had gone to the same school and stayed together right up until her senior year. Clearly the breakup had left scars, and if he didn't want her to pry, he wouldn't, either.

But he did wonder. He wondered about the guy who'd hurt her so badly that she really hadn't dated since coming back to Darling. He thought about what Aiden had said about her being asked out and turning the guys down flat.

And he wondered why, after all this time, he'd been the one to break through that barrier, even just a little. It was impossible to think that he was the only one since college, though. He suspected she'd just been very discreet. Unlike him . . .

"Is this enough?" she asked, showing him the pile of diced tomato.

"Perfect. Let me heat up the shells and then we'll be ready."

Buster woke up when he heard the clattering of plates and cutlery, so Oaklee finished setting the table while Rory went to find Buster some supper. The conversation while cooking had been interesting. She'd never realized that Rory had even noticed her in that way in high school. Or that Cam had made him promise such a thing. She'd always known he'd looked out for her, but this was different.

She wasn't sure how she felt about having a protector. On one hand, it made her feel cherished and secure. On the other, she could take care of herself. Always had.

Jeff's abandonment had been the worst thing to ever happen to her, and look how she'd got through that? All on her own.

And yet knowing that Rory had always been there, ready to step in if needed, was a nice feeling. Like she mattered to someone. And perhaps that was what had been missing for a long, long time. The feeling like she really mattered.

"Are you ready?" Rory asked.

"Can't wait," she responded, turning in her chair.

He brought a platter of tacos to the table, along with a roll of paper towels to serve as napkins. "It's going to get messy," he advised, putting the plate down on the table. "And I don't have real napkins."

She laughed. "It's perfect." Each taco was loaded with beef, lettuce, tomato, cheese, salsa, and a dollop of sour cream. She carefully chose one from the platter and held it over her plate. "Cheers," she said, and took a first crunchy bite.

He was right. He did make good ones. It had to be the spices in the meat, but the flavor exploded in her mouth.

"Okay?" he asked.

"Delicious."

And messy. Clearly they weren't out to impress each other, because shells crumbled and bits and pieces of taco fell onto plates or down chins and there was definitely no elegant way to eat them. Rory drank water and then grabbed a beer from the fridge and added pickled jalapeños to his second taco. She stayed away from the hot peppers.

They ate until the platter was empty. "Oh gosh,"

Oaklee said, leaning back and patting her belly. "I am really going to pay for that later."

"I take it dessert is out, then?"

"I did bring some." She pointed at the tote bag by the door. "Fresh doughnuts."

"And you left them in the bag? With Buster around?"

"It's zipped."

"You know what he can do to a bag. I heard all about it the first day you had him."

She frowned. "True enough. Probably not smart to leave them there. Maybe we can eat them a bit later, though? I really am stuffed."

"Sure."

She went to the door and dug the bag of doughnuts out of the tote, then took them to the kitchen. "Here," she said, holding them out. "Chocolate ones covered in toasted coconut."

"A woman after my own heart."

He took the bag and put them up in a cupboard, because, he said, that way Buster couldn't sneak them off the counter. He turned to her. "So. What would you like to do now?"

She wiggled her eyebrows. There was nothing else she could think of doing except making light of things. If she didn't, she'd get caught up in memories of the other night. The thought of taking it a step further scared her to death.

He laughed. "How about a movie? We can see what's on or put in a DVD."

"That sounds okay. It's still early."

She chose a comedy from his stack and they sat together on the sofa. Buster came in and curled up on the floor by their feet. Halfway through, Rory disappeared to the kitchen and came back with two doughnuts, the bottoms wrapped in another piece of paper towel to catch the coconut crumbs. As the movie progressed, Oaklee found herself with her feet on the end of the sofa and her back resting against Rory's shoulder. Good heavens. They really were snuggled up watching a movie together. Like a couple.

A ripple of unease slipped up her spine. This was comfortable. Too comfortable. She could get to like this a little too much, and this wasn't what they'd talked about the other night on the Green. That conversation had been about wants and needs. Not this. Not . . . normalcy.

It was far easier to think about sex with Rory than this sort of intimacy. This was more dangerous by far. A cuddly Rory, laughing at some dumb humor, was more threatening to her status quo than even the sexy, oh-so-competent man in her bedroom just two days ago.

"You okay?" he asked, and she felt his head move close to hers as he tried to look into her face.

"I'm fine. Just thinking. And a bit tired."

"You got tense all of a sudden. Here." He shifted a bit more, and used his right hand to cup the back of her neck. His fingers massaged the muscles there, the touch warm and firm. "How's that?"

It was heavenly. And Rory was just a little too perfect.

"You don't have to," she said, shrugging her shoulders a little. "I'm just tired. I should probably go when the movie's over."

He reached down for the remote and hit the pause button. "What's wrong?"

"Nothing." She pasted on a smile. "Truly. I think the long hours have just caught up with me. I got all warm and comfortable and . . ."

"And what?"

She wished he wouldn't push. She sat up, out of his embrace, and turned on the sofa so her feet were flat on the floor. "Okay, we talked about being honest the other night, so the truth is, this feels a bit too much like a 'couple' thing, and I wasn't prepared for that."

"And it freaks you out."

"Doesn't it freak you out?"

"What do you want, Oaklee? Would you rather I pinned you up against the door to my bedroom and tore off your clothes? Maybe we could roll around on my bed for a while and go all the way. And then you could get up, put on your clothes, and go home like it wasn't something really important."

Her mouth dropped open. "I can't believe you just said that."

He ran both hands through his hair and heaved a sigh. "Me, either. But we've both been thinking about it, right?" He looked over at her, his brows pulled together, a look of consternation marring his face. "Look, I know you were afraid before. I saw it on your face, and that was why I held back from making love to you. But just now . . . it hit me. You're more afraid of snuggling on a sofa than you are of dealing with this attraction thing we've got going. So if that's what you'd rather do, I'm game."

There was a challenge in his voice she didn't expect. And he'd nailed her reasoning so perfectly that tears sprang into her eyes. "Don't make it sound like that. You make it seem like I don't even care about you. That's not true."

He let out a huge sigh, and silence fell between them for a few moments. "I'm sorry. I'm frustrated, too. Maybe this was all just a huge mistake."

And the fact that he was voicing the option of backing away completely scared her. Everything scared her right now. Being with him, being without him, her own sudden feelings . . . not a damned thing made sense.

"This was supposed to be a fling," she declared.

"I know."

"It's not working very well."

"I know that, too." He sighed heavily. "I underestimated the difficulty in being casual about a physical relationship when it's with someone I actually know and care about."

"It's difficult to separate the two. I know. I've been having the same problem. I can't act like it doesn't really, well, mean anything."

"Which is why I made the comment about the bedroom. I'm sorry about that, Oaklee. It was uncalled for."

She turned to face him, nerves churning in her stomach. "If I thought it would be that simple, I'd tell you to try it and see where it led. But it's not just me. It's not simple for you, either, is it?"

He shook his head.

Oh, they were both in so much trouble. And part of her wanted to just leave it alone and move on. But another part—the part that had known him for the better part of a decade—wanted to reach out to him.

"Do you want to tell me why?"

"Why what?"

"Why you're so afraid? Why you never go on more than a handful of dates with any one woman, generally all very public, never with any emotional attachment? How many have you had over for tacos?"

Troubled eyes met hers. "None."

Which already told her she was special. She didn't want to be special, so why did the knowledge somehow make her feel warm inside? Could she be any more confused?

She never really wanted to get too personal with anyone, but this was Rory, and right now, she couldn't walk away. Part of her wanted to. It was like muscle memory, trained to recognize a certain stimulus or situation. Only this muscle was her heart, and it remembered what it was like to give, and invest, and be burned so badly it felt as if it might never recover.

She'd loved Jeff. Heart and soul. Despite their differences, despite the signs that they were growing apart rather than together. And right now her heart's memory was telling her to stay uninvolved. Not to put it in that precarious position of caring too much again.

But she couldn't walk out on Rory. Because she knew if the chips were down, he wouldn't walk out on her. That counted for something.

She touched his knee. "Maybe it's time for you to talk to me," she suggested. "Or someone. It has to do with the woman in college, right? The one you never talk about but everyone knows exists?"

His deep blue gaze touched hers. "Of course it does. And the only person I've talked to is Aiden."

"Surely your family—"

"Just Aiden."

"Oh." She was surprised at that. The Gallagher clan always seemed so close.

"I didn't want their pity. And I sure as hell didn't want to talk about it. I still don't."

Whoever this woman was, it was clear he wasn't over her. Oaklee was in no position to judge. Or to push. "Then don't," she replied, rubbing his knee. "If it hurts too much, don't. But if you need to get it off your chest, you can do that, too." She hesitated, wondering how much she could share. How honest she could be with him. "Rory, maybe we need to leave the physical side of things alone. And the cozy couple thing . . . that's led us to this kind of strange moment. Maybe that's not right, either. Maybe what we need to be is friends. I think, for both of us, that we can maybe trust friends when we can't trust . . ."

She nearly said "our hearts." Instead she finished, ". . . something deeper."

His gaze delved into hers. "I'm not sure you and I will ever be just friends."

"Then maybe Buster and I should go."

She didn't want to, though, and that surprised her. Normally she avoided heavy conversations, deep feelings, anything that spoke of conflict. It was so much easier to keep to the surface of emotion by smiling from the wrists down, writing an upbeat post or keeping life limited to 140 characters. Always being sunny and positive, always focusing on the next exciting thing was like a drug hit. It was easy and it felt good.

But it did mean that she never really had to deal with anything heavier than "Is it going to rain on our town event on Saturday."

That she wanted to stay, that she wanted to be a friend to him right now, said something important. She wasn't sure exactly what, but she felt as if it marked a change in something.

He was frowning at her. "I don't even know where to begin," he said.

"What was her name?" she asked gently.

"Ginelle," he answered, and he sat back against the sofa. "You want to know why I don't get my heart involved anymore? It's because Ginelle took it and ground it to dust under her heel, and then walked away."

Holy shit. Oaklee swallowed and tried to keep her expression neutral, but that was a pretty blunt and awful statement to make. "Clearly she broke your heart."

"Yep." At his declaration, his face hardened. The expression reminded her of when kids got called out for doing something wrong and they adopted a defiant facial armor rather than show how the censure affected them. Rory, for all his devil-may-care smiles and outwardly easygoing ways, was stubborn. And hurt.

"And you really loved her."

His gaze met hers. It was diamond-hard and so, so unrelenting. "I did. With everything I had. I would have given her everything." His lips curved in a cold smile. "I came this close to offering it to her." He lifted his hand and put his fingers close together. "But before I could, she ended it."

"Why?"

"What?"

"Why did she end it? What did she say?"

"That she didn't really love me. And if she was going to spend her life with someone, it needed to be someone she truly loved."

Oh, God, he had to have been gutted. "How long had you been together?"

"Two years."

"And you were going to propose?"

"I still have the ring. I didn't have the heart to take it back. And now . . . well, it's a reminder. A cautionary thing if I ever find myself being a fool again. Much easier to keep it casual and light. No commitments. No hearts."

"Except this got messy." She pointed between the two of them.

"Yeah." His facial muscles relaxed a bit. "Because I know you. And I care about you. And right now we're dealing with this physical thing and it's making it all muddled and difficult."

"We were fooling ourselves with those rules, weren't we?" she asked.

"I think so." He leaned his head back against the sofa and closed his eyes. "If I'm being honest, I think it was a way to justify what we wanted to do. To convince ourselves we could just . . . not be emotionally involved. But I can't, Oaklee." His eyes opened and he turned his head, looking at her. "I can't with you. We go back too far. I like you too much."

It was odd how she could feel relieved and deflated all at once. "Maybe it's good we didn't sleep together, then," she said quietly. *Sleeping together* felt a bit like arguing semantics right now, though. They'd come close. And she'd let herself be very, very vulnerable with him, both emotionally and sexually.

"I trust you," he said, his voice low and soft. "I can't say that about very many people, you know?" He chuckled a bit. "I talked to Aiden about this a while back. He told me to try a few things. I have to say, the first two solutions failed. His third was honesty. I guess that's where we are right now."

"I trust you, too," she replied. "And that in itself is a rarity."

"So where does that leave us?"

"Friends?" It sounded so cliché. So . . . predictable. But maybe that's what they were supposed to be in the end.

"Friends," he echoed. "Sounds boring."

What it sounded like to her was safe. There was a lot to be said for safe. "You know, maybe this is just the right time for us to be grown-up friends. On our own, without thinking of you as Cam's best friend or me as the little sister. Just adults, who live in the same town, who like each other." If he was into honesty tonight, she'd add a little to the mix. "Truthfully, Rory, I don't have many friends that I really trust. I could probably use one."

Other than Emily, Buster was really the best friend she'd had in years. And that was saying something. None of her college friends had stayed in touch. They'd all gone on to their own shiny lives. By shutting herself off from real relationships, she'd left herself very alone.

Going to bridal showers and collecting wedding invitations, but nothing with any real meaning.

"It might be for the best."

"You do make great tacos." She tried lightening the mood, offering a smile.

"I'm sorry, Oaklee. I didn't intend for the evening to be like this."

"Me, either. But this is good." She winked. "Maybe not as good as . . . well, you know. But smarter. I should probably take Buster and head home."

"Probably."

She got up from the sofa and called the dog, waking him from his sleep. Rory followed her as she collected her tote bag, and hooked Buster to his leash. Rory slid on a pair of shoes. "I'll carry him downstairs for you."

"Thanks."

Rory carried Buster down the stairs, then set him down and held the leash as they walked slowly to her car. When they got to her car, he helped Buster into the back, and then shut the door. "Drive carefully on the way home," he said softly.

"I will. Thank you for everything you've done for him."

"It's my job."

"It's more than a job for you. It's who you are." She smiled up at him. "Thanks for dinner."

"Thanks for doughnuts."

She opened the driver's side door. "Is this going to be awkward, Rory?"

"It doesn't have to be." He reached out and rested his hand on the doorframe. "Maybe we can go for a walk again. As friends. You can bring Buster." He thought for a moment. "The school Fall Frolic is coming up. Ethan's made all of us promise to go. You could bring Buster."

"I'd probably go on behalf of the town anyway," she said. "That might be nice."

"All right, then."

She got in the car and he shut the door. "See you later, Oaklee."

"You, too, Rory."

She drove away from the clinic, feeling incredibly off balance. Nothing had gone right tonight. As she got closer to her apartment, she realized it was because neither she nor Rory knew what they wanted. All they knew was that it involved each other.

Once at home, she helped Buster out of the car, took him to do his business, and led him inside.

"Well, buddy, it's just you and me," she said, unhooking the leash and giving him a pat. "At least there's nothing confusing with us. We're pretty simple, huh." She knelt down on the floor and gave his head a brisk rub. In response, he nudged up against her shoulder and wiggled happily, nearly knocking her over.

She'd fought caring for Buster at all and had only agreed out of obligation. Now she had to confess that she was dreading the day that he found his forever home.

"Do you like it here? Huh, buddy?" She ran her hand down his smooth back. "Tell you what. I'm gonna give it one more shot. One more post looking for someone to adopt you. And if no one answers it, it'll be a sign. You'll stay with me. How does that sound?"

His tail thumped against the floor.

She grabbed her phone and clicked away with her thumbs.

@OakleeC_Darling: This handsome guy is 100% healthy
and ready to adopt. Look at that face! Contact Darling Vet
Clinic.

She tagged the hospital and also the animal shelter,
and added a new pic of Buster. Then she got ready for
bed and patted her leg, getting Buster to follow. She
helped him up onto the bed and watched as he circled
on his blanket and flopped down, then waited for her.

She got beneath the covers and Buster left his blanket and crept up the covers and snuggled next to her.

And she just put her hand on his coat and closed her
eyes.

CHAPTER 11

Oaklee and Emily took Oaklee's car to Burlington for their sushi date. Oaklee was relieved to get out of town for a while, and when they hit the highway a sense of freedom flooded her. "I'm glad we're finally getting together," Oaklee said, looking over at Emily. "I feel like it's been forever since we caught up."

Emily nodded, her dark ponytail bobbing, and smiled. "Me, too! The café's been crazy. And Willow's offered me a manager position. I'm sorry I've been MIA. We've actually just started interviewing new staff."

"You're happy with the promotion?" Oaklee couldn't imagine working in food service full time. She'd done her share at coffee shops and some waitressing in college. It hadn't been bad work, but it definitely wasn't something she'd wanted to do on a permanent basis.

"Oh gosh, yes!" Em's smile was wide, and her dark eyes sparkled. "I love The Purple Pig, and Willow's a great boss. I know I'm not going to get rich there, but I like it, I really do. I like the cooking and I like the people." Her grin went a little lopsided. "Well, most of the time."

Oaklee laughed. Being in the service industry did mean dealing with the odd complainer. Just Emily's luck that she was cute and friendly. All she had to do was smile and say something sweet, and the grumpiness evaporated.

They got to the restaurant and ordered miso to start, then a platter of assorted rolls to share. They were about a third of the way through the platter, and Oaklee had just popped a sweet potato roll into her mouth, when Emily casually asked, "So were you going to bring up the dog? And Rory Gallagher?"

Oaklee nearly choked. A grain of rice came away from the roll and lodged in her throat, and she frantically chewed and swallowed to avoid coughing. Emily waited patiently while she took a big drink of water and then pressed a hand to her collarbone.

"I nearly died," Oaklee said.

Emily laughed. "Hardly. So seriously. You keep *me* in the dark? I know I've been busy, but gee, Oaklee."

Guilt slid over Oaklee. "Okay, I know. I just wasn't sure what to say. I change my mind about what I want five times a day."

"You've never let a guy get under your skin like this. Not since Jeff."

Oaklee put down her chopsticks, her appetite waning. "I don't know what to tell you, Em. I've known Rory a long time. You know I had a crush on him in high school. But that was all it was. Now, though . . . I like him. A lot. And it scares me to death but I can't seem to help myself. Seriously, I'm boomeranging all over the place."

"And the dog?"

Oaklee sighed. "He's much easier, now that he's settled in. But he's not staying, you know?" She frowned. "I live in an apartment with a tiny front yard. He's cooped up all day. He needs a place to run around and chase squirrels and snooze in the sun."

Emily dipped her roll in soy sauce and then popped it into her mouth. "I think," she said thoughtfully, chewing, "that you're scared of Rory and in love with the dog. Or maybe the other way around."

Impossible. Of course it wasn't the other way around. There was no way she was in love with Rory. "It's not like that. It's because we're friends, and neither of us wants to be in a relationship, but we like each other so it gets in the way."

"Have you tried friends with benefits?"

Oaklee just looked at her.

"Okay, we'll mark that as a failure. Unless you want to share details."

"Not really." She looked around. "At least, not here."

"Damn."

When Oaklee laughed again, Emily shrugged. "I could use some excitement. Even Willow has more drama in her life than I do, and she's the queen of Zen."

The waiter came by and removed their plates, and then returned moments later with two little bowls of mango ice cream. Oaklee put a spoonful in her mouth and sighed in appreciation. "This trip was worth it just for the ice cream," she admitted.

Emily dipped her spoon, but before she took her bite

she looked at Oaklee, her gaze shrewd. "Sweetie, I know you're afraid of committing to anyone. Of caring too deeply because you don't want to get hurt. Jeff didn't just leave you. He humiliated you. He disrespected the years you'd had together." She put her spoon back down. "I mean, what kind of guy leaves a bride at a Vegas chapel, for God's sake? He's a selfish ass and I'd like to kick him to next Tuesday. But I digress." Her eyebrows smoothed a bit as her frown relaxed. "What I'm trying to say is, maybe it's time. Because it's clear to me that you care about Rory a lot. Maybe he's the one worth taking a risk for again."

Oaklee bit down on her lip. Was Emily right? This was the first time she'd been emotionally involved since the wedding that wasn't, and she'd had no choice in the matter. Her feelings for Rory were out of her control. They just . . . were.

"Every time I feel us getting closer, I panic. I never want to feel that way again, Em. And I'm not sure I can move past it."

"You've got to, honey. Or you're going to be alone forever, and we both know that's not right. Just think about it. You could do a hell of a lot worse than Rory." She finally ate her spoonful of ice cream. "Believe me. I know all three Gallagher boys and he's the hottest of the bunch."

Oaklee laughed then, and scooped up some ice cream. But as they finished their meal and made their way back to Darling, she was just as conflicted as before. Emily hadn't said anything that Oaklee hadn't thought at least once over the past few weeks. And Emily was right. What was Oaklee going to do, be alone forever? In her head she knew that was a ridiculous thought.

But she really wasn't sure how to bridge the gap between where she was now and a committed relationship—with Rory or anyone else. Right now the only "relationship" in her life that was easy was the one she shared with Buster. And that was only because his needs were simple, and so was his loyalty.

Rory hadn't really been looking forward to the Fall Frolic. He was the bachelor uncle, and while he adored Ethan's boys, Connor and Ronan, he found being at this sort of an event a challenge. He'd done a few of these types of things with Ginelle and Kyle, and when he went to kid events with his family, it served as a painful reminder.

But he wouldn't miss it because Ethan was his brother, and he was raising his boys alone, and that was a huge deal.

There was a dunking booth set up, and all sorts of food and games. As he wandered into the fray, which was on the Green, he caught sight of Oaklee and Buster. Buster's limp was pretty much gone, and he was pulling on the leash, nearly tugging Oaklee along behind him. Rory laughed. For a long time Oaklee had seemed perfect and poised and utterly in control. But after the last month, he'd realized that she had her flaws and foibles. Watching her trot behind a stray mutt, her hair flying in the fall breeze, somehow made him happy.

Later in the afternoon Ethan rounded up the family for an announcement. Rory was surprised to see Willow Dunaway at his side. They'd been seeing each other for a while, but a few weeks ago something had happened and Rory had figured whatever had been between them was over. Now, though, the two of them looked absolutely radiant. And the boys looked happy and contented, too.

When Ethan announced that he and Willow were going to have a baby, Rory nearly swallowed his tongue. He'd had no idea that their relationship was like that. Their parents were utterly surprised and went forward to give Willow and Ethan huge hugs, and ask about the pregnancy. Rory congratulated them as well—obviously congrats were in order since they seemed happy about it. Aiden, Laurel, and Hannah hung back, clearly unsurprised by the news. Laurel and Willow were best friends, after all, and Hannah was a good friend to them both as well, particularly since she had her real estate office in the same building as Willow's café. Added to that, Laurel and Aiden were also expecting. Talk of babies dominated the conversation.

He was the odd man out. Single, out of the loop, no kids. He caught Hannah's gaze and she shrugged, but her smile was wide. Too wide.

Rory just kept thinking about Oaklee, and how she'd pulled away the other night, and how they'd agreed that they should be just friends.

The shitty thing was that he didn't actually agree with her. He'd be the first to admit that the idea of a relationship scared him to death. But he was also starting to realize that this single life was getting a bit stale. He wanted more.

Sadly, it wasn't all up to him.

He caught up to her—and Buster—about an hour later,

as the Frolic was in its third hour. He stopped and bought a bag of popcorn, then touched her shoulder as she spoke to the mayor and his wife. "Hello, Oaklee. Brent. Mrs. Mitchell."

"Dr. Gallagher." Mrs. Mitchell smiled at him. "What brings you by a school function?"

"Ethan's boys," Rory replied, smiling. "We all try to show up to these things if we can."

"Your family's really close like that," Oaklee said, and he felt her warm gaze on his face. He smiled at her.

"We try. Ethan's had a rough few years. Besides, the boys are really something. I'd like to say trouble, but they remind me of what we were like as kids. And of course, we were angels." He smiled brightly, and everyone laughed.

"Oaklee was just telling us about her dog, here," Brent said. "He's quite a pooch."

"She's done a terrific job fostering him. Especially since she'd never really had a pet before. Buster's recovery has been great."

"Have you found a home for him yet?" Mrs. Mitchell asked.

"Not yet," Oaklee replied, and Rory detected a hint of hesitation in her voice. "His picture's been up on the shelter website, and the clinic site, and I've posted in the usual places. I don't think he was cared for very well at his last home. Otherwise someone would have come forward, you know?"

"Well, he certainly is a handsome boy now." Mrs. Mitchell reached down and gave him a scratch behind the ears. Buster sat and leaned his head into the scratch, blissfully happy.

"He was malnourished when he came in. It's amazing what good food and some love will do for a dog," Rory said.

"Not so different than a man, eh, Rory?" Brent asked, and everyone laughed.

"I was going to go for a walk," Rory said. "Oaklee, would you and Buster like to come along? I'd like to have a quick look at his leg, too. It looks like it's coming along nicely since the cast came off."

"Sure. I'll see you in the office tomorrow, Brent. Nice to see you, Mrs. Mitchell."

"You, too, Oaklee. Brent keeps saying what a great job you're doing with the town social media."

Rory stepped away from the couple, and he and Oaklee started off down the path. "How about somewhere else?" he asked. "There's such a big crowd here. And Buster seems overly excited."

"He nearly pulled my arm off, trying to catch some huskies earlier. The barking was unreal." She rubbed her shoulder. "Nearly pulled my arm out of the socket, too."

"I don't think he ever learned good manners. It's been up to you to teach him. I think he's done okay."

"Thanks."

They left the Green and walked up Main Street, past the colorful businesses with potted mums out front on their doorsteps. "So, do you want to hear my news today?" he asked.

"Sure. Beats mine. I have nothing. Same old same old, day in and day out."

"Ethan and Willow just announced that they're having a baby together."

She stopped, right there in the middle of the sidewalk. "You're joking."

He shook his head, still a bit shocked from the news himself. "As you can imagine, totally unplanned."

"What are they going to do?"

Rory shrugged and started walking again, and Oaklee and Buster kept step with him. "Well, I don't think they're getting married right away or anything. But they're definitely doing this together."

Oaklee pursed her lips. "Wow. I guess sometimes life really does throw curveballs, huh? I had dinner with Emily the other night. She said Willow was making her the manager of the café and was considering expanding."

"I don't think that's going to happen now. But they seem really happy."

He felt Oaklee's gaze on his face and he turned his head. Sure enough, she was looking at him. "What?" he asked.

"I think this is harder for you than you let on."

His stomach went strangely cold. He'd deliberately left Kyle out of the conversation the other night. There was only so much sharing he'd wanted to do, so what was she getting at?

"Nah," he answered, keeping his voice light. "It's not like I'm desperate to settle down or anything. It didn't work out for me, but good for them, you know?"

There. That sounded convincing.

"If you say so."

They stopped at the ice cream shop and each got a soft cone. The day had a fall crispness but was still warm, and when Oaklee got to the bottom of her cone, she offered the tip to Buster. He munched on it happily.

"Did you walk over to the Frolic or drive?" Rory asked. He was hoping she said walk. He'd like the chance to walk her home, say good night properly, without there being any drama or weird atmosphere.

"I walked. Went home and got Buster first. It's so great having him without his cast. We've taken slightly longer walks each day, and he seems to be doing fine." She smiled up at him. "Good as new."

"Better," Rory answered, loving the happy look on her face. When he'd suggested she foster Buster, he'd thought she could use the company. Pets had such a way of enriching people's lives even when it was unexpected. He wasn't sure how to explain it, but there was an openness to her face now, a contentment that hadn't been there before. Buster had needed her, but she'd needed him, too. He just hoped she realized it and maybe adopted him herself. Permanently. Clearly the dog loved her, too. As they walked along, Buster kept looking up at her, so happy and anxious to please.

When they reached her place, Rory decided not to follow her to the door. They'd decided to be friends and if he were going to keep to that deal, he needed to keep himself out of temptation's way. He was smart enough to know that temptation lay just beyond her front door, so at the bottom of her driveway he halted. "There," he said brightly. "Back home safe and sound."

Her gaze met his, and he saw the questions there. Questions he didn't want to answer; it was better if they kept things just on the surface. The appearance of just friends until it was easier, and absolutely true. Still, he saw the indecision and braced himself against it. He didn't want to spell out why he wasn't walking her to the door, or explain why giving her a good-night kiss, however light, was a bad idea. Instead he knelt down and gave Buster a really great pat. "You go in and get your supper and be a good boy," Rory commanded. "Yes sir. Oh yes. That feels good." He'd started to rub Buster's ears and the dog pressed into his hand, ecstatic at the touch.

"You don't want to come in?" she asked quietly.

"I think I'd better go. I've got to check on the animals tonight, and take the clinic dogs out for their nighttime ritual." He smiled at her. "But it was nice getting ice cream with you."

"A very friend-ish thing to do," she agreed.

Which all sounded good except nothing had changed for him. He did want to go inside. He wanted to kiss her again. Feel her in his arms. See where things led. But she couldn't even make it through a whole movie, cuddled on the sofa. She wasn't ready, and he was smart enough now to know he was never going to force someone into pretending to care more than they did.

"It was. I had a good time."

Now it was getting downright awkward. He lifted his hand. "So. See you later, you two."

"Bye, Rory."

He turned away and started walking back toward the Green and the parking area where he'd left his car.

This wasn't what he wanted. Hands in his pockets, he trudged his way along the path and let out a huge sigh. The stupid truth was, he wanted more. He hadn't, not until the night he'd kissed her. But now he did. He wanted the crazy chemistry simmering between them. He wanted cozy movie nights, curled up on the couch together, and long walks, and talks. Oaklee was probably the only woman he trusted to not be casual with his heart. She'd already shown that. He'd be willing to move forward, but she wasn't. He didn't know why, though he suspected it had something to do with Jeff and their breakup.

As he reached his car, he gave a small, self-deprecating laugh. Wouldn't his brothers get a kick out of this? After all, traditionally it seemed to be the women who got fanciful ideas of relationships and intimacy and the guys who tried to avoid that sort of commitment.

And he'd lived up to that image for quite a while now.

But it wasn't him. It had never been really him. And now he was falling for someone who didn't want what he had to offer. And he wasn't at all sure he was ready to offer it anyway.

What a kick in the pants.

Oaklee scanned through the pictures she'd taken with her phone today. There were lots that were great for the town Facebook page, so she created an album and did as much tagging as possible. The proceeds from all the activities and sales were going to benefit the elementary school, so she made sure to tag the school and the principal as well. A few she shared to Twitter. And a few she kept on her phone just for herself. One was of Buster, but a handful were ones she'd snapped of Rory when he wasn't looking. Getting popcorn. Standing with his mother, Moira, who was nearly a foot shorter than he was, but from whom he'd gotten his dark hair and impish smile.

Standing alone, the wind ruffling his hair, looking just a little bit lost.

Yeah, that one got her every time.

She wanted to let him in. Wanted to so badly. But each time she got close, she got scared. She didn't want to get hurt again. Worse, she didn't want to hurt him. He'd been hurt enough.

Still, she took the picture of him and his mom and sent it to him through a Facebook message. "Took this today," she typed. "Thought you might like it. You look like your mom."

It was a half hour before he answered her, and she was sitting on the sofa, watching TV with Buster when the notification sound dinged.

"Aw, thanks. I like this one. Will send it to Mom. She says she doesn't see me enough and forgets what I look like."

Oaklee chuckled. "Mom guilt," she typed back. And then she thought maybe *she* should pay a visit to her folks. Since coming back to Darling, she'd been determined to be independent. But her childhood had been a good one, if a little chaotic. With her hand on Buster's head, she wondered if she'd actually distanced herself from everyone who'd cared about her. Emily had hinted at it at dinner the other night. A visit every few months to her folks was a pretty poor track record.

"Does your mom lay it on thick?" he asked.

She bit down on her lip. "No. Not like yours, I don't think."

"I'd complain but . . . Mom." He added a smiley emoticon.

Oaklee frowned and her breath caught. For the first time since returning home from college, she really and truly missed her mom. She'd never elaborated on what had happened with Jeff; she'd been too embarrassed and too hurt to tell the truth. Maybe it was time.

Before she could change her mind, she called up her parents and invited herself for dinner on Friday, after work.

And she made sure to include Buster in the invitation. No one had stepped forward to claim him or adopt him, and she was starting to consider him part of the family.

CHAPTER 12

The Colliers lived in an older part of Darling, part of the original town on the north side of the creek, in a fairly small yellow saltbox-style home with white trim. Oaklee had gone home to her apartment and fed Buster, then packed him up into her car and drove over, grabbing a small bouquet of flowers from the market on the way.

The outside of the house was deceptively tidy. Oaklee knew that it was because her dad loved small engines and gadgets and puttering, so there was no question that grass would be cut and shrubs trimmed. The trouble came from having a small garage and a full basement since he couldn't seem to throw anything away because it might come in handy someday. It was hard to argue against, because more often than not he'd dig around in his stash and find exactly what he needed to fix something.

The inside of the house smelled like roast chicken

and something else spicy, like cinnamon or ginger. Oaklee's stomach rumbled—she'd had a quick yogurt parfait for lunch. "Hello? Mom? Dad?"

Cheryl Collier came around the corner, her hair more gray than blond these days, but still up in a ponytail. "Oaklee? You're here early." She stopped when she saw Buster. "So you really did do it. You have a dog."

A smile split her mother's face, surprising Oaklee. "Well, it appears I have. But by accident, really. Literally."

"So I heard."

"You did?"

"I follow you on Twitter."

If she'd said she'd confirmed the moon was made of green cheese, Oaklee wouldn't have been more surprised. "Since when do you have Twitter?"

"Since your dad and I got smartphones a while back. Bring him in. I'll find a bowl to put some water in."

She followed her mom into the house. A laundry basket with folded laundry sat at the bottom of the stairs, and a coat hung from the back of the kitchen chair. In the living room, a pile of store flyers were piled messily on the coffee table, held in place by two different coffee mugs. But the floor and counters were clean, with the exception of some dirty dishes created by the cooking of supper. It was tidier than she ever remembered it being.

Besides, maybe Cheryl Collier wasn't the world's best housekeeper, but the house felt welcoming. Lived in. Like home. Oaklee found she'd missed it, and swallowed against a lump in her throat. Why had she resisted visiting so much?

"Is Dad home for supper?"

"Oh, another ten minutes or so. I was just going to put the vegetables on and make the gravy."

"Can I help?"

Her mom looked over and smiled. "It's been so long since you were over, I'm just excited. I've got it covered."

Oaklee thought back to Rory showing up at her apartment, and the horrible frozen pizza, and the other stuff she usually ate because she didn't really know how to cook. "Mom, how did you learn to cook?"

Cheryl laughed. "Don't you remember when you and Cam were growing up? Boy, we lived on frozen crap, didn't we?"

"Yeah. I never really minded, though." She had been young enough, she'd never known the difference.

"I spent so much time at the rink with your brother, something had to give. I'd never been a great cook, so it wasn't a big thing to give up. Since he left, though, and then you went to college . . . I started cooking a bit more. Learning. Watching some shows and buying cookbooks."

"You did?" Oaklee made Buster sit while her mom turned on the tap to fill up a plastic dish for him.

"Sure."

"Do you . . . well, do you think you could teach me? Because I suck in the kitchen."

Her mom burst out laughing. "Well, that's a little like the blind leading the blind, but okay. What do you want to know?"

"Let me help with the rest of dinner. Tell me how you made the chicken. What to do with the vegetables."

"I can do that. Is your dog safe to let off his leash

now? He doesn't look like he's going to tear the place apart."

No, indeed. Buster was happy as anything, sniffing around the kitchen as far as the leash would let him, curious but not crazy. "Probably." She reached down for his collar. "I'm letting you off. You mess up, and it's right back on again, you hear?"

He licked her face.

"Gross, Buster." She wiped it off and unclipped the leash.

While Buster made himself at home on a rug in the living room, Oaklee stepped up to the island in the kitchen and joined her mom. "So, what's next?"

Together they peeled potatoes and carrots, covered them with water, and put them on the stove. Then her mom took out the roast chicken, put it on a plate to rest, and showed Oaklee how to make gravy from the drippings. She was whisking the gravy around and around, trying to keep it lump free, when her father got home.

"Hey, dumpling," he said, giving her a quick kiss on the temple.

"Hey, Dad."

Buster trotted over to say hello, and her father gave him a pat on the head. "Your mother said you got a dog. How's that going?"

"Good." She smiled. "Unexpected. And the first few days were trial by fire. But good."

"Go wash up," her mom advised. "It won't be long now."

While Oaklee's father left the kitchen, her mom told her about turning down the vegetables and how long they'd need to cook. Then they set the table and Oaklee learned how to properly carve a chicken. She mashed the potatoes and drained the carrots and put a salad that her mom had made earlier on the table. By the time everything was ready, she was feeling quite accomplished. She'd even asked about cooking times for the chicken, and what her mother had put on it to make it smell so good and brown so beautifully.

After dinner, she and her mom took Buster for a short walk down the street and back. When they got back home, they sat on the small front verandah in a pair of plastic Adirondack chairs. "Your dad'll be watching the news," her mom said. "But we can talk out here. It feels like we haven't really talked for ages."

"I know. And that's my fault."

"We kind of gave up asking you over all the time. You seemed to really want your independence."

Of course her parents had wondered about her. "I didn't mean for you to feel . . . I don't know, Mom . . . rejected."

"We did, some. But you're a big girl, Oaklee."

"I'm sorry about that." Oaklee sighed and leaned her head back. "I guess I just really wanted to be on my own." More than that, for the first several months she'd been back home in Darling, she'd been licking her wounds. She hadn't wanted anyone to know what had really happened between her and Jeff.

"You finally ready to talk about it?" Her mom looked over at her. "Because I think this has a lot to do with Jeff, and whatever happened between you. Particularly since you've never said."

"We broke up during spring break of the last year of college." Broke up was such a bland term for what had happened. What would her mom say if she admitted that she'd flown to Vegas for a quickie wedding? That she'd spent what little money she had left on a white dress and a single rose to carry up the aisle? That when she and Jeff had left their hotel room that morning, his last words had been that he'd see her at the chapel at four o'clock?

And that she'd waited for over two hours, sitting in the lobby while other weddings took place, wondering where he was? Scared to death something had happened to him? With a horrible sick feeling in the pit of her stomach? And then a single text message, blowing it all to hell, saying he wasn't coming and was taking an earlier flight home.

"Broke up? That doesn't really say much, sweetie. I think you got your heart broken. But what I don't understand is why you pulled away from the people you care about. Who care about you. Your dad and me, and Cam, too."

She bit down on her lip. "Truth is, Mom, I wasn't just heartbroken. I was humiliated. I was . . . crushed. And I didn't want to talk about it with anyone. I didn't want anyone to know the true story because I felt like such a fool. I still do."

"What could have been so bad?"

Oaklee looked over at her. "How about spending my last dollars eloping to Vegas and being left at the altar?"

At any other time, the shocked look on her mother's face would have been comical. Her eyes widened and lips dropped open while she stared at Oaklee with shock. "Left at the altar?"

"Yep. And had to check out of the hotel and fly home

alone. Keeping the original flight because I had no money to change it."

"Oh, honey."

"I'd blown whatever cash I had left. Cam lent me a few hundred bucks to get me through the semester with some spending money. Then I came home and started working right away."

"And you never said a word to us."

"I didn't know how. I didn't want pity, and I was still sorting through all my own feelings. I was so humiliated and embarrassed. The last thing I wanted to do was talk about it. With anyone." She looked at her mother. "I loved him, Mom. We'd been together since our junior year in high school. Wasn't I right to think he'd keep his word, after all that time?"

Her mother's face hardened. "Of course you were. What an asshole."

Oaklee laughed, surprised at the plain speaking from her mom who usually chose tamer words. "Oh, God," she said around her laughter. "I needed that."

"Well, honestly," her mom said, frowning. "What kind of guy does that?"

Oaklee's laughter faded and she sighed. "I don't know, Mom. And I know, deep down, that I wouldn't have wanted to marry someone who didn't really want me. At the same time, it was a shitty, shitty thing to do, and it's embarrassing. I'm just glad the people of Darling have never got ahold of it." She gave her mom a sad smile. "Look at Laurel. She came back home and all people could talk about was poor Laurel and the details of her divorce. I'm really glad I didn't have to deal with that, too."

They sat in silence for a while, then her mom spoke. "If you ever get married, no eloping, you hear? We'll have a real wedding, with you in a white dress, and flowers, and bridesmaids, and a real reception. None of this sneaking away."

Oaklee's heart warmed at the stern tone in her mom's voice. "Okay."

"Why did you want to elope, anyway?"

"It seemed romantic at the time, and, well, rebellious. And even though I was nearly broke in the end, so much cheaper than a big wedding. We talked about it, and how we were coming out of college with loans and how being together was what was important." She swallowed against a lump in her throat. "What a joke."

"Aw, you were young and idealistic. Next time you'll be smarter."

Oaklee thought of Rory for a minute, and the ball of confused feelings that she had for him took up residence in her stomach. "I don't think so, Mom," she said quietly. "I'm not really interested in setting myself up for a fall like that again."

But her mom merely waved a hand in her direction. "You will be. When the right one comes along. Trust me."

Instead of being consoling, the words made Oaklee's spirits plunge. If what her mother said was true, that person wasn't Rory. The other night had proved that. She couldn't even cuddle during a movie without freaking out.

"I don't know, Mom. I just don't."

"Well, at least now you have your dog." Buster was sitting next to her mom, looking every inch the handsome mutt. "And you don't have to avoid us, either. I've missed you. Maybe you can come around a little more often."

"I'd like that." And she would. It didn't stop the heavy feeling from settling over her, though. She wished Victoria had been at the clinic that night instead of Rory. Wished they could have just gone on the way they were, two single people in the same town, without having shared walks and kisses and feelings. It just made things messy and confusing and painful.

It wasn't supposed to feel this way. If she ever needed a sign that Rory wasn't the guy for her, this was probably it.

"I think I'll take Buster home and call it an early night," she said, getting up from her chair. "But thanks for dinner and the cooking lesson." She tried a small smile. "I'm a horrible cook. Not much of a housekeeper, either. But I'm getting tired of living that way, so . . ."

Her mom laughed lightly. "Now that there's just your dad and me, things still get a bit messy but not as much as when you were kids, I was working, and running you guys around to different things. Maybe domestics should have been more of a priority . . . but I'm awfully proud of the people you and Cam have become. So . . . I don't think I'll go to my grave wishing I'd cleaned more or served less frozen lasagna."

Oaklee smiled. "Thanks, Mom. Though to be fair? Frozen lasagna's pretty gross."

They laughed a bit and Oaklee shook Buster's leash. "All right, big guy. Let's go say bye to Dad and get going."

She drove home in the semi-dark, feeling both better and worse about things. Better because she'd finally told her mom what had happened with Jeff and the world hadn't ended, and her mom hadn't been all pitying and overly sympathetic—Oaklee wouldn't have been able to stand that. She'd never had time for big dramatics or floods of tears. But tonight had also made her think. First of all, if Rory didn't seem like The One, he probably wasn't, if what her mom said was true. And second, maybe the fault lay with her, because that was one of the things Jeff had criticized her for in the end. He'd called her cold and practical and incapable of deep feeling.

When she got home to her apartment, there was a message waiting for her on her phone.

"Hi, Oaklee? It's Christy at the vet clinic. We got a call late this afternoon from someone who claims that Buster is their dog. Can you call me back if you get this before eight? We're closed after that tonight."

She checked her watch. It was eight-fifteen. She picked up the phone anyway, and went through the motions of hitting caller ID and the talk button.

She got the answering service, and while she was tempted to call Rory to see what was going on, she resisted. There was a good chance that whoever was making the claim was wrong. After all, why wouldn't they have been looking for him before now?

But she was unsettled enough that when she went to bed, she didn't even bother with the extra blanket at the foot of the covers. Instead she patted the spot next to her, and Buster crawled up and lay by her side, his chin resting on her arm.

"They'd better have some good proof," Oaklee muttered, but remembered what she'd told herself when she'd made that final post about him. That if no one came forward, it was a sign.

This was a sign, too. And it wasn't the one she wanted.

The family was from a town over an hour and a half away from Darling. Throughout the day, Oaklee told herself over and over that it was incredibly unlikely that Buster was their dog. How would he have gotten so far from home? She alternated that thought with some righteous anger. Buster had been skin and bones when she'd found him, and his coat had been rough and dirty. Rory had said there were rub marks on his neck, as if he'd been tied and left. If that was the kind of family that had owned him before, there was no way she was going to let him go back.

They'd agreed to meet at the clinic. She was glad, because the staff would be there to attest to his health when he'd come in—the accident notwithstanding. She also trusted them to know the right questions to ask.

And if she were surrounded by other people, she'd be able to hold her shit together. She wouldn't embarrass herself in front of a crowd.

"Come on, buddy," she said, trying to ignore the sick feeling swirling around in her stomach. She clipped on his leash and he jumped out of the car, tongue hanging out from panting. He sure didn't like driving, even though she always made sure he was comfortable and that she drove carefully without sudden turns or stops to scare him.

Rory met her at the door, his eyes soft and understanding. "Don't look at me that way," she said under her breath, issuing the warning. "I told you from the beginning that I was only fostering him until we found him a forever home. Besides, I'm not convinced these people are the real deal."

"They're pretty convincing, Oaklee. Just to give you a heads-up."

She lifted her chin. "What do you mean?"

"I mean they have family pictures. And they brought their kid with them."

Oh God. There was a kid? Her heart sank further, dropping right to her toes. "I still have a lot of questions."

"I know. Anyway, come on in. They're waiting in one of the private waiting rooms. I didn't want to discuss this in the main one, you know?"

She appreciated that. He held the door while she went in, Buster trotting happily behind. Rory led the way down the hall and opened a door. They stepped through.

"Sparky!"

The shout nearly deafened Oaklee, who took a step backward. But not Buster. He lunged forward, pulling on the leash, meeting what appeared to be a six- or seven-year-old boy right in the middle of the room. He jumped and then stuck his nose right in the boy's face, licking him from chin to cheek.

She looked at Rory. He had that sad, understanding expression again and she averted her eyes.

"Oh, Sparky." There were giggles. The boy was on the floor, and the dog was rolling around with him. It would have been cute if the situation were different. A sense of finality washed over Oaklee. Buster was not her dog. He never had been, and he never would be.

"Hi. We're the Blakes. We can't thank you enough for all you've done for Sparky."

A man stepped forward. She wished he'd looked . . . dirtier. Meaner. But he looked like a perfectly normal, suburban man, with his normal, soccer-mom suburban wife beside him. Her eyes were full of tears. "Yes, oh my. It really is him. I can't believe it. Casey has been so desperate to find him."

Oaklee couldn't smile. She tried, but it just wouldn't happen. "I'm surprised that I've had him for over a month and this is the first you've come looking. We posted his picture on the site and shared it all over the day after I found him."

Mr. Blake nodded. "We never thought to look this far from home, really. At first we thought he'd taken off and we'd find him close by, or at our local shelter. But then . . . well, a few neighborhood dogs went missing, and we wondered if maybe he'd been stolen." He knelt down in front of boy and dog, who were still playing on the floor. "I'm just so glad he's safe and healthy."

"Oaklee's done a terrific job caring for him." Rory stepped into the conversation.

"Right. And so has Dr. Gallagher. Did you know, despite his accident, he was underfed and had sores on his neck? Like he'd been chained a lot. Do you chain your pets outside, Mr. Blake?"

"Oaklee," Rory chided gently.

She heard the desperation in her voice, but she couldn't help it. "I'm sorry, Rory, but I need some assurances that he's going to be well looked after. You know what he was like when I brought him in. When did you say he went missing, Mr. Blake?"

The accusation didn't seem to fluster the man at all. "April," he said quietly, meeting her gaze. "We'd actually given up hope of getting him back, and saw his picture when we started looking at nearby shelters to get another dog. When we saw the picture, we knew. It breaks my heart to think of someone misusing him, Miss . . ."

"Collier," she replied, trying to keep her voice even. With every passing moment she was more sure that this was Buster's—Sparky's—family. He was not hers. He had never been hers. And deep down she'd always known it.

Mrs. Blake reached into her purse and pulled out a picture. "Maybe this will help," she said softly, handing it over. "It's Sparky and Casey at Christmas last year."

The dog was wearing a goofy Santa hat and a Christmassy collar. Casey's grin was huge, and he wore a matching hat. They were sitting beneath a very perfect Christmas tree.

She couldn't break up a boy and his dog. She knew that. There wasn't even a question of it. She handed the picture back and smiled weakly.

"As you can imagine, I've grown quite . . . fond of Buster. I mean, Sparky." Her voice wobbled a little but she steadied it. "But I don't think we can argue with this." She pointed toward the floor. The welcoming ruckus had quieted, and Casey lay on the floor and the dog had his head right on the boy's stomach. Like it was exactly where he was supposed to be.

"By any chance," she asked quietly, "does he sleep on your son's bed?"

Mrs. Blake smiled sheepishly. "Well, when we brought

him home, we said no way. And then . . . well, it happened, and we didn't have the heart to say no." She reached over and took her husband's hand. "When he was first gone, it was horrible trying to get Casey to sleep at all."

Oaklee nodded. "He wouldn't settle until he was in bed with me, either."

And at that last bit of insight, she consciously began the process of shutting off her emotions. If she didn't, she was going to cry right here in front of all these nice people. In front of Rory. And that just couldn't happen.

She looked over at Rory, and at Christy, the assistant, who was standing in the doorway. "Is there anything I need to do as far as paperwork or anything?"

Rory shook his head, his eyes sad as they looked at her. She looked away and kept her chin up. "I can go back to my place and get his things. Do you mind waiting?"

The Blakes shook their heads together. "We still have everything from before," he explained. He looked down at his son. "Casey wouldn't hear of us getting rid of anything. So we're set. We're just so, so grateful to you, Miss Collier. You just can't imagine."

No, no, no. She would not let their sentimentality get to her. "Hey, it was my accident. I'm just very glad he was okay so that your little boy can have his best friend back."

There. That was as sentimental as she dared to be. She pasted on a smile. When uncomfortable silence spun out, she gave a shrug. "I was only fostering him until we found him a good home. This is even better because it's his real home." She looked at Casey, and felt she was getting to the point where she was going to have to make an exit or embarrass herself. "You've got yourself a great dog there, Casey. I'm sure you'll be glad to get him home again."

"I sure will," he answered, and he wrapped his arms around Buster's neck and squeezed.

In her heart, way down deep, she knew that this was absolutely the right conclusion to the mystery of Buster. It was a little boy and his dog, for God's sake.

She knelt down and handed him the leash, pausing for one brief moment to rest her hand on Buster's soft fur around his ears—the only goodbye she'd make. "Take really good care of him," she said, and stood.

Rory cleared his throat. "All right. Let's update his file and get him ready to go."

"I've got to get back," Oaklee said, her insides quivering. If she waited much longer, her lip would be quivering and she wouldn't be able to see very well. "Thanks, Rory, for looking after this."

He put his hand on her arm as everyone filed out of the room and headed toward the main waiting room. "Are you okay?"

Oh Lord, why wouldn't he just let her go? She smiled brightly. "Of course. This is what the plan was all along, remember? I told you I didn't want anything permanent. No commitments. I'm not even a dog person."

How she managed to get through all those lies she really didn't know.

"You don't want to say goodbye?"

She laughed a little. "It's fine, Rory. He's going home with his family. Best kind of outcome we could have hoped for."

She gave the family a little wave and a smile as she

left, and walked steadily to her car, not rushing. Just a regular walk, to her regular car, and she'd make a regular drive home.

Which was fine until she went to back up and saw his car blanket on the backseat.

Her lip began to quiver. Defiantly, she shifted into drive and headed out of the parking lot toward the road. Turned toward town and then to her subdivision. Two small tears leaked out of the corners of her eyes, but she clenched her teeth and kept going, parking in her driveway, gathering up her purse, walking to the front door.

But once she was inside, she let it all go.

CHAPTER 13

The emotions she'd held back for the better part of an hour slammed to the surface, stealing her breath.

She took great gulps of air, trying to breathe, but it was nearly impossible through the sobs that bubbled up and out. She took a step forward and stepped on Buster's Kong toy, and the reminder sliced into her like the blade of a knife.

She dropped her handbag to the floor. She'd never have to worry about her strap being chewed again, or her clothes being strewn around the house, or stepping in an unexpected puddle in her kitchen.

And instead of making her feel any better, it all just made her feel worse.

"Buster," she whispered, and leaned back against the door. She couldn't even see through her tears, so she simply let herself melt against the door until she was sitting on the floor, crying.

The last-ditch effort of posting his doggy profile had

been her final attempt at denial. To show that she hadn't started to love him. To tell herself that she really didn't want to keep him, or be his forever home. But she had. Oh, she had. Somewhere along the way she had finally opened her heart and let herself love again. It didn't matter that he was a dog and not a person. It didn't matter that it had been a short amount of time. She'd brought him home reluctantly, but she'd been a goner from the first night when he'd snuggled close to her on her bed. She'd been enough in that moment, and it had done something to her on the inside. Something wonderful and healing.

He'd never snuggle there again. Or put his chin on her knee as she sat on the sofa. Or play with his indestructible toy or his Kong or stand by his bowl, not so patiently waiting for his supper, clicking the steel with his toes.

The house felt so empty. Just so very, very, empty.

This was why she didn't love anymore. It hurt too damn much when it was ripped away. And it was always, always ripped away.

After twenty minutes of sobbing, she got up from the floor and made her way to the bathroom for tissues to blow her nose. Her eyes were puffy and red, face blotchy from crying and not a lick of makeup left. The tip of her nose was raw from wiping it on her sleeve—she'd have to go change her shirt—and the ache in her heart had spread to her whole body. She stumbled into the bedroom and got out her fuzziest pair of pajamas, a pair of cream-and-pink flannel sleep pants with a super-soft fleecy pullover. The only thing she wanted to do tonight was curl into a ball on the sofa and grieve.

When she got to the sofa, she spotted Buster's "bed," the soft blanket Rory had brought over that first night. Disregarding the dog hair, she grabbed it and pulled it onto the sofa with her, holding it close in her arms.

Why could she not manage to hold on to those she loved? Why did it feel as if they could just . . . leave without a backward glance? Jeff certainly had, with a horrible text. Hadn't their five years together deserved more than that? And Buster . . . he'd walked into the waiting room, had seen that little boy, and forgot all about her.

Her lip quivered again. He was a dog. She knew he hadn't done it on purpose. But it didn't stop the hurting, or make her feel less forgettable.

And then came the knock at the door.

She knew who it was. No one else would just pop in unannounced. Besides, she didn't actually think she'd fooled Rory all that much with her *oh, everything is fine and dandy* routine. She peeled herself off the sofa and went to the door. Sure enough, when she looked through the peephole, Rory stood there, his brown jacket zipped up and a worried frown marring his smooth forehead.

She opened the door.

The alarm on his face was instant, and then his expression softened. "Oh, honey," he said quietly, then came inside and put his arms around her. "I'm sorry."

That started a whole new flood of tears.

She did fine if no one touched her, or used that particular gentle tone. Rory had done both. Her face was pressed against the soft fabric of his jacket. It smelled like fresh air and fall leaves. Rory's arms were strong and sure, holding her close. "I know," he murmured against her hair. "It's hard to let them go."

She drew a shaky breath. "It isn't supposed to be. Why does this hurt so much? It's so silly! He's just a dumb dog!" A fresh sob escaped with her exclamation.

"Because you loved him, Oaklee. And he loved you too. It showed every time you guys did something together."

The words didn't help. "Don't say that!" It was bad enough thinking she'd gotten overly fond of a dog she'd only agreed to foster for a short time. Thinking that maybe Buster had also got fond of her, too, made everything hurt worse. "He was a good dog but he was never mine. He walked into that room and saw that kid and that was it."

"And that sort of thing is really, really great. But not great for you, not at this moment."

His hand moved over her hair, soothing, consoling. "It's so empty here, Rory. Everything is so empty." She pushed out of his arms a little. "This is why everything was always a mess in here. The chaos covers up the empty spaces. I know that's seriously messed up. I do, because I'm the one determined to keep it empty even though I hate being alone. I hate the loneliness and I'm so goddamned afraid to ask for anything more."

"Why?"

Her eyes filled again. "Because it hurts. Because it's not real. And in the end, you're left standing alone surrounded by a world made up of couples and lovers, and wondering what the hell you did that was so wrong, that made you unlovable."

His eyes looked confused for a moment, and she realized what she'd said. But it was true. Nothing had been worse than standing there waiting in the wedding chapel, except the exact second that she realized Jeff would never be coming. And for two years she'd avoided dealing with it. Tonight she couldn't run away anymore. "I loved him, Rory. I didn't want to. He made me so mad. But I did, and now I'm sad and hating myself just a bit for being so stupid."

"Come here," he said quietly, and he tucked her into his embrace again. "We can't always be happy. And we can't always hold ourselves back from caring. What sort of life is that?"

"I'm just not sure that it's worth it," she said, her voice muffled against his chest. "Oh, Rory. He won't be panting stinky dog breath on my face in the morning or be waiting at the door when I get home or begging for scraps of my horrible food."

"I know, sweetie."

"I always knew he had to have been somebody's baby. But with every day that passed, I guess I started thinking of him as my baby."

Rory squeezed her tighter. "It's amazing how they can make us love them so much. Maybe because they ask for so little, and they give unconditional love in return."

But it wasn't just Buster that hurt tonight. It was the ache, deep down inside, that had been building for over two years. She was so, so tired of being alone. Of shutting herself away. And tonight, while she was vulnerable and bleeding, Rory was here, holding her, hugging her. She hadn't called for him to come. He'd just come because he knew she needed him.

She let her arms go around him and let out a long, slow breath of surrender.

His palm ran over her back, soothing, comforting. After a few minutes, he kissed her temple, his breath warm through her hair.

"Rory," she whispered.

He drew back a little and looked into her face. She knew she had to look horrible. She had never been a pretty crier, and tonight had been a full-on ugly cry. She still felt incredibly fragile, but he put a finger beneath her chin and lifted it, so she was looking into his eyes.

"Here," he said gently, and brushed back a chunk of stray hair that was stuck to her wet cheek. "Don't cry anymore, Oaklee. I can't stand it when you cry."

"I never cry," she asserted, but her voice came out weak and shaky. "Not until tonight. Tonight I just . . . I can't pretend any longer, Rory. I'm so, so alone. And I've made myself this way and don't know how to get out of it in one piece."

"Shhh," he soothed, his thumb grazing the top of her cheek. "You don't have to find all the answers tonight."

She closed her eyes, felt moisture on her lashes, focused on the texture of his thumb as he caressed her face.

"You're not alone," he murmured, just before he put his lips on hers.

The sweetness of the contact reached in and touched her so deeply that two tears slipped from her closed eyes.

This kiss was different. It wasn't simple chemistry or need, which sat on the surface of feelings and made them easier to ignore. Tonight she was more open, and

unable to shut herself away again. Tonight she felt bare
and vulnerable and desperate for an anchor to keep her
from drifting away. That gentle and steadfast Rory was
that anchor only made it better. She kissed him back,
putting all she had into it, and the connection was deep
and strong. His fingers wiped at the tears stuck in her
hair just above her ears while his tongue plundered her
mouth with a thoroughness that stole her breath.

"Don't be sad," he whispered.

"Just hold me," she murmured back, and she reached
for the zipper of his jacket and slid it down, giving it a
little pull at the bottom to unhook it from the mecha-
nism. She spread it open and nudged his shoulders, so
he'd drop his arms and she could get his jacket all the
way off. Beneath it he wore a Henley shirt in a khaki
brown, utterly masculine and surprisingly soft.

"Whatever you need, Oaklee."

"I need you."

His hand traced over her shoulder. "Be careful what
you ask for. I might just give it to you."

She met his gaze. "I'm not stopping you."

He kissed her again, then drew back and looked her
fully in the face. A look of tenderness swept over his
features. "You're so sad. And your eyes . . ."

"I know. I'm an ugly crier. Never mind . . ." She had
to be incredibly unattractive and unappealing right now.
And maybe being so forthright was a mistake . . . but
anything was better than going back to being alone.

"You're beautiful," he whispered, tracing his thumb
beneath her eye. "Maybe more beautiful than before."

She wanted to ask what he meant, but was afraid that
the answer would be a little too much to handle. Emo-

tions were high right now. She had to finally admit that she cared for Rory, not in a scratch-the-itch kind of way, or a friends-with-benefits agreement . . . but Rory, her high school champion, her crush, her friend.

"You're beautiful, too," she said, and kissed him back.

Rory tasted salt on her lips and the soft, smooth skin of her face, and his heart constricted.

This wasn't sex for fun. It wasn't satisfying a craving or a physical need. This was Oaklee, and all he wanted right now was to take her pain away.

This wasn't just about Buster. He'd known for weeks that she held herself back from caring too much; he just didn't know why. Tonight her heart was open, and he saw past the walls she'd built around herself. What he saw was beautiful, and he wanted to show her how beautiful.

He took his time, kissing her thoroughly, exploring her mouth and listening to her sighs as she melted against him. Her fingers dug into his shoulders, strong fingers that had clutched Buster's leash tighter than she probably realized. Her knuckles had been white, her smile tight with effort to keep her feelings from showing. But he'd known, and his heart had gone out to her for having to say goodbye.

In a lot of ways, he was responsible for her feeling such pain right now. And he wanted to make it better.

He slipped his hand beneath her pullover, the material feather-soft against his skin. When he encountered her bare breast—no bra—he was surprised, pleasantly so. The tip hardened against his palm and she moved slightly, pressing into his touch. The kiss deepened, and her hands slipped beneath his shirt, moving over the skin of his back, the nails lightly tracing a path from waist to shoulder blade. He shivered with pleasure.

And still they remained upright, at the edge of her living room.

She let out a breath, shuddered in his hands, and he made an executive decision.

He swept her up in his arms, one arm beneath her knees and the other under her shoulders. Her arms lifted instinctively and clasped around his neck, even as she made a soft, surprised sound in her throat. Feeling gallant and manly, he carried her to her bedroom door and waited while she opened it, then went inside and gave it a shove with a foot. The door latched with a definitive click.

He put her down on top of the covers, and then reached for the hem of his shirt and pulled it off over his head, dropping it on the floor. Her eyes widened and her pupils dilated, and he joined her on the bed, kissing her, pressing her body into the mattress, moving against her in an anticipatory dance.

"You're so warm. So hard," she breathed, lowering her chin and nipping his shoulder with her teeth.

He gasped at the sharp little pain, which only added to his arousal. He reached and touched, lifted and tugged on clothing until she was naked and pliant beneath him. God, she was beautiful. Even with her tear-stained face, he'd never seen a woman so gorgeous. Her hair spread over the pillow, and the soft light through the blinds highlighted the curves and dips of her body from her pink-tipped breasts to the tiny swell of her abdomen, to her long, sleek legs.

Oaklee. The pain-in-the-ass teenager, turned vibrant, smart, beautiful woman. And she wanted him. The hungry look in her eyes told him so.

He reached into his back pocket for his wallet, and took out a condom. He tossed it on the pillow beside her, then reached for the button on his jeans.

They were going to do this. He was going to make love to her . . . be inside her . . . and he couldn't remember ever wanting anything more in his life.

Her hand slid over her own body and he nearly lost feeling in his legs.

And yet they took their time, touching, exploring, savoring. Her fingers were small and strong, and to his delight, a little bit tentative, like she wasn't taking any inch of him for granted. When had he last felt this cherished? When had he last felt this sense of absolute wonder? Every sensation begged to be acknowledged, and he did his best to absorb every sweet stimulus. How she looked, sounded, felt, tasted . . . the scent of her, soft flowers and woman. When the time came, she opened the packet herself.

He paused, his weight resting on his hands, looking into her eyes, poised at her entrance. Once he moved forward, there would be no going back. With other women this had been the natural progression and there'd been no hesitation. But not with Oaklee. This was more. His heart was involved this time, and there was no sense pretending it wasn't. The time of self-delusion was over.

He cared about her so, so much.

She shifted beneath him, moving her hips, nudging him closer and issuing a silent invitation. He inched forward; her eyes widened and her tongue slipped out and swiped across her bottom lip. Another inch . . . sweat beaded on his forehead, half from heat and half from trying to exercise such restraint.

And then he shifted his hips and it was all the way. They held that way for a moment, looking into each other's eyes, and something shifted inside his chest. It tightened and squeezed, and somehow expanded at the same time. She bit down on her lip, and her lashes fluttered closed just for a second.

Never had he been more aware of a woman.

He started to move, and Oaklee lifted one knee and hooked her heel against his bottom, levering up to meet his thrusts.

"Rory," she breathed, her head thrown back, exposing the delicate column of her throat. He leaned forward and swept his tongue up the tendon in her neck, then fastened his mouth on her breast, wanting to hear her say his name again. She did, as well as a gasp that made him feel about a million feet tall. He moved to the other breast and she met him stroke for stroke. He felt her muscles bunch and tense, and he moved faster, harder.

"Rory," she moaned, writhing in his arms. "Oh God, Rory. I just . . ."

She couldn't say any more. She came apart in his arms, calling out one long, beautiful, indistinguishable syllable.

He couldn't hold back any longer. Her legs and arms clung to him as he let himself go.

And when the haze behind his eyes cleared, he met Oaklee's gaze and felt himself fall.

CHAPTER 14

Oaklee woke at three in the morning and stared at the ceiling.

Rory lay in the bed beside her, his eyes closed, breathing soft and regular. She felt limp as a dishrag, and knew she should have that happy, boneless feeling that came after great sex. Instead she just felt . . . tired. Worn out. Confused.

And it wasn't that the sex hadn't been good. It had been . . . amazing. Possibly transcendent. Never in her life had Oaklee felt so treasured and so beautiful. Not that she had much experience. There'd only ever been Jeff before Rory. And if she admitted that to him, he'd probably run for the hills. He was far more experienced, and having only one partner before him? He'd see that as something big. It would carry far more weight in their relationship than it otherwise might.

Relationship. Is that how she saw them now? A knot formed in the center of her chest.

What was bothering her was both the why behind what had happened, and the possibility of what might happen in the future.

Neither was good to think about. Sex out of desperation was not a good thing. And the future? What sort of future did they have, or did she even want? It was all so overwhelming.

Rory snuffled in his sleep, rolled over, and his foot crept over to her side of the bed and slid along her calf. Still, he slept on, his breathing deepening, as if the simple contact had given him comfort.

And still she stared at the ceiling, her heart pounding painfully, her body still and stiff. She'd made love to Rory . . . let him make love to her . . . because she hadn't wanted to be alone. Because she needed to fill the space left behind by a silly mutt with funny eyebrows. The thing was, she could fall for Rory in a heartbeat, and that was dangerous. He could have the power to hurt her. And tonight she'd realized something awful. In the two years since Jeff's betrayal—and she did consider his abandonment a betrayal—she hadn't healed. Hadn't moved past it. She was broken. And she was also smart enough to know that broken people were poor bets when it came to relationships.

She didn't want to hurt anymore. And she didn't want to be responsible for hurting someone else, and after last night she was pretty sure she might hurt Rory. Their connection had been deep and profound, surpassing words.

And yet she couldn't escape the idea that she'd somehow used him. Oh, what a mess. Her mom had always said that sex complicated things. At the time, when she was sixteen, it had been said as a caution against moving too fast, or not thinking things through. She was twenty-four and she'd forgotten the lesson.

She lay awake until six, when the night sky began to lighten and gray, watery light filtered through her curtains. Rory had spent the night in her bed; the only time she'd ever shared it before was with Buster. Her eyes watered, thinking about him. She'd loved him. It was a bit of a relief to realize she was actually capable of loving again, but it hurt so badly.

At six-fifteen, her alarm went off.

She rolled over to shut it off, the sheet slipping off her skin. Rory shifted, and she felt him stretch behind her, a change in the bedding as his legs extended and his arms moved above his head. She closed her eyes for a moment and imagined what he looked like, all sleepy and manly.

"Good morning," he said, his voice crackling.

"Hi," she answered, pulling the sheet back up to cover her breasts. She rolled back over and stayed on her back, but turned her head to look at him. "It's just after six."

"I slept like the dead." He grinned and shifted to his side, resting his head on a bent arm. "I think you might have had something to do with that."

She tried to smile and wondered what he'd say if she admitted she'd been awake for three hours, fretting over what they'd done.

"I'm glad you slept well," she said. "I've got to hit the shower. It's the Chamber of Commerce meeting this morning. Laurel's hosting at the Ladybug and I promised to go early to help set up."

"You did?"

Oaklee nodded, her discomfort growing. It was impossible to avoid the Gallagher family in Darling. Laurel and Hannah had businesses, and Ethan and Aiden were both first responders. Then there was Claire who'd interned at the office, and Willow Dunaway, who owned the café and was carrying Ethan's baby. The only family member not in Oaklee's sphere of work existence was Claire's twin, Cait.

Now if things became weird and awkward with Rory, it would be weird and awkward with all the Gallaghers.

"Laurel admitted she's still feeling a bit morning sick. I told her I'd stop by The Purple Pig and pick up part of the catering order and help her set up tables and chairs."

"That's nice of you."

"The Chamber tends to be that way. Everyone helps each other."

"Right."

Unease tightened her throat. So far they'd covered her morning meeting but hadn't said a word about last night. She tried a smile. "So . . . you're welcome to anything you can find for breakfast. I'm guessing you need to be going to work, too."

His gaze was penetrating. "Sure."

Her nervousness doubled, and she was sure he could either see right through her or was trying hard to figure her out. She didn't like either option.

"Thanks for coming over last night." She softened her voice and tried to find some sort of emotional middle ground. "I was so upset about Buster. I'm going to miss him horribly."

"I know," Rory replied, and he reached out and

stroked her hip, on top of the covers. "I'm sorry if fostering him was a mistake. I know I pushed you into it."

She'd been aware of that, and wished she could put some of the blame on him, but she wasn't exactly sorry she'd done it. Buster had added something to her life that had been missing. "I was mad at first, but then it was nice to have someone here waiting for me. Relying on me and just . . . company. That's not the problem. The problem is me. I let myself get too attached. I started to think of him as mine. And when no one came forward . . . I made assumptions. Getting that call was like getting hit by a truck, but I'll get over it."

She would. That was what she did, after all. Pull up her socks and move on. And if it was a little bit empty, well that was life, wasn't it? She'd find something else to do. A cause. A volunteer position or something to occupy her time.

"After Ginelle broke up with me, I had a cat. I only had him for six months—he had feline diabetes, and I knew his kidneys would only hold out so long. But no one else wanted him because he was so sick, and I felt like we had something in common. We'd both been pushed aside. That cat got me through the worst time of my life, and when I had to let him go, I grieved. So you don't have to pretend with me, Oaklee. I'm a vet. I get it. I love animals, and I work every day with people who love their pets deeply. It's okay to mourn a little."

"I'll keep that in mind." She wanted to change the topic, and wondered how to discreetly extricate herself from the bed without giving Rory a full view. "But I really do have to hop in the shower, Rory." She tried a cheeky smile. "This was kind of a surprise addition to my agenda."

She sat up in the bed and realized if she leaned to the side, over the edge, she could just reach her robe. She snagged it and tried shoving her arms in the sleeves without flashing him too much.

"Are we going to talk about last night?" he asked, and guilt rode a cold path down her spine.

"Sure," she responded easily. "But maybe when we're not so rushed and have to get to work, you know?"

"You're sure you're okay?"

"Of course." She slipped out of the bed and belted the robe around her waist. Truthfully, she couldn't wait to get in the shower, and hoped he would be gone by the time she got out. He'd want answers to questions and she wouldn't have the ones he wanted. Besides, it would be better to wait, wouldn't it? To let the dust settle, and see how they really felt about things?

She faced him at the bathroom door. "Do you need anything in here before I turn on the shower?"

He looked at her for a long minute, during which she felt utterly transparent and selfish. He probably wanted an invitation to join her under the hot spray, but that would only complicate things more. Or breakfast together, or at least a good-morning kiss.

But then she looked down and saw a dust bunny containing Buster's fur and her heart ached. She looked at Rory, remembered the tenderness he'd shown last night and the ache grew. She couldn't do this. Couldn't feel this much. Right now she needed a tactical retreat to regroup.

His gaze cooled. "Naw, I'm good, thanks. You have a good meeting. I'll give you a call later."

"Sounds good."

She went into the bathroom and closed the door, then turned on the shower. But before she got in, she closed her eyes and let the awful feelings sweep over her. Why was it they were so good together and in tune, and then every time they pushed a boundary, it got awkward and strained?

She stepped under the hot spray and sighed. It was because she was a big old chicken shit. And he was too, really. And they had to figure something out soon, because this two-steps-forward-one-step-back thing meant that someone was going to get hurt.

Rory was out of sorts for the whole of the day. He went home and showered and shoved a piece of toast in his mouth for breakfast, grunted at the animals that were kenneled at the clinic, snapped at the staff, and stomped around whenever he wasn't in an exam room with a client, where he forced himself to be calm, patient, and pleasant. He noticed the sidelong glances from the assistants and also that they avoided asking him any questions. But when one of the newest techs asked a newbie question, he snapped at her and said something to the effect that she should have learned that at school and to step up and show some initiative.

He knew he needed to apologize, but he just wasn't in the headspace. Oaklee had done to him what he'd done to women in the past, and he hated himself for it. She'd been pleasant as anything, but she'd also distanced herself from him utterly. No emotion. No promises made for later, just a noncommittal "we'll talk."

The problem was, this wasn't casual for him. Not

anymore. Not since he'd seen her crying over Buster. He'd pushed for her to foster the dog because he'd thought it would be good for her. But he'd underestimated the cost of when she'd have to give him up. And he'd wanted to give her the love she so desperately needed.

And in the process, there'd been a moment last night where they'd looked into each other's eyes and he'd just known. The reason he'd been holding himself back was because he'd been waiting for her.

He was falling in love with her. With his best friend's sister. With a girl who'd grown to be a capable, strong, fun, caring woman.

And she wasn't falling for him in return. Damn, that hurt. And he didn't know what to do about it.

Christy finally came up to him as he was counting out antibiotics to give to a patient. "Hey, Dr. Gallagher."

"Hi, Christy. What's up?"

She paused, and at her silence he stopped and looked over at her. She looked half angry and half frightened. "What is it?" he asked.

She took a deep breath. "I've been here the longest so I'm the spokesperson this morning," she said, her voice soft but determined. "You've made Lexi cry. I don't know what happened to put you in such a bad mood today, but you can't take it out on the staff."

Heat rushed to his cheeks. Partly because he was being taken to task by a woman two years older than he was, and a member of his staff. And partly because he knew she was absolutely right.

"I'm sorry. I know I need to apologize. I've been trying to get myself in a better frame of mind first."

"I don't know what happened, but this isn't like you, Rory." She switched to his first name. "You're always the easygoing one. You never growl at us. And a bit of a bad mood is one thing, but when you start snapping and being a shit, it's not okay. She's new and she had a simple question."

"I know," he replied, thoroughly chastised. "It's been a crappy day, but that's not your fault, or anyone else here. I'll apologize. And try harder to be less of a 'shit.'" He smiled a little.

"Good. Your eleven o'clock is in exam three. Have fun expressing his anal glands."

He raised an eyebrow at her saucy tone, and she shrugged. "Call it karma for today," she said, and then headed back to the front desk.

Oaklee stopped at The Purple Pig and picked up boxes of muffins, cookies, and fancy breads to take to the garden center. Emily was behind the counter, dressed in a pair of skinny jeans and a tunic-style sweater, covered by an apron with the Purple Pig logo. "Hey, girlfriend."

Oaklee tried a smile, and hoped Em's radar wasn't operating at a hundred percent today. "Hey. I came by for the stuff for the Chamber meeting. Is it ready?"

Em nodded. "Boxed it up myself. Hang on. I'll help you get it to the car." She smiled at a customer, handed over their change, and then slipped into the back to retrieve the bakery boxes. She handed three to Oaklee, then went back for three more and they made their way out to Oaklee's car.

Once she'd shut the car door, Oaklee smiled at Em.

"So, I hear Willow's expecting. Is that going to affect you at all?"

Em shrugged. "Not right away. I'm slowly taking over the managerial duties, so when the time comes, it should be a pretty smooth transition. She'll still be around to help with the administration bits. It does give me some job security."

"Does this mean no expansion of the café, though?"

"It does. Willow still has the lease on the space next door now that the food bank is renovated after the fire. She's using it to open a yoga studio instead."

That was news. And welcome news, too. Other than a few classes open through the recreation department, there wasn't much in Darling for fitness facilities.

Em's gaze sharpened. "So, how did you hear? Willow told me, but said they'd only spoken to immediate family."

"Oh. Rory. We went for a walk after the Fall Frolic. He was pretty surprised."

Em's expression sharpened. "So, how are things going there? You've been very quiet since our sushi date."

"It's a long story, and I need to get over to the garden center." She really didn't want to get into it now. She was still feeling pretty fragile, and this was the kind of conversation that was best held over a bottle of cabernet.

"You're not . . . a thing?"

"Oh, well. Not really." Oaklee tried to brush off the question. Last night definitely constituted a thing. And here she was, once again, running away with her tail between her legs.

Emily's face fell. "Oh. You know, hearing Willow talk about him, I think the whole family would love to see him settle down. I know you're not ready for that, Oaklee, but I was kind of hoping you guys were going to try to make it work. I want to see you happy."

But no pressure, Oaklee thought. "We've been friends for too long," Oaklee explained. "And I imagine Cam would blow a gasket."

Except none of this was because of Cam or despite him. It had nothing to do with him, really, other than giving their relationship history and context. Last night had changed a lot of things. Last night they'd met as equals. As a man and a woman.

"Anyway," she continued, "I should get going and help Laurel set up. Tell Willow to come talk to me about the yoga studio. The town account can help spread the word, give some linky love, all that stuff."

"I will. Have fun at the meeting."

The warm welcome was continued at the garden center. Laurel had started the Ladybug when she moved back to Darling after her divorce. Now married and expecting her first child, she met Oaklee at the gate looking a bit pale.

Clearly she wasn't feeling one hundred percent. Oaklee parked close to the chain-link gate and hopped out of her car. "Did someone call for a muffin delivery?"

Laurel smiled. "I could use a muffin. I just lost the toast I had for breakfast." She smiled sheepishly. "Here I thought I was going to escape the worst of morning sickness. It's kicking my butt."

Oaklee had no idea what to do or really say. This was almost as bad as the spring and summer and all the weddings and baby showers. She was surrounded. But this was also Laurel. Rory's sister-in-law. It was somehow different. Or perhaps she was different. There wasn't really a lot of time to think about it, and for that she was glad. Keeping busy kept her from freaking out any more than she already was.

"Let me bring these in and I'll help you set up."

Laurel smiled. "That'd be great. George is already here, setting up a few tables for the food. But I want to move some things and set up chairs under the canopy. It's such a nice morning and I know it's crisp, but outside there's the scent of the fall flowers and fruit." The Ladybug was also selling some locally sourced produce, like pumpkins and apples. The fruity, pungent smell came from heavy wood bins piled with the fruit.

"I can definitely help with that." She was glad she'd worn trousers and a sweater repetition, with ankle boots rather than heeled shoes. It was a slightly more casual look than she wore to the office, but it would serve her well today.

For twenty minutes Oaklee helped George set up the tables. George was Laurel's right hand at the garden center, a former veteran and until recently, homeless citizen of Darling. Sometimes it was strange, seeing him in jeans and his red work shirt with the ladybug crest on the chest, when he'd used to sit on the corner, looking for food. She didn't know his story, but she knew that Laurel giving him this job had been life altering. He carried himself proudly, and while quiet and somewhat shy, he smiled at her a few times and they spoke about the best way to set up chairs. George even moved several tubs of mums and fall arrangements so that the whole area looked welcoming and warm.

Laurel reappeared carrying an extension cord and a

bag of paper cups. "I borrowed the big percolator from the women's group at the church," she explained. "If you can help me get it set up, we'll nearly be ready." A bit of the color had come back into her cheeks. "George is going to man the store while we're meeting. It hasn't been super busy lately anyway."

Her eyes clouded with what Oaklee perceived to be concern. "Do you need some marketing help?" she asked Laurel. "A social media campaign or something? We can talk about those things today, since fall and Thanksgiving promotions are on the agenda."

"That would be great. I've been wondering about Halloween and the pumpkins . . ."

"I'm sure we can come up with something. Ryan, the town's promotion guy, is coming to the meeting, too. I know our jobs are to promote the town's tourism industry, but our small businesses are all part of that." She leaned in. "I also know that most small businesses can't afford to hire someone to do their marketing and publicity. This is what the Chamber is for, Laurel. So no one has to go it alone."

The words hung in the air for a moment, holding an importance that Oaklee hadn't expected.

She'd been going it alone. Until Buster. Until Rory.

"That sounds great," Laurel said with a smile. "I can't afford for the business to struggle too much, you know? I'll have a new baby during our busiest season next year, and so I'll have extra manpower costs."

"I know we can come up with some good ideas." She reached over, grabbed a blueberry muffin, and took a bite. This morning's yogurt hadn't quite cut it as far as fuel, but she'd been too nervy to think about eating more. "If you like, I can help you brainstorm. Or you know who else is really good at this kind of thing? Claire. I bet you could even get her to do some work for you for free, as part of her college credits or something."

Laurel's face brightened. "That's a great idea! Thanks, Oaklee. You're a gem. Really glad you're seeing Rory, by the way. He's needed someone like you to shake him up a bit."

Oaklee's face froze mid-chew. She forced the bite of muffin down her throat. "Um, what do you mean?"

Laurel's face pinkened. "Oh, I'm sorry. Aiden just told me he'd had a talk with Rory a while back, and then we've seen you around together, and . . ."

Laurel's gaze met hers. "Shit. I've really stepped in it, haven't I? Did something happen between you two?"

Something had happened all right, but not the way Laurel meant. For weeks Oaklee had been able to avoid having this sort of conversation with Rory's family; now with one Chamber of Commerce event she was on the hot seat.

She had a hard time meeting Laurel's eyes. "We're just friends, that's all. He helped me when I hit the dog last month, remember? And we've known each other a long time."

"Right. The dog. How's he doing? At the Frolic we saw you being dragged along by him." Laurel laughed.

"He's back with his family. I was only fostering him." She struggled to keep her voice light, but it was a reminder that tonight when she went home there would be no Buster. No Rory. This was what happened when you got too close, too involved. Stuff *hurt*.

"Oh. Well, happy endings all around, then." Laurel

smiled and turned her head as a car crunched over the gravel drive. "And I think our first Chamber member is here. I'd better get that coffee going. It takes a while for it to brew."

Oaklee mingled through the coffee klatch portion of the meeting, where everyone chatted and caught up and was social. Normally she was on her game, getting people to commit to different things, coming up with plans for this and that, even taking notes on posts and tweets she'd want to send out about certain events or sales. Today, though, she was a bit off balance. Maybe it was lack of sleep. Maybe it was a bit of numbness, too. But she was relieved when the social hour was over and she could sit and listen as the committee chair went through the agenda. She took notes about Halloween sales and concerns, fall specials, fundraising ideas from food bank drives to specials at the local barbershops and salons for "Movember." Nothing really caught her attention until Hannah Gallagher got up and spoke about a Christmas charity event she wanted to run to support the local library and state literacy programs.

It was big enough, juicy enough, that Oaklee was intrigued. It was a good cause and would need volunteers. And she needed desperately to be involved in something rather than sitting around and overthinking. When Hannah suggested a day of programming followed by a fancy dinner and silent auction event, Oaklee knew this was right up her avenue.

She raised her hand, and when Hannah nodded in her direction, she said, "Count me in as a volunteer, Hannah. I'd love to help you put this together."

Hannah's gaze brightened. "Fantastic, Oaklee. We

can speak afterward. If anyone else wants to help out and be on a planning committee, let me know. Even if you don't want that much of a commitment, we'll need volunteers on the day. Even sparing an hour would be great."

The meeting ended and Oaklee felt more like her normal self. It was important to keep busy. To keep grounded. The whole mess with Rory felt like an out-of-control spiral, a mixed mess of emotions, like she'd suddenly lost her focus but had it back now, sharper than ever.

Hannah approached her as she was helping fold up the borrowed chairs. "Hey, thanks for volunteering. I'm so glad you did. You're so good at getting the word out, and with ideas . . . this is going to be great."

"I'm happy to help. And it's such a good cause." Oaklee smiled up at her. "Hit up your sister, too. Depending on your event date, she'll be home from school and she's sharp. I already told Laurel she should ask for Claire's help with garden center promotion and brainstorming stuff."

"You've really been a mentor to her, you know," Hannah said, smiling.

"Me? God, no. I was where she is not that long ago. I've got a long way to go before I can be a mentor."

"Don't be silly. She told us all that she looks up to you and you're the best thing about working in the town office. If she knows you're involved, she'll be on board." Hannah laughed, and then her smile softened. "And you and Rory . . . I'm so glad that's become a thing."

"It's not a thing." Oaklee's voice sharpened, and then she sighed. "I'm sorry, Hannah. I didn't mean to snap.

But Laurel said something similar. Does the whole family think that Rory and I are some hot item or something?"

Hannah looked at her closely. "Oh, dear. It's the real deal, isn't it? No one gets this angsty and defensive when it's not serious."

Oaklee and Hannah were not particularly close, but they were similar people. Ambitious, driven, and possibly a little bit pushy, but in what Oaklee hoped was a persistent and not a pain-in-the-ass kind of way. "This is awkward," she admitted. "Rory's your brother. And he's great. He's really, really great." He really was. That was the problem. "But we both have a lot of baggage to get through. I don't think it's going to work out." At Hannah's concerned expression, she lifted her hand. "It's okay. He's fine, I'm fine. Really. We tried it, but neither one of us is ready for anything big." She met Hannah's gaze. "I hope that doesn't change things for the charity."

"Of course it doesn't." Hannah shook her head. "And I'm sorry I stuck my nose in your personal business. I didn't realize it was . . . complicated." She pursed her lips. "Rory's been talking about you a lot, and he hasn't ever done that since he came back from school. He was nursing such a broken heart. Losing Ginelle and Kyle was such a blow. We were just hoping he'd finally moved past it."

Ginelle and . . . Kyle? Who the heck was Kyle?

"I didn't realize you knew," Oaklee said cautiously.

Hannah tossed her red hair over her shoulder and her expression hardened. "I think Aiden knows. They were roommates for a long time. And Rory never told me, but I knew something was up. His happy phone calls and e-mails stopped coming. All of the family knew was that he'd been seeing someone and apparently it hadn't worked out. I wasn't happy with that." She smiled a little. "He's my baby brother. I wanted to know about the bitch that hurt him."

Oaklee felt a bit cold, and it didn't have anything to do with the autumn chill. What would Hannah say if she knew about last night, and the way Oaklee had acted this morning?

"Oh, my."

Hannah laughed. "Don't worry, I didn't hurt her. I just asked a few questions. Talked to a few of his friends and then one day I saw her. She and her son were coming out of the college daycare. Then I got it. He'd fallen for her and for her kid. Of course he was going to need time to get over that. Rory always was a real softie. Look at what he does for a living. I was really hoping that he'd finally let someone in. It's about time, you know?"

Oaklee was reeling from the news and trying to act like she'd known all long. "He's definitely tender-hearted," she said weakly.

"Yeah. Hannah's gaze softened. "But you know, sometimes people just aren't ready to move forward. And sometimes they get a giant shove forward when they think they aren't ready, and it ends up being the best thing. Look at Laurel and Aiden. And Willow and Ethan. Man, I'm so glad to see Ethan happy again."

"Me, too," Oaklee agreed.

Hannah was quiet for a moment. "Okay, what's wrong? Did I say something wrong? I'm always doing that. I go full speed ahead and forget to be tactful."

Oaklee hesitated. "This is awkward, because he's your

brother, you know?" Oaklee wiped her hands on the front of her trousers. "I care about Rory, Hannah. I always have. It doesn't mean it'll work out." Particularly since he'd told her about Ginelle, but had left out the very telling detail that she'd had a child. That was a big deal. Of course Rory would have been devastated. He'd probably envisioned a family. She already knew he adored his nephews and was good with kids. This Ginelle must have really done a number on him for him to resort to dating-site hookups that were meaningless in the years since.

That he'd started to move past that—with her—scared her to death.

"And I'm sorry if I've put you in a tough spot."

Oaklee tried to make light of it. "Oh, just you and Laurel." She sighed. "But it says a lot that his family cares so much. I know he's a good guy. And the last thing I want to do is hurt him." She met Hannah's gaze. "I gotta say, the comment about finding the bitch that hurt him scared me a little bit."

Hannah smiled. "Nah, I like you. Regardless of whether or not you're in love with my brother."

Oaklee choked, letting out a strangled little cough that made Hannah laugh. She really liked the Gallagher girls, and Laurel, too. Maybe it was time she started making a few more friends. Let her world become a little bit bigger.

"Well," Hannah said, patting Oaklee's back, "I can see that scared the living hell out of you." She laughed. "Maybe my brother's finally met his match. Or maybe you have. Either way, I'll be in touch about the literacy fundraiser. I think this is going to be fun."

Oaklee nodded, still trying to ease the tickle in her throat, and with a wave, Hannah went on her way.

But then Oaklee was left with time to think, even as she folded up chairs and helped stack them for someone to pick up later. Why had Rory given her the protracted version of events when he'd confided in her? Clearly he hadn't been ready to share. Neither of them was. And perhaps that was what was needed most of all. Perhaps laying it all out there was the only way to move past the two-steps-forward thing. They always ended up back-tracking or regretting what they'd done. Or trying something that didn't work, like the "let's see where this leads" attitude.

Being cavalier about it had been a big, fat failure.

Was she ready? She'd already run out on him today. Could she possibly explain it all to him? And if she did, would he be truthful with her, too?

CHAPTER 15

Rory didn't call that night. Oaklee waited. She tried to read. Tried to work on some stuff from the office, since she'd missed the morning because of the meeting. But she was distracted, unfocused. She wondered if she'd ruined everything this morning, and she wondered if it was for the best. In addition, the apartment seemed so quiet and cold without Buster there, filling it up with his company, his snores, and his big eyes and bushy eyebrows.

She put the laptop aside and found a box in a storage closet. In it she put Buster's blanket, his bowls, and the Kong toy that Rory had bought for him at the beginning. By rights, these things belonged to Rory. He'd paid for them out of pocket. There was also a partial bag of food in the closet that was no longer needed. Surely they could use it to feed the dogs at the clinic, or could give it to someone, perhaps another foster owner.

She cried a little, packing it all up, but reminded

herself that Buster hadn't died. He'd gone home to be with his real family. That he was most likely happy and fed and well-loved at this moment. Even if he couldn't be with her, she was glad for that.

And he'd taught her something important about herself, too.

She was at least capable of loving. And yes, it hurt like hell. But she'd worked so hard at numbing those feelings, at shoving them down, that she'd truly started to think she wasn't even capable of any deep feeling. She was. She really was. At least it hadn't been taken away from her.

Now the big question was whether or not she *wanted* to care about someone or something, and not if she could or not.

The box of Buster's stuff sat in her kitchen for two more days. She'd gone over to her mother's for dinner both days, and learned how to make spaghetti sauce and a chicken and rice casserole. But by Saturday she was sick of seeing the box, sick to her stomach knowing that Rory hadn't even called her back after their night together. Not that she'd given him any encouragement, but he'd always at least sent her a message or . . . something.

He had. He'd taken the initiative more than once. And what had she done? Gone along with it. Going for walks, tacos and movies, the Fall Frolic . . . all his idea. Both of them so hesitant and scared of putting themselves out there that they hadn't even gone on a real date. They'd skirted around anything official. Even his family, who seemed to know that there was something going on, didn't know much of anything. Just that there was . . . something.

She looked at the box of stuff once more and decided that maybe what was needed was some dealing with stuff head-on. And maybe that meant apologizing for running scared and trying a new and revolutionary thing called going on a date.

Oaklee picked up her phone and held it in her hand for a moment. For Pete's sake, she went after what she wanted ninety percent of the time. No indecision, just making up her mind and jumping in. She'd done it with finding this job, renting the apartment, in her day-to-day duties. The whole reimagining of the town's tourism campaign had been her idea, and she'd had to strong-arm Laurel and Aiden into agreeing. But the moment she was faced with anything in her personal life, she'd backed off and run scared. Been swamped with indecision and second thoughts.

Damn, she was tired of it. And if this thing with Rory wasn't going to work, she at least wanted to know. Wanted to clear the air and move on. She'd handled herself poorly.

And then she decided not to dial, and typed instead.

@OakleeC_Darling: Looking for a good place for a date night around Darling, VT. Any suggestions? @DrRoryG

She'd found his new Twitter handle and tagged him in it, and she sat up straighter on the sofa as suggestions began popping up. The Foxborough Inn for dinner. A club in Burlington, dinner and a movie, tweeted by a restaurant that had a menu fixe plus tickets special. Go Karts . . . that sounded fun and intriguing, too.

She replied to them all, little comments to give them a bit of a boost. There was a dinner theater, a historic walk, and a corn maze and haunted house set up for the upcoming month as Halloween drew near. That one seemed kind of Rory's style, but she knew she'd hate the haunted house, so she let it alone and just gave it a retweet. Miniature golf, bowling . . .

Oaklee stopped at that one. An indoor sports bar, only about thirty minutes away, that had a mini golf course, a driving range simulator, bowling, pool, and an arcade racing game. It sounded like huge fun, and even though she wasn't sporty, this wasn't really sports. She hit retweet and tagged him again.

> @OakleeC_Darling: RT Sam's Sports Bar for great games and food! What do you say, @DrRoryG?

The twitterverse seemed to pause for a moment, and then a tweet came in.

> @SamsSportsonSouth: Yeah, @DrRoryG. You gonna say yes or what?

Oaklee laughed out loud. Three more tweets came in, all tagging Rory and asking if he was going to go.

> @DrRoryG: Are you asking me out on a date? Really?

> @OakleeC_Darling: Yes. On a date.

> @DrRoryG: Funny.

Oaklee frowned. Wow, was he really that pissed? Her notification sound pinged and she looked down. He'd dm'd her. "You're asking me on a date over Twitter? This is weird. Oaklee, after the other morning . . . this is messed up."

She typed back, her heart in her throat. "I freaked out. And you didn't call. But I also realized we'd never actually gone on an honest-to-goodness date. Maybe we should try it."

Meanwhile, her Twitter feed was blowing up. All asking Rory if he was going to say yes or not, and why hadn't he answered?

Her dm window flashed. "I don't know, Oaklee."

Her heart sank, but she took a deep breath and squared her shoulders. "Okay. It's up to you. I just wanted to . . . try. I don't like how we left things."

"Me, either."

There was a pause, then he sent, "I'm taking a bit of a beating on Twitter."

She laughed. "Then say yes. Chicken wings and beer and kicking my ass at mini golf. Come on, Rory. It's just a single evening. If nothing else, let's patch things up instead of leaving everything on a sour note."

"Okay."

"Okay?"

"Yes, fine. Tomorrow night."

She immediately went back to her Twitter feed.

@OakleeC_Darling: He said yes! Pick you up tomorrow at six, @DrRoryG.

The resulting cyber-teasing directed at Rory made her grin from ear to ear. Maybe this wasn't love. Maybe . . . just maybe it was. Maybe making love to Rory at such an emotional time really just caused her to freak out and withdraw. It was understandable, wasn't it? But the truth was, for the last month, she felt as if she'd been living in someone else's skin; a bit too small, confining and uncomfortable.

And now she understood what held him back a little bit better. She wished he'd told her himself, but she hadn't been that open with him either.

It had taken getting hurt again, losing something she cared about, to make her realize that she could survive it. And it had taken Hannah's words at the Chamber of Commerce meeting to remind her that she was stronger than this. Better than this. And she could apply what she'd learned in her professional life to her personal life.

She spent all her working days hustling for things for other people. Now she'd try going after something for herself.

She'd thought for a long, long time that Jeff leaving her at the altar was *her* humiliation. But the truth was, it was *his*. He'd been the coward. He'd been the one to propose, to make plans with her, to fly with her all the way to Las Vegas, and he'd been the one to drink champagne as they booked the chapel.

She'd been the one to show up. Just like she'd shown up for Buster. Like she'd shown up for her job and more recently, reconnecting with her parents.

She'd been so determined to not get hurt like that again that she'd missed that crucial distinction.

But no more. Maybe what Rory needed . . . maybe the reason he hadn't called, was because he needed someone to fight for him. She hadn't been prepared to.

She wasn't sure he was prepared to fight for her, either, but one of them had to take the first step.

Rory saw Oaklee drive into the clinic parking lot and wondered what the hell he was doing.

He hadn't wanted to be charmed by her unorthodox way of asking him out on a date, but it was just so *Oaklee* that he couldn't say no. Using Twitter as a dating service? She had to have known other people would get in on it—including people from Darling. For someone so worried about appearances, she'd been very public. And cute, dammit.

She started to move from her car to the back stairs of the clinic, and he realized she had a big box in her hands. Frowning, he went to the apartment door and trotted down the stairs to meet her at the bottom. The box contained a partial bag of food, with the top folded over and over, and Buster's bowls and toys. She met his gaze. "You provided them. I figured you'd know someone else who could use them. Or if they're from the clinic, they should be returned."

Her voice was steady, he noticed. "How're you doing without him?" he asked.

"It's hard. It's lonely. But when I feel down I remind myself that he's with his family and getting lots of love. That's what's important, right?"

Rory nodded, a wave of affection rolling over him. Sometimes she confused the hell out of him, but damned if she didn't have a big heart.

He took the box from her hands. "I'll put this upstairs and then we can go, okay? Do you want to take my car or yours?"

She smiled at him. "I invited you. I'll drive. If that's okay."

"I think I'm secure enough in my masculinity to handle it."

He ran upstairs and deposited the box inside the door, and then jogged back down the stairs and met her at the bottom. She looked cute tonight, in jeans and little brown boots and a red jacket with a woolly scarf wound around her neck.

They drove the half hour to the bar, and parked in a lot that was about two-thirds full. Neon lights lit the outside, with the word SAM's continuously lit and then flashing bowling pins that gave the appearance of tipping over.

Rory hadn't been to a place like this in ages. Not since he'd been in college. He and Aiden and Ethan tended to do the real thing, and go play a round of golf or head to the driving range. Or the batting cages—they'd all played ball at one time or another growing up. And this wasn't exactly the kind of place he'd bring someone on a first date.

Another indication that Oaklee was different. And that worked in her favor.

They stepped inside the door and music beat from big speakers, more on the rock side of things than pop. A bar was set up in the middle, with tables all around, where people sat and enjoyed drinks and food. The place itself was huge, accommodating several activities. Cheers went up from every corner when someone made a good shot or won a race. Lights flashed and it gave the impression of a carnival, only without the cheap stuffed animals for prizes or games of chance.

"What do you want to do first?" she asked. "Tonight's on me."

He remembered her talking about money when she'd taken in Buster, and he didn't feel comfortable letting her pay for everything. "You don't have to do that. I know you're going to say you asked me, but—"

"But nothing. It's fine, I promise. Besides, the games don't look that pricey. She went to the arcade car racing and grinned. "Fifty cents apiece for a round. Wanna go?"

How could he say no? They waited a few minutes for two chairs to open up side by side, and then he slid into one and she sat in the other. She handed him a couple of quarters.

Once his money was in, he quickly picked his car and they chose their track. He looked over and grinned at her car choice—a Skyline. She wasn't messing around. She flashed him a smile and winked. "Ready?" she asked.

He nodded and she hit the Start button. The timer counted down from five . . .

And then they were off. There was no time to look over at her; he was too focused on keeping his car on the road as they snaked around turns. Once he went into the guardrail and she zoomed past him, laughing and sending a little trash talk his way. But then she went around a corner, drifted, and went right into the rock wall. Then he laughed and flew past her car. And so they went, lap after lap, until it was the final lap and he was slightly in the lead. "I've got your ass now," he taunted, taking the final turn.

But he accelerated too soon, the back end of his car spun out, and she zipped by him, speeding the last hundred yards to the finish.

"You were saying?" she asked, and gave his arm a nudge. "That right there? Bragging rights."

There was no one waiting for the game, so they played another round, which Rory won, and then a third to break the tie. Halfway through the last lap, Oaklee hit the rail and spun herself around so she was facing the wrong direction. It cost her so much time that she lost.

"Who has bragging rights now?" Rory asked, grinning. A group was waiting to play at this point, so they got up from the chairs and moved out of the way. "You did better than I expected, you know," he said.

She chuckled. "You and Cam used to play *Gran Turismo*, do you remember?"

He nodded. "For hours. We used to talk about the cars we were going to get when we were older and had bags full of money."

"I used to play, too. Just not with you because you guys used to kick me out of the family room."

"Why am I not surprised?"

They moved on to bowling next, where Oaklee wiped the floor with him. Her small hands looked dwarfed by the giant bowling balls, but she sent them down the lane with determination and scored several spares. Her cheeks were flushed with exertion and laughter, and she looked absolutely beautiful. She'd taken off her coat and scarf and wore a simple top in navy blue, which brought out her eyes and set off her blond hair. He was so distracted that he totally messed up his next shot and sent it into the gutter.

When they finished the game, they decided to get some drinks and food. Rory found a small table in a corner, and Oaklee sank into it with a laugh.

"Okay," she said, brushing her hair back from her face. "I totally think this was a great idea. I'm having so much fun!"

"Me, too," he said, accepting menus from a harried-looking waitress. "I was doubtful, but . . . yeah." Her eyes twinkled at him in a way they hadn't in the last six weeks. "You're different tonight," he said.

"I am? How?"

"I don't know. More relaxed. Something."

She leaned forward a little. "I think maybe we went about this the wrong way," she said, and put her hand on his arm. "We did this thing where we were very determined to not date. And then we'd get all . . . datey. And it made everything confusing and screwed up, and then we'd run away. So I thought maybe we could hit a reset button and do something fun. No pressure. Just kind of normal, without all the extra . . . I don't know . . . context we seemed to bring to everything."

It made sense, except it was very hard to backtrack, especially after they'd slept together. Still, he didn't want to ruin the night. They were having fun. Maybe she was right. Maybe going back to the beginning and starting again was for the best. They'd both freaked out after he'd spent the night. She'd run away and he'd . . .

Well, he'd figured out that he was falling for her. Knowing she didn't quite feel the same gave him room to breathe. His own feelings he could deal with; he'd been doing it ever since Ginelle had left him. The last thing he needed was for Oaklee to start professing her love or something. Their last encounter had simply reinforced what he'd already known: that taking it slow had nothing to do with how fast he might fall for her.

Going back to square one meant buying a little more time before he really had to deal with the possibility of an actual relationship. To get used to the idea without breaking into a cold sweat.

They ordered a basket of hot wings and a plate of nachos and Rory got a beer since Oaklee was driving and was sticking to soda. Before long their fingers and lips were orange with hot sauce, though the sour cream from the nachos helped cool things considerably. Drinks were refilled, and then Rory picked up the bill for the food. "Let's do it this way," he said, reaching into his back pocket for his wallet. "You can pick up the tab for all the games, and I'll pay for eats."

"You do remember that I'm the one who invited you," she reminded him.

"I know. But if we really want to keep it casual and fun, isn't it better if we both pay a bit and have it . . . well, equal?"

She gave in, and he paid for the food and drinks. But then she was ready to go again, so they hit the golf simulator, which she was terrible at, and then mini golf, which she was much better at. Her putting skills far outweighed her drives, and she jumped up and down as she hit a ball up over a bump, through a windmill, down the other side, around a curve, bumping off the sides, and then watched it drop with an audible *plop* into the cup.

"I did it! I got a hole in one! Suck it, Gallagher!" She did a little victory dance that was delightfully awkward, and he couldn't help but start laughing. And then it took him four tries to get his ball through the windmill and another two on the other side to get it in the cup.

The final event of the evening was pool, and she took

out a five-dollar bill and put it on the cherry table as they sorted out sticks and chalked the ends. "Five bucks to the winner," she said, challenging him with a competitive glare.

"You're on," he said. He'd played a decent amount of pool in college, particularly when he'd been with Ginelle and an evening out at the bar with the guys meant shooting a game or two rather than trying to pick up girls. "We're two-all for events tonight, so Sam's Sports Champion goes to the winner of the game."

She took out a coin. "Flip to see who breaks?" she asked.

He won the break so he set up the balls, stepped back, lined up the white ball, and let it fly.

He sank a solid, and the game was on.

When he first missed, she stepped up to the table, called her ball, lined it up, and dropped it into the side pocket.

She wasn't going to suck at this. She might even make it a game.

He couldn't help but notice the way her jeans and top fit against her body as she angled herself over the table, pulled back the cue, and banked another ball off the side and into a corner pocket. Damn.

After three balls, she missed one and it was his turn again. And on they went, neck and neck, until it was her turn, she sunk her last striped ball, and set herself up for the eight.

And missed.

A small group had gathered around the table, sensing a decently competitive game, and one of the guys cheered Rory on. "Come on, man. Show her who's boss. Right in the corner."

Another guy elbowed the first. "Naw, man. She can take him."

He looked over at Oaklee. Despite her missed shot, she was grinning from ear to ear. Damn, this was fun.

He focused on the ball. Lined up. Drew the cue back a few times, reconsidered his angle, kept it the same, and finally hit the ball, just hard enough to have a gentle bank off the side and send the ball rolling toward the bottom right corner pocket.

It died an inch from the hole.

Whoops went up from the spectators as he stared at the ball. Not only had he missed, but all she had to do was tap it gently and it would drop, ending the game. She slipped by him, and leaned in close to his ear. "Couldn't quite get to the finish, huh?"

Heat rushed through his body, and when he looked at her, her eyes were dancing at him. Minx.

She tapped the ball, and then reached for the ten dollars from the bet, folded it, and tucked it into her bra. Wasn't she the saucy one tonight?

A couple of the guys clapped her on the shoulder, and Rory saw another woman send her a wink. They gave up the table and put away their cues, and Oaklee laughed out loud at him. "How's your masculinity now?"

"A bit bruised, but recoverable," he said. What he really wanted to do was show her exactly how intact it was, but kissing her right now felt like the wrong time. They were taking baby steps, after all, and having such a good time that he didn't want to do anything to screw it up.

She checked her watch, then looked up at him. "I have to work tomorrow. Would it be okay if we headed back to Darling?"

"Unless you feel the need to utterly humiliate me again, that's fine." He grinned at her. "I had fun, though. We should do this again."

"I agree. And the food was good. I want to try that Kitchen Sink appetizer thing."

He'd seen that, too. A giant platter containing six different kinds of appetizers. Another table had ordered one and it was too much for two people, but it had looked incredible.

They got their jackets and headed out into the cool night. Rory got into her car and watched her as she got in and put on her seatbelt and started the engine. He wasn't quite sure how he felt about the evening. It had been fun, so fun. But it had only showed him how much he cared for her, and how there was a depth to their friendship . . . for lack of a better word . . . that made everything between them resonate a little bit deeper.

She drove toward Darling, and then took a detour away from town, out toward the lake. "You don't mind if we go somewhere to talk for a bit, do you?" she asked. "I want to show you something."

His stomach knotted. The night had been so perfect. Talking . . . well, with their history, that was just going to complicate matters.

Dammit.

Oaklee looked over at Rory's profile in the dim light of the dash. Her question hung heavy in the air around them.

His jaw had tightened, and nerves began tingling in her stomach and down her legs. She shouldn't be anxious about this, except she was. She wanted to tell him the truth about Jeff, and why she was the way she was, and she hoped that it would prompt him to open up about Ginelle and her son. That first night on the Green they'd agreed to honesty, but neither of them had been truly honest with each other. If they were going to begin again, this was the starting point.

"I thought you had to get home?"

She shrugged. "I do. But it's only ten. I don't think staying out a little longer will break my curfew."

She smiled, but he didn't really smile back.

As she drove down Frontage Road, she slowed near a stand of pines. "Right around here," she said quietly. "This is where I hit Buster. Oh, he scared me so much." She glanced over at him, thinking of the words "the truth, the whole truth, and nothing but the truth." "My phone buzzed and I picked it up to see who was messaging me. Next thing I knew, there he was, and I couldn't stop fast enough."

Rory's eyebrows went up. "You were texting?"

She nodded. "Yes, I was. And I haven't since. And I know I was incredibly lucky that I didn't kill him, or someone else, or myself. What I wanted to say was, that night a lot of things changed for me. At the time it was horrible. And all of it was hard, but hitting Buster with my car was exactly what I needed to give me a wake-up call."

"My first column was about car safety with your pets." He shook his head. "You must have been shitting your pants when I suggested it."

"My guilt complex did make an appearance," she replied, smiling softly. "And if I'm being totally honest, a big part of why I agreed to foster him was because I didn't just hit him, I hit him because of my own inattention."

"So now where are we going?"

She smiled a little. "My thinking spot. Who is it that has one of those? Winnie the Pooh? I seem to remember something like that from when I was a kid. Mine's the public beach at the lake, though I stay away from the public part and usually go to the left of it, down past the picnic area. When I really want to ponder life's mysteries, or get away, I need to get out of Darling to do it. I love our town, but it can feel a bit close sometimes." She turned off the main road, onto a smaller one that led to the lake. "I don't know what it is, whether it's the fresh air, or the trees, or the water . . . but this is my favorite place to go."

"We used to come out here as kids. Be jealous of all the boats on the water, because our family couldn't afford one. Not with six kids to bring up."

She pictured it in her head. The Gallaghers were loud and boisterous but loving and fun. It made a lovely picture in her head. "I only had Cam, and he was always playing hockey," she confessed. "It made me a little lonely sometimes. I either sat at the rink with my mom and dad, or stayed at a friend's place on the weekends. I'm stupid proud of him, of course, but I'm always a little jealous of families with lots of kids."

She'd never admitted that to anyone before. And she was so undomestic, it felt strange to think of being a part of a big family. But it felt a little bit right, too.

The parking lot was completely empty; unsurprising since it was a Sunday night in October. Oaklee parked facing the water, the surface a flat, black pool surrounded by the hulking shapes of spruces, pines, and hardwood trees still flaunting their fall colors, undiscernible now in the dark. Still, she rolled down the window and let in the cool air, leaned her head back, and took a deep breath.

"It is nice out here," Rory said beside her. "So, this is your thinking spot. Did you bring me here to do some special thinking?"

She rolled her head to the side to look at him, and offered a sideways smile. "You mean like parking?"

She wasn't sure he was going to smile back, but he finally did, just a soft curving of his lips.

"Maybe a bit like parking," he said. "But . . . I'm not that easy on a first date."

She laughed then, ending on a sigh. She liked him. She really, really liked him. As a person. As a friend. And as a friend, she was going to confide in him and try to make everything right instead of being afraid.

"I brought you out here because I wanted to tell you something I should have told you a long time ago. At least when we first started . . . well, seeing each other is probably the best descriptor." She ignored the voice in her head that said she should protect herself and remain quiet. She couldn't live this way forever. "We said we were going to be honest, but I wasn't honest with you. I wasn't even really honest with myself."

"O . . . kay," he answered, and she heard the caution in his voice. This wasn't easy, for both of them. But they couldn't go on the way they were, spinning their wheels. And she was just smart enough to know that if she didn't deal with this now, it would follow her in her next relationship attempt, and so on.

She needed to rip off the Band-Aid. For strength, she thought back to when she'd told her mother about the elopement, and what her mom had said.

The only thing Oaklee had done wrong was trust the wrong man.

"On spring break of my final year of my degree, Jeff and I concocted a plan to get married. We'd been together since high school. We were nearly done with our degrees, both of us were carrying some student debt, and we figured we had all the answers. We decided to do a spring break wedding and honeymoon, and caught a great last-minute deal to Vegas. Flight, hotel, you name it. I bought a white dress that I could wear again, picked up a rose, and went to the chapel to wait for him."

She had Rory's complete attention; she felt his gaze stuck on her profile. But she couldn't meet his eyes just now. She didn't want to see the dismay or pity. She just wanted to be honest.

"I was so excited, Rory. It felt risky and grown-up and amazing and adventurous. Our college years were coming to a close, and all I could think of was that we were getting a jump on the next stage of our lives, together. We'd stayed together through high school, all through college. We'd made plans. Oh, there were signs, and I missed them all. Or if I did see them, I thought it was just stuff that we could overlook because we'd been together for so long. We're talking five years." She looked over at Rory now, and he was watching her intently but she couldn't read the expression on his face. "I'd been with the same guy for five faithful years. Five years of sharing dreams. Of making plans. Of talking about our future careers and ten-year plans."

She swallowed against a painful lump in her throat.

"What happened?" he asked gently.

"I went to the chapel, in my white dress, with my rose, excited beyond belief. I was in Vegas! It felt surreal. I was getting married. I'd be leaving the chapel with a ring on my finger and a husband. I was on top of the world. And then it was fifteen minutes to our appointed time and he wasn't there yet. And then ten, and five, and the appointment came and I was still there alone. I was starting to get really worried, you know? I'd seen Jeff that morning, and he'd gone to plan some things, and to give me time to get ready. He had said he'd meet me there. I came up with all kinds of scenarios. First it was maybe he couldn't get a cab. Or there was heavy traffic. Then when he didn't answer his phone I thought maybe he'd been in an accident. Meanwhile, couple after couple came and went, happy and excited. And I waited, and waited, and waited . . . trying so hard not to cry, not to panic . . . not to let anyone see that I was dying inside. It never even occurred to me that he wasn't actually trying to get to me. I was certain that something terrible had happened to him. He'd been robbed, mugged, hit by a car . . ."

She bit down on her lip. And reminded herself that trusting someone did not make her stupid. She'd maybe been blind, but not stupid.

He reached over and touched her hand, gripping the steering wheel so tightly that her fingers cramped.

She let out her breath. "I finally got a text, two hours and twenty-three minutes past our scheduled time. It said, and I quote, 'I can't do this. I'm sorry. I'm already on a plane. Sorry, babe. This's on me.'"

A laugh bubbled out of her throat. "Can you imagine? 'This's on me.' That's how you end five years of fidelity, of growing up together? Of loving each other?"

Rory let out a growly sound. "Jesus. I knew you guys had split. I knew he'd broken your heart. But I didn't realize he'd been such a . . . such a . . . douche," he finished.

Oaklee laughed harder, this time out of amusement and not disbelief. "Oh Rory, that's so perfect. He really was a total coward about it. I mean . . . yeah, I probably would've cried. It wouldn't have been a really calm conversation, but I deserved better than that. In person. Maybe before I'd spent money on a dress, and a plane ticket, and the wedding license . . ."

"What did you do?" Rory asked.

"I walked out of the chapel with my head held up and my eyes dry. And I never cried. Not once. Not packing my things, not staying in that room all alone for the next two nights . . . you see, we'd bought an all-inclusive thing including airfare. I wouldn't get any money back if I'd left early, and would've had to pay extra to change my flight to an earlier time. I spent my two-day honeymoon alone in my hotel room because I couldn't afford to do anything in Vegas and I couldn't afford to leave."

"I'm so sorry," Rory said. "Getting stomped on like that . . . I can't believe he did that. He always seemed like a good enough guy, you know? Even Cam thought he was okay." Rory straightened. "Does Cam know about this? Because he'd be really upset that you'd been treated this way."

"Which is why I didn't tell him the whole story. It

was mid-season, and they were on a playoff run. The last thing I needed was for him to fly out and beat the shit out of Jeff and then go back with a broken hand or some stupid thing. I just told him we'd broken up, and that I was okay, but short of cash. The trip tapped out all my savings," she admitted. "Cam lent me five hundred to get me through to the end of the semester. That was all I'd accept, though he said I could have whatever I wanted."

"Because he cares about you. And he has more money than he knows what to do with."

"I'm not about to take advantage of that."

"I know."

She leaned her head back against the headrest. "So I've spent two years single, determined to spend it alone, while being incredibly lonely. And then Buster comes along, and for the first time since Jeff bitch-slapped me with reality, I let myself care. I was going to keep him. If no one had come forward, I was going to take down the ads and adopt him myself. And when his family showed up and took him away, it felt just like going through that breakup all over again. In my head I know that sending Buster back to his family isn't the same thing, and my pain was probably disproportionate. But I hadn't felt anything in so long. And then you were there with your sad eyes and strong arms, and I just had to cling to someone to make it okay again."

She turned in her seat. "And when I woke up in the morning, I was so scared. So scared, Rory. Because I care for you. Because I'd let myself be weak again. And all I could do was try to protect myself."

Silence fell in the car. Finally, Rory said, "Why are you telling me all this now?"

She looked over at him. "Because I'm tired of spending so much energy to protect myself. And I want to be able to trust someone again, but I don't know how. All I know is that out of anybody in the world, I feel like I can trust you the most. So instead of leaving things as they were, with all my mistakes, I wanted to start with a clean slate. Total honesty, and a first date that was just fun. Ground zero for you and me. I had a really good time, you know? And I think now, if we can have total honesty between us, we might have some idea where to go from here."

"Right."

His face seemed tense, though it was hard to tell in the dim light. "Are you upset that I told you?"

He turned in his seat. "No, of course not. I'm honored that you trusted me with that, especially if you've never told anyone else."

"Just my mom, but not quite as much with the details. Moms don't like to hear the deets about how their daughters' hearts get crushed into dust, you know?"

He laughed a little, a tight, uncomfortable sound. "Or about their baby boys, either."

"Yours doesn't know about Ginelle, you said." She started the subject, hoping he would come clean. Be as open with her as she was with him. Then they could really start at square one.

"There's not much to tell. We were together, and then we weren't." He shrugged. "She didn't love me enough. Kind of like Jeff. It does make it hard to trust anyone again."

She'd basically poured out her soul tonight, and had hoped that he wouldn't still hold back. Maybe he just needed a little more encouragement. Some understanding. "Yeah," she said softly. "We just handled it in opposite ways. I stopped dating completely. And you went for the casual but no-strings plan. But after a while, it doesn't work, does it? I think that's what the last month has taught me. I can't run away from it anymore. I'll only move on if I face what happened head on and find a way to put it behind me and put my faith in someone again."

"You make it sound so easy."

Her heart softened a bit, and she put her hand on his knee. "It's the hardest thing I've ever done, Rory. I don't know why I wasn't enough. Or why we grew apart, only that we did. And I have no idea if I'll be enough for someone else, and I'm scared to try. But this isn't working so . . . I think I have to switch things up. Tidy my house and let my life get messy, rather than the other way around."

"Maybe. Maybe I have to stop trying to control everything. I'm just afraid of getting sucker-punched in the love department again."

"I know you are. She must have hurt you very badly. It's hard to lose what you thought was your future, when you're thinking about becoming a family."

If that wasn't a lead-in, she didn't know what was. She'd all but said it for him, except leaving out the word "Kyle."

His eyes gleamed at her in the moonlight. "Yes, it is. But tonight was a good start, I think. I had a lot of fun, and I'm glad we talked. Let's just . . . take it slow and steady. See where it leads. Maybe we can go out again next weekend."

Oaklee's heart sank. She'd taken a risk, and it hadn't

paid off. At all. Sure, maybe another date was a victory, but it wasn't the objective. The objective was trust with the truth. Trusting each other with their hearts might take a lot longer, but she'd invited him to share, and he'd shut her out.

"That would be nice. Do you want to pick the place this time?"

"Sure. I'll text you this week. Unless you want to promo it on Twitter."

She smiled a little and started the car again, rolling up the window against the cold air. "Naw, just pick it," she said, without a whole lot of enthusiasm. "I'd better get us back to Darling. Since we both have to work in the morning."

The drive was quiet, and it seemed to take forever to reach the clinic. Oaklee put the car in park but didn't get out; it wasn't like he needed a walk to the door, and she wasn't even really feeling like she wanted a good-night kiss. It would just be a sad P.S. to a night that had started brilliantly and then fizzled out at the end.

"Thanks for a great night," he said, unbuckling his seatbelt. An awkward pause formed inside the car, and finally he leaned over and kissed her cheek. She closed her eyes, absorbing the light touch, wishing for things that she thought would probably never be. The taste of disappointment was strong as he pulled away and reached for the door handle.

"Drive safely," he said quietly, and she smiled at him through the light created by the overhead bulb.

"I will. Good night, Rory."

He shut the door and lifted his hand in a farewell wave.

Oaklee drove home feeling let down, but strong. She'd done it. She'd opened herself up to someone and the world hadn't come to an end. She'd faced disappointment and she was still standing, though feeling slightly bruised from the encounter.

She was stronger than she'd given herself credit for, and she'd continue to be, even if Rory kept himself locked away in the same old patterns.

CHAPTER 16

Wednesday night, everyone gathered at Ethan's for supper. While Moira had hosted many a weekly family dinner for the whole Gallagher clan, times were changing. Now Ethan and Aiden were both in committed relationships, and lately they'd taken to sharing host duties. It was great for the family, and as Ethan said, it meant the boys could enjoy everyone's company and then get ready for bed as it was a school night and they wouldn't wake up completely cranky the next morning.

As Rory parked on the street outside Ethan's house, he wondered if this also meant that Christmas mornings were going to rotate from house to house as more babies were in the picture.

Kyle would have been a year older than Connor now. If things had worked out the way Rory had planned, they would have grown up as cousins. Instead Rory found himself thinking about the boy nearly every day. After two years, it didn't hurt as badly, but he still missed

Kyle's dark hair and freckles and cheesy grin. In fact, he thought maybe he missed that more than he missed Ginelle.

With both girls away at school and everyone else coupled up, Rory and Hannah were the odd ones out. As such, they found themselves seated together in the living room with their plates on the coffee table, since Ethan's dining table seated six, and Ethan, Willow, the boys, and Aiden and Laurel filled the chairs. Their parents, John and Moira, sat in patio chairs in the kitchen, with foldable TV trays in front of them. Willow had made two large vegetarian lasagnas and salad, with a whole loaf of garlic bread. When Rory looked over at Connor and Ronan, both of their faces were covered in tomato sauce. He grinned.

"Those two are going to be so much trouble," he said to Hannah.

She nodded. "They already are. And so damned cute it's hard to be mad at them. Ethan told me that last week he caught them by the rose bushes, peeing, and seeing whose could go farther."

Rory nearly choked on his garlic bread crumbs. "Oh, Lord."

"Sound like someone else we might know?" She lifted an eyebrow.

"I know." He sighed, feeling unsettled. He'd been feeling this way since Sunday's date with Oaklee. Something just wasn't sitting right. The first part of the night had been simply amazing. So fun, so relaxed. And then she'd told him about Jeff and he'd been unsure of what to say, and then it had felt like she was waiting for him to say the right words and when he hadn't, they'd gone home and left things off balance yet again.

Maybe they should seriously stop beating a dead horse and just move on.

"What's going on with you, little bro?" she asked, cutting into her pasta.

"I dunno, Han."

"This have something to do with Oaklee Collier? The whole town knows she asked you out online last week. How'd that go?"

He shrugged. "I guess okay. We had a lot of fun at first. We both just have a lot of baggage."

"Funny," Hannah said casually. "That's what she said to me, too. Baggage."

Rory put down his fork. "When did she say that?"

"The morning of the Chamber of Commerce breakfast."

He remembered that morning. It was the morning after he'd spent the night, when she'd gone running scared. "What else did she say?"

"Not much. Just that you both had trouble trusting or something." She frowned, as if trying to remember. "I think she worries about you, you know? Because of Ginelle and Kyle."

She said it so casually that he did a double take. "What?"

Hannah met his gaze evenly. "You thought I didn't know? I've known all along, honey. I'm your big sister." She smiled a little. "I have no personal life. And when you dropped off the family radar, I figured something had gone very wrong."

"You knew?"

He kept his voice low, because other than Aiden, no one in the family knew. And that was how he'd wanted it.

"Once I figured out you were going to be okay, I waited for you to tell us. When you didn't, well, I do have some boundaries." She smiled softly. "I figured you wanted your privacy."

His stomach twisted, and his appetite fled. "And you talked to Oaklee about it?"

"Yeah. She opened up a bit, you know? And said you both had hurts to get over. The only woman you've ever been serious is Ginelle. It wasn't a hard deduction to make."

Oh, God. He closed his eyes. Okay. Maybe no names had been spoken. Because this was not something he wanted Oaklee to hear from his sister. Damn it all. "Did you actually use those words, Hannah? Did you say their names?"

Hannah frowned. "I don't know. I think so." She hesitated. "She does know about them, right? Because she seemed unsurprised."

He put his forehead on his hand. "She knew about Ginelle. She didn't know about her son. Goddammit, Han."

"You didn't tell her?"

"No."

Hannah put her plate on the coffee table. "Damn, Rory. I'm sorry." She let out a big breath and twisted her fingers together. "I need to learn how to shut my mouth. My big mouth spilled the beans on Willow's pregnancy, too. I thought she was going to kill me."

Rory felt sick to his stomach. Oaklee had told him all about Jeff the other night. About why she'd been so hurt, about why her trust had been so broken. It hadn't just been a breakup but a betrayal of the worst kind. At least Ginelle had been honest and hadn't let it get to a wedding day before heading for the hills.

And Oaklee had opened the door for him to share. She'd said something about losing the hope for a family. All he'd needed to say was Kyle's name. That he hadn't just lost the woman he loved but a boy he considered a son. And instead he'd offered her nothing. He'd held on to that secret, tight to his chest, because the simple truth was he wasn't sure anyone would understand the emptiness he'd felt at losing a kid that wasn't his. He hadn't seen Kyle be born. He hadn't changed his diapers or walked the floor with him at night. But he'd fallen for the boy, and he'd pictured him and Ginelle giving Kyle brothers and sisters, and them all growing up together. He'd helped Kyle learn to zipper his coat and how to hold a baseball bat; had gone to the father-son picnic at preschool and picked him up when Ginelle's classes had run late.

The week before Ginelle had broken it off, Kyle had asked if he could call Rory "Dad." And after the breakup, Rory'd had no rights to assert. There was no visitation. No calling to see how he was. Ginelle had insisted that a clean break was best.

Keeping Kyle a secret had become a habit. Except now Aiden knew, and Hannah had known all along. And Oaklee knew too, and had given him a chance to explain. To start them off on even ground.

For the second time, he felt as if he'd failed some sort

of test, only he hadn't known he was being tested and had no idea what the rules were. This was why beer and hockey were simple. They were straightforward and didn't leave you full of self-doubt in the morning—unless you drank too much or were cheering for the Montreal Canadiens. That was a deal breaker for any self-respecting Bruins fan.

"I'm sorry, Rory," Hannah said softly. "I didn't know."

"I know. I'm mad right now, but I'm mostly mad at myself. Oaklee was trying to start over. I ruined it all because I wasn't honest with her."

Someone made a joke at the table and the resulting outburst of laughter was loud and jolting. He was tired of being alone. He could go on and on about being fine and having the life he wanted and wasn't it great to be a bachelor, but deep down this was what fed him, what kept him going. Family. He wanted one of his own. He wanted to bring his kids to a family dinner, and wipe their hands and faces, and kick them outside to play in the backyard with their cousins. He simply hadn't allowed himself to hope. And when he had, even briefly, he kept screwing it up and then saying he wasn't ready or she wasn't ready, when the truth was he was too scared to go after what he wanted. In case he lost it again.

But if he kept on this way, he'd lose anyway because he'd never try for it in the first place. And that was the worst way to lose—by not trying.

"Can I do anything to help?" Hannah said, her voice low and contrite. "I hate that I might have messed this all up. Do you want me to go talk to her?"

"No." He looked at her sharply. "No offense, but no. Besides, I have to clean this one up on my own."

"Don't go now," Hannah advised. "Wait and think about what you're going to say. Oaklee matters, Rory. I can tell. And I think she cares for you more than she lets on." She looked down at his plate. "Finish your dinner. Hang out here with the family." Her gaze met his, and he thought he saw a flicker of something . . . sentimentality, perhaps? But Hannah didn't do sentimental. "Our family is pretty awesome," she said quietly. "It grounds me. Maybe you should let it ground you for tonight."

He put his plate back on his lap and picked at the lasagna. "Hannah?"

"Yes, sweetie?"

He didn't mind her calling him that. She was four years older and she didn't mean it in any sort of condescending way. "Do you ever feel left out? Like the rest of the family gets 'it' but something doesn't quite fit right? Like someone else's shoes, and the arch is wrong or the heel's worn on one side?"

"All the time," she whispered, and she touched his knee. "The twins are still so young. Ethan and Aiden . . . they've figured it out. But I haven't." She raised an eyebrow and sent him a small smile. "And at this rate I think you're going to get it before I do."

"It's hard being single in a world populated with pairs."

"Or people who seem convinced you should be in a pair." She picked up her plate, too. "I don't want to be with someone just so I'm not alone. It's all or nothing with me. And in Darling . . . well, I'm not stupid. I think I scare the hell out of the male population, and the ones I don't scare think I'm too high maintenance."

Rory smiled, a wave of affection rolling through him. "Aw, Han, you're not high maintenance. You just won't settle. Some guy's going to come up to scratch and sweep you off your feet."

"Maybe," she said, with a little chuckle. "Or maybe not. Maybe I'll just be the crazy aunt who always has a secret stash of candy at her house."

"You're forgiven," he said quietly, nudging her shoulder with his. "Truth is, I should've told her. That I didn't is no one's fault but my own. Though I wish I'd known you'd knew the truth all along."

"If you ever want to talk, I'm here."

"Thanks, Han. I did finally tell Aiden last month."

"Seems Oaklee has created all kinds of trouble."

"More than you know."

Hannah laughed, and reached for her water glass. "Finish your lasagna. Then you can have cake. It's chocolate zucchini, I'm told."

He made a small gagging sound, but laughed. It would be delicious, like all of Willow's dishes.

And he sat back and finished his meal, enjoying the time with his family, and thinking about what he needed to do for his next step. He was pretty sure humble pie was on the menu.

Oaklee hadn't heard from Rory since Sunday night when she'd dropped him at his apartment. It was now Thursday, and they were supposed to have a date on Friday, and he'd said he was going to text her with details.

Twenty-four hours was not a lot of notice. And since their date hadn't ended well, she was even more put out about the noncommunication. Maybe Rory wasn't that keen on fixing things between them. Maybe her big revelation had put him off, made her too much bother, have too much baggage.

Deep down, she'd hoped he'd decide to come clean and trust her. But he hadn't, so she put on a pair of sweatpants and a T-shirt, got out the cleaning supplies, and went to work on her apartment. She'd never be a terrific housekeeper, but she was improving. Not because she enjoyed it, but because she didn't want to go back to being the pathetic, lonely person who cluttered her house with shoes and laundry and dirty dishes just so it looked like her life was fuller than it was.

So she dusted, and vacuumed, and shoved her hair up into a messy ponytail, cleaned the bathroom, and scrubbed the kitchen. And when it was all done, she rather liked the look of it.

Then she took a jar of the spaghetti sauce that she'd made at her mom's out of the fridge, heated it up, cooked some tortellini she'd picked up at the market, and had a real dinner with a glass of wine. Maybe it was for one, but if no one else was going to indulge her, the least she could do was indulge herself. Willow would call it "self-care." Oaklee smiled at the thought. She could do worse than emulate Willow Dunaway. The woman was the queen of serenity.

She dropped a cheese-filled circle of pasta on her shirt, and scooped it off, popped it in her mouth, and stared at the stain in dismay. At least it was an old shirt. She could always pretreat it when she did the laundry, and hope that the stain came out.

Instead of changing, she merely took a sip of pinot

noir and speared two more pieces of tortellini with her fork while sitting cross-legged on her sofa.

She'd just swirled the last disc through the remaining sauce when there was a knock on the door. Immediately her thoughts went to Rory, but she'd have to stop that. Maybe she'd have to actually invite other people over at some point, so that random knocks didn't come with a preconceived identity. Like Emily. They needed a girls' night in really soon. Single girls unite and all that jazz.

"Coming," she called, putting her dirty bowl on the end table and pushing herself up from the sofa.

She looked through the peephole. It was Rory. And she was in sweats, with a ratty ponytail and a spaghetti stain on her shirt. Fantastic.

She opened the door a little. "Hi. Did we get our wires crossed? I wasn't expecting you."

"I know." He shoved his hands in his pockets. The evening was cool, and his breath formed clouds in the air. "I wanted to talk to you."

"I'm kind of a mess, but come in."

She stepped aside.

Rory stepped inside and stopped short. She followed his gaze and realized that her place was actually pretty spotless. "I cleaned tonight. You can actually see my carpet."

"Sorry. I didn't mean to stare."

"It's fine. Have you eaten? I have leftover pasta."

He shrugged. "That's okay. I'll get something later."

"It's real food, Rory. Not out of a can. I bought the pasta at the market and made the sauce at my mom's earlier."

"Then . . . okay. I guess."

She heated the leftovers in the microwave, then sprinkled some Parmesan on the top. It gave her something to do, because she really didn't know why he was here. Except to talk. And he wasn't really doing that.

"Have a seat," she offered. "I'll just tidy the mess."

While he sat at the counter on one of her high stools, she put away the rest of the leftovers and ran some water in the sink for her dishes. He tasted the pasta as she went into the living room to retrieve her dirty bowl. "Hey, this is good."

"Thanks." She smiled at him, then got him a glass of water from the fridge dispenser. "I'm trying to broaden my horizons a little. My mom is helping me. I've actually learned to cook a few things that are edible."

"That's great, Oaklee." He looked around, then looked at her. "I think you're farther ahead on the 'get your shit together' scale than I am."

"It's not a race," she offered, but didn't say anything else. He'd had so many opportunities over the last month and a half to tell her about what was holding him back. It might have been easier if he'd told her nothing at all, but instead he'd opened up just enough to make her feel badly for his broken heart, without letting himself be truly vulnerable. Oaklee resented it just a tiny bit. Mostly because of what it said to her: that Rory didn't trust her enough to be honest.

He finished the food and put the fork in the bowl with a quiet clatter. She took it from him and put it in the dishwater, then scrubbed it out and put it in the rack to dry.

"What were you doing when I got here?" he asked.

"I'd just finished eating and was having a glass of wine," she replied, feeling cautious. She had no idea why Rory was here, but expected he'd get to it eventually. "You want one? We can sit on the sofa if you want. Then you can tell me why you're here."

"I think you know why," he said, following her into the living room. "And no, I've got my car. My water'll do fine."

She sat on her end of the sofa and picked up her glass. "So? We didn't have plans, so I'm assuming you came by to tell me something."

"Are you mad at me?" he asked. "You're usually not so . . . cool."

She sighed. "Not mad, exactly. Exasperated is probably a better word."

"Why?"

"You first. You're the one that drove all the way over here, after all."

"Okay." He took a sip of water, cradled the glass between his hands. "I came to tell you about Kyle."

Her hand paused in midair, halfway to her mouth. "I see." She didn't quite, but maybe something she'd said on Sunday had resonated with him. Either way, she'd hear him out.

"You know who he is," he stated, a question that needed no answer.

"Ginelle's son. Because she was a package deal."

He nodded, and she felt sorry for him. He looked so sad. So lost. She let go of some of her defensiveness and turned toward him. "You loved him, too, didn't you?"

"I did." He met her gaze, and she'd never seen that particular look of pain in his eyes before. It made it difficult for her to remember that she needed to be strong and sure, when she wanted to pull him into a hug and tell him in didn't matter.

"More than Ginelle?" she asked softly.

"Not more. As well as. I can't think of one without the other. They'd become my family. I wanted a life with her, and more children. And I already loved Kyle as my own. God, he was a sweet kid. Reminded me a bit of Aiden, actually. A bit of a practical joker, but had a heart of gold underneath. Ginelle and I were both in the vet program, and I was going to ask her to marry me, and then bring her home with me after graduation. Her and Kyle, and then I figured I'd live and work wherever was best for us as a family. We talked about opening our own practice. I went to Kyle's hockey games that last winter . . . God, he was funny, all wobbly on his skates at first, and a helmet that made him look like a bobble-head." He laughed a little. "We spent evenings together, the three of us. I'd help tuck him in. Gin and I would study together . . . it was damned near perfect."

It was hard hearing him talk about loving another woman so much, particularly now that Oaklee's own feelings were involved. She wondered if he'd felt this way the other night when she'd talked about Jeff. But he hadn't really acted jealous or proprietary at all. Instead he'd acted as if her confiding in him was terrifying.

What did they have if they couldn't share openly and honestly? She knew the answer as sure as she was breathing. Eventually they'd go down the same path that they'd already traveled. A distance would grow between them until one of them—or both of them—were unhappy and ready to move on.

She couldn't do that again. And she didn't want to see Rory go through it, either. From the beginning, their friendship had been too important to be careless with. Now she had to make the choice to not take the easy way out and sweep their troubles under the carpet.

"So you lost both of them," she said quietly. "Not just the woman you loved, but the family you thought you'd have. And a little boy you loved, too."

He nodded, and she saw him roll his lips together as he swallowed. "I talked to Hannah yesterday," he admitted. "And it came out that she'd mentioned Kyle to you."

"So that's why you're telling me now?"

He nodded again. "I should have told you before. You shouldn't have had to hear it from my sister."

"But you didn't."

"No, I didn't. I didn't even know Hannah knew. The only person I ever told was Aiden."

"He knows about Kyle, too?"

Rory nodded, looking abjectly miserable. "Yes."

She was quiet for a minute, not immune to his pain, trying to keep her focus on what this meant for them. "Rory, would you have told me if you hadn't found out from Hannah that I knew?"

He lifted his gaze. "I don't know," he confessed.

"Then we have a problem," she murmured, her heart heavy. "Rory, I told you I wanted to start over, and not just by having a fun, official date, but by being honest so we could move past our personal baggage and maybe find a way to be together. I gave you lots of opportunities and lead-ins. And I didn't expect you to be honest if I wasn't, so I told you about Jeff and how hurt and humiliated I was, and how things have changed for me.

That was trust, Rory. For the first time in what feels like forever, I trusted you with everything. I've told you secrets. I've let you in on my biggest fears, I've let you hold me when I cry, which I never do, and we made love. I don't know how many more ways to show you that I'm in this. That you kept this from me . . . it hurts. And it shows me that you're not ready to trust me in the same way."

"I'm trusting you now."

He was, and yet it didn't feel quite right. "Except that you're trusting me with something I already know. There's not much risk involved there."

Silence fell. It was several moments before Rory lifted his head and sat back on the sofa. "You're right. You're totally right. And here I thought I would be the one having to convince you. Truth is, Oaklee, the thought of trusting someone still scares me. Even you. When Ginelle left, I tied my brain into knots trying to figure out why. Why I wasn't enough. Why she didn't care enough. After two years of loving her, loving her son, giving her everything I had, it hadn't been enough. Maybe you and I could make it work for a while, but what if I'm not enough for you, either? Will you walk away like she did?"

"You want guarantees."

"I know it's unreasonable. Hell, look at Ethan. While all this was going on in my life, he was losing his wife. How could I possibly come home looking for sympathy?"

"And yet Ethan's happy again. So why not you?"

"I don't know."

"Maybe you need to stop looking for guarantees and

having everything planned out. I lived like that once and it still didn't work, so we have two choices. We can either jump in and hope for the best, or we can play it safe. Sunday night was me jumping. I had hoped that you would jump with me, but you weren't ready. You're still not, Rory. And I can't twist myself into knots trying to force you to be. That's not fair to either of us."

His water was probably warm by now, considering how he was cupping the glass in his palms. He moved it around and around, while once more the awkward silence spun around them.

"You got strong," he remarked quietly. "No retreating. No running scared."

"I'm still scared," she admitted, her breath catching. "I'm just not running."

"I need some time to think." He put his glass down on the coffee table. "Is that okay?"

"Of course it is." If she'd been anticipating any big declarations tonight, his last line doused her hopes. "I said I wanted to start over by having a normal date, and with honesty. It doesn't mean we have to move fast, Rory. But it does mean that we need to be open with what we're each dealing with. It's the only way we're going to move past our problems and have a hope of making it."

He nodded, then looked over at her, tilting his head sideways. A small smile touched his lips. "You're bossy," he said, and some of the tension between them softened.

"I just realized that I missed being loved. That I missed loving other people. And that I'd thrown myself into my work but I've been a bystander in my own life. When I had Buster here, I couldn't hibernate anymore.

I had to think of him, too. And he gave love back to me. Even for such a short time, he was accepting and loving and I need more of that in my life. Me being bossy? That's just my way of saying this is too important to get wrong a second time."

"You're right."

"I know."

He laughed suddenly, and she smiled at the sound. As much as this conversation hurt, her confidence grew because she knew it was necessary and right. If anything, she was fighting for them. Maybe, once he'd had time to think, he'd be able to see that.

"I should go. But thank you, Oaklee. For dinner. For letting me talk, and for listening."

"Of course I listened." They got up and she walked him to the door. "You've got to trust someone sometime, Rory, or you're going to be lonely your whole life. And that's not for you. You have too much to give."

He put his hand on the doorknob, then turned to look at her. "Can I kiss you?" he asked. "I just . . . I should've on Sunday, and not just kissed your cheek. I promise I won't ask for more. But I want to kiss you so badly."

She wanted it, too. Instead of answering, she stood up on tiptoe and touched her lips lightly to his, in a soft, lingering contact that made her heart weep. Maybe this would be goodbye. Maybe it wouldn't. But it was definitely the sort of kiss laden with hesitant possibilities and unanswered questions.

She backed away and rested on her heels. "Good night, Rory."

"Good night," he replied, and his gaze touched hers,

the brief connection deep and strong. Then he slipped out the door.

Oaklee shut it and locked it behind him, then pressed her head against the cool steel. She'd been strong throughout the whole conversation. Strong and uncompromising, when all she'd really wanted to do was crawl onto his lap, into his embrace, and tell him it was okay and they'd figure it all out.

A tear slid from the inside corner of her eye and down the side of her nose, and another, before she gave a big sniff and lifted her head, squaring her shoulders.

She wasn't giving up on him yet. Not really. She was just going to give him the space he needed to sort things out. She just hoped that when he did, he'd find his way back to her instead of ending it all forever.

CHAPTER 17

The colors deepened on the trees, a bright combination of reds, golds, and yellows. In addition to fall planters, businesses along Main Street added pumpkins, gourds, and ghouls to their decorations, in preparation for Halloween. Oaklee worked on a fall promotion with several local businesses, and then amped up the fall tourism campaign for the "leafers"—the cars and bus-loads of people who travelled through New England this time of year to enjoy the fall colors. Claire's idea of looking for Kissing Bridge success stories had been brilliant. Oaklee started featuring couples on the town Facebook page on Mondays, Wednesdays, and Fridays. She also met with Hannah about the holiday charity event, and they started planning an agenda and brain-storming events. Hannah, to her credit, did not mention Rory's name, but kept the entire meeting businesslike.

It was all very busy and positive, with the obvious

absence of communication with Rory. Two weeks had passed and not a peep. No date, no text, no nothing. Oaklee tried to keep busy to help with the sting of rejection, but she wasn't always successful. Still, she would be. She had gotten over Jeff. She'd grown up a lot . . . and she could move past this, too.

She was sitting in The Purple Pig on a Wednesday evening, having a pumpkin latte and a cinnamon roll, when her phone buzzed with an incoming notification. She unlocked her screen and had a peek. She wasn't expecting to be tagged by Rory.

> @DrRoryG: So @SamsonSouth is a great place for a date. Not their fault I messed it up with the girl. @OakleeC_Darling

Her lips dropped open. Was he . . . actually apologizing in public? To her shock, Sam's immediately retweeted and added, "Anything we can do to help?"

Her thumbs were poised over the keypad, but she couldn't type anything. She didn't know what to say. But she didn't need to. Rory kept tweeting.

> @DrRoryG: Thanks @SamsonSouth, but this is on me. I let my baggage get in the way of something great.

Holy shit. He didn't just say that.
And it didn't stop there.

> @DrRoryG: Best thing to happen to me in years. @OakleeC_Darling is sweet, generous, amazing. I'm an idiot.

@LaurelLadybug: Yes you are, @DrRoryG. We think you should fix it.

@MtrMama: Hey @DrRoryG, are you the guy she asked out a few weeks ago? I was rooting for you two.

@DrRoryG: Yeah, @MtrMama, that was us. Told you I was stupid.

@SamsonSouth: Grovel, son. @DrRoryG

Oaklee laughed at that, and took a sip of her latte. Damn, this was entertaining. And she was getting a warm sensation all over, knowing that Rory was sitting somewhere, perhaps in his sterile, personality-less apartment, talking about feelings on social media.

More people started commenting, offering advice. Some reiterated the idea of groveling. A few said she wasn't worth it, man, because women just complicated things and suggested beer, hockey, and cars. A few kind souls asked what happened.

And then someone asked if she was reading.

@Darlings_Finest: Where is @OakleeC_Darling anyway? You getting all this, Oaklee?

@OakleeC_Darling: I'm listening.

A Twitterstorm of "She's here!" set the feed on fire. She had never expected a grand gesture on Rory's part. He was so private. For him to do this . . .

@OakleeC_Darling: Are you drunk, @DrRoryG?

@DrRoryG: Sober as a judge.

Her heart took up a strange beat, fluttering against her ribs as she gripped her phone. What on earth was he doing?

@DrRoryG: You see, Twitter, I didn't trust her with my heart. I had it broken a while ago and don't like to talk about it. I shut her out.

@DrRoryG: She believed in me and I disappointed her. Because I'm scared. Big ol' lily-livered coward, right here.

@DrRoryG: Problem is, I love her.

Oaklee nearly dropped her phone.

The feed went wild, people freaking out that he'd actually said he loved her. She saw Laurel post again, a simple, "*sniff*" reply. Darling's Finest, which she assumed was someone on the police force, was a little more succinct in their reply and suggested he "nut up" and go tell her. A few more accounts she didn't recognize voiced the opinion that if she didn't come around after that, she didn't deserve him.

Oaklee simply stared at the screen. He loved her. She knew people could often say things online that they couldn't say in person, but to even type those words . . . Rory wouldn't have done it as a game or if he didn't really, truly mean them.

He loved her.

Her lip wobbled. He *loved* her.

Emily came over and put her hand on Oaklee's shoulder. "We're closing in ten, sweetie, but you stay as long as you want." She gave a squeeze. "I can't believe he's doing what he's doing," she said gently, and lifted her phone. "You did it, Oaklee."

"Did what?" Dazed, she looked up into Emily's eyes.

"You became more important to him than the fear. Now do us all a favor and don't throw away the opportunity. Rory is a great guy and we're all rooting for you guys to make it."

"You are?"

Emily nodded, smiling sweetly. "One thing I've learned about Rory. He jokes and teases, and he used to serial date and be a real good-time guy. But I haven't seen him around town with one of his dates since the two of you started up. I've seen him with his furry friends and besides, he's got to be great to make you care so much about him. He loves you. If you love him, too, grab on to it and don't let go."

Oaklee's eyes misted over. She pictured Rory, and his crooked smile, and a warm, all-encompassing certainty washed over her. It was like her mother said: When it was meant to be, she'd know. And perhaps what she'd really needed was to know that he loved her to be truly sure.

"Thank you, Em."

"Anytime."

She looked back down at her screen, and had to scroll back up to see a lot of the responses. Many of them asked her where the hell she was and did she love him back, for God's sake?

Her hands shook as she sent a response.

@OakleeC_Darling: DMing him right now

And then she sent the direct message, her heart pounding so hard she could hear it in her ears. "What are you doing?" she typed. "This is crazy."

The response came back immediately. "Not hiding. Being honest. If you can move past your broken heart, so can I. I wanted you to believe me, so . . . I made sure there were witnesses."

She gave an emotional chuckle as her thumbs flew over the letters. "You sure did. I love you, too, Rory. We have so much to talk about, but that seems like a good place to start."

There was a pause, then, "Meet me at the Kissing Bridge in ten minutes."

"Okay."

It was the only answer she could give.

She shut off the phone, ignoring the questioning masses they'd just left hanging in the middle of their drama. Instead she grabbed her purse and headed for the ladies' room, while Emily shut and locked the front door and turned off the *Open* sign. She hurriedly swiped on a little more mascara and freshened her lipstick, then took her hair out of its clip and shook it out so it fell over the collar of her suede jacket and down her shoulders.

"Wait," Emily said, coming forward. "You're going to meet him, aren't you? It's written all over your face."

Oaklee nodded, her insides shaking with both nervousness and excitement. "He sent me a DM to meet him at the bridge," she said, and even her voice trembled a little.

Emily disappeared into the back for a second and came back with a little square of chocolate. "Okay, so it's not a breath mint, but when he kisses you you'll taste like chocolate. Open up."

Oaklee obeyed and Em popped the square into her mouth. It was dark and rich but not so dark that it was bitter. Emily grinned. "Okay, sweetie. Go get him. Love you."

"I'm freaking out," Oaklee admitted.

"Don't. Just go. Tell him how you feel and just be in the moment. Okay?"

"Okay."

Emily let her out the door and Oaklee took a deep breath before crossing the well-lit Main Street for the park. She normally didn't walk alone at night, even though Darling was a pretty safe town. But in a few minutes she'd see the bridge, and he'd be there. She knew he would.

And he was. Already waiting, standing by the hand railing at the bottom of the arc, wearing ripped jeans and a battered jacket and with his gorgeously thick hair mussed on top, as if he kept running his hands through it. She paused for just a moment, looking at him, and he shoved his fingers through his hair, just as she suspected.

He was nervous, too.

She stepped onto the path leading to the bridge, her boots making a soft crunch on the gravel. He looked up, and their gazes locked.

And then he moved, and she moved, both of them striding purposefully to the other, meeting about fifteen feet from the bridge and straight into each other's arms.

She pressed her face against his jacket, wrapped her arms around his ribs, and held on.

"Oaklee," he said into her hair. "I love you, Oaklee."

She nodded, even as tears stung the backs of her eyes. "I love you, too. Scary as hell but here we are."

He stepped back and cupped her face in his hands. "But if we're scared, we're scared together. And you were so right. So right. We need to be honest about how we feel, even if it's scared. Because that way at least we're terrified but loving each other together." He kissed her forehead, her eyelids. "I know there aren't guarantees, but I can promise that I'll never do to you what he did. That's not the kind of man I am. You're safe with me, Oaklee. I hope you know that. I'll do everything I can to not let you down again."

She gripped his jacket in her fingers. "You didn't let me down, not really. You just weren't ready. I know it's hard. I'm still afraid. But Emily said something to me tonight that makes so much sense I don't know why I didn't see it before."

"What's that?"

"That you—and me, too—have got to a place where the love we have for each other is bigger than the fear we have of being hurt. Oh, Rory. I've known you since puberty. And I always knew I could rely on you if I needed help. I know you aren't Jeff. You couldn't possibly be. You were my hero back then. Now you're just . . ." She looked up into his eyes, bit down on her lip. "Now you're the man I love. The man I trust."

"I trust you, too," he said, brushing her hair off her face. "Because after what we've both been through, I know you wouldn't say it if you weren't sure."

Oh, God. This was just . . . amazing. So perfect. A frozen moment in time where Oaklee felt invincible and strong in her femininity and in her future.

"Come here," he whispered, sliding his hands down her arms to twine his fingers with her. Then he moved away, out of their embrace, and he tugged her the short distance to the bridge.

Their boots made clunking noises as they trotted over the arch to the apex. Then they stopped, looked out over Fisher Creek, the reflection of the moon and the tree branches in the water. The sky was lit with a million stars, and Rory held her cold hands in his as he turned her to face him.

"Seeing as you work for the town, you know the legend of the bridge," he said softly. "A love that lasts forever. I don't know if it works or not, but I'm willing to take a chance and say that I want it to."

Forget past gestures, forget even the excitement of running away to Vegas. This moment, this simple minute in time where she looked in Rory's eyes and he looked in hers while standing in the middle of the town icon . . . this was the most romantic moment of her life. Because she knew what it meant to him. Knew how open and vulnerable he was right now, and what he was giving her. Himself. There was no greater gift.

"I want it to, too," she whispered, squeezing his hands. "And this is as good a place as any to say I love you, and that I want our love to last for a lifetime."

She turned so that her lower back was pressed against

the wall of the bridge, and he stepped closer and kissed her, his lips warm while his face was cold against hers. She lifted her hands and put them flat on his chest as she kissed him back. They'd had many kisses already, but this one was the best, because all the others had been questions and this one felt like the answer. Maybe there would never be guarantees, but there were promises, intentions, wishes. And right now she wanted to feel this way for the rest of her life.

And just when their lips were about to part, he put his arms around her and lifted her up so that her toes didn't touch the ground anymore.

When he put her down and the kiss ended, she looked up at him and felt a happiness that had been missing for so long. "So where do we go from here?" she asked, taking his hand in hers. "What's next?"

He grinned. "That part's easy. I never took Ginelle home with me, you know? The family never met her. I think I was too afraid of jinxing our relationship or something, and she was never really pumped to come with me. She always wanted to go see her family, and so that's how we did it. I don't want to be like that. If you're with me, Oaklee, you're with *me*. I'm not going to hide you away until there's this perfect, plannable moment. Family dinner is at my mom and dad's this week. I want you to come. With me. As my girlfriend."

Oaklee nodded. "I'd love to."

Rory ran his hand over his hair again, and Oaklee wondered why, and if he was agitated again. "What is it? You do that when you're nervous."

He smiled at her, a big, wide smile, and his eyes full of wonder. "I'm not nervous. I just realized that I'm freaking happy. Really, really happy. Oh my God, what a feeling."

She laughed, and hugged him, and they ended up kissing again.

"Can I walk you home?" he asked, when the kissing got a little intense for being in public, even if the park was empty.

"I'd like that a lot," she replied, and hand in hand they left the bridge and followed the path on the Green to home.

Rory looked at his phone the next morning, and ran his finger over the screen to see what notifications he'd missed overnight. When a tweet with a picture caught his eye, he tapped it and opened it.

"Oaklee. Sweetie, you've got to see this."

She rolled over in the bed and rested on an elbow. "See what?"

He angled the phone over, and she sat up a bit. The photo was from last night, on the bridge. The bodies were mostly silhouetted, but there was no mistaking the pose. "Oh my God. That's us!"

He nodded.

"Who took that? Oh jeez . . ."

He patted her leg. "It's okay. I think we ended up with our own fan club last night. Listen to this." He read the content of a bunch of messages. "Okay, so where did our lovebirds go? Is this going to work out? Why did this go so quiet? Hope she's said it back." He chuckled. "Someone agreed with that poster and said that it took big 'nads to say I love you online.'"

She grinned. "I nearly fell off my chair at the café.

Why did you do it publicly, anyway? You're more the show-up-on-my-doorstep type, you know?"

He smiled. "Because I wanted to show you that how I felt was more important than protecting myself. And that I was willing to take a risk for us."

"It was a smart strategy," she admitted, and winked. "At least, I think it turned out okay."

He nodded, still scrolling. "Okay, so the picture was sent from . . . from the Darling town account. That's weird."

She took the phone from his hand and frowned. "The town account? But only a few people have access to that. Me, Ryan, and . . ." She looked up at him. "And Claire. But how?"

"Let me see. Maybe there's more."

He scrolled through his e-mail. There was one from Ethan, with an attachment.

Hey, bro. So nice work on the public declaration last night. It's about time. Oaklee was at the café when the Twitterstorm happened, and mentioned going to the bridge to Emily. And because Emily is wonderful and nosy, she intruded on your moment a little bit and took the picture that I've attached. She sent it to Willow, who sent it to Claire, thinking that your adoring public would like to see how the evening ended. So if you see it from the town Twitter account, you can blame your little sister. There are tons of congratulations there for both of you. We've all enjoyed this maybe more than we should.

I've kissed two women on that bridge, Rory, and

both times it was the best decision of my life. I'm happy for you, and happy for Oaklee.

A lot of guys say that love makes you soft. But it doesn't, Rory. It makes you stronger. It brings out all the good parts. And you already had a lot of great qualities, so I expect from now on that you will be a much better little brother.

He added a little smiley face after that, and then signed it, simply, *E.*

By the time he finished reading, Oaklee was already on her phone, reading through the messages and grinning. "Oh my goodness. We were quite the spectacle last night."

"And inadvertently, the best tourism campaign to come out of the office all season," Rory answered, nudging her elbow. "Claire posted the pic. Ethan said she and Willow and Emily were in on it together."

"She's going to be doing my job before I know it," Oaklee answered him. "But today, I don't care about work, or advertising campaigns, or social media stats. This is what I'm interested in, right here." She slid over closer, beneath the blankets, and cuddled up against his side.

"Hmm. I could be interested in that, too," he said, and he threw his phone onto the floor and took her in his arms.

CHAPTER 18

Oaklee had never been to a family dinner as loud and welcoming as the one at John and Moira Gallagher's home.

It was on Saturday night, and the place was decorated for Halloween for Ethan's boys and for the trick-or-treaters that would be around in a week's time. Strings of purple lights were draped over the deck, and ghost-like figures danced in the trees leading up the drive. The lights over the front door had orange bulbs, casting an eerie light over everything, and pumpkins lined the steps, waiting to be carved closer to the day.

"Wow," Oaklee said, climbing the stairs. "This is cool."

"Mom even dresses up each year in her witch costume to hand out candy. Though last year she scared Ronan." Rory chuckled.

They went inside and Oaklee realized they were all there. All the Gallaghers, even Claire and Cait.

The noise in the kitchen was thunderous, but when Rory and Oaklee walked in, the volume increased as welcomes were shouted out. Hannah came over and gave her a quick hug, and so did Willow, apologizing briefly for aiding and abetting the publication of the picture.

"It's okay, Willow. To be honest . . . I'm glad you guys did it." She leaned in so only Willow could hear. "It was really romantic. Not that I'll ever forget it, but the pic is lovely."

Then she looked up at Claire, who was grinning at her from across the room. "You," she said sternly, "on the other hand, are not off the hook. Away at school and using the town account? Tsk tsk, Ms. Intern."

Claire shrugged. "I told you that night at the Suds and Spuds that you had a thing for him. Was I right or was I right?"

"At the Spud?" Rory heard the last and came up to her and put his arm around her waist. "Wait. The night I was there with . . . what was her name again?"

"Patty," Claire and Oaklee said together.

"Right. Well, Claire, you and Patty were sharing a brain cell, because when I drove her home she told me I was more interested in Oaklee than I was in her."

Oaklee turned around, her mouth open. "You never told me that!"

"A strategic omission," he said with a shrug, and then plopped a silly kiss on her mouth.

"Eeew," came another voice. This one was Aiden, who was grinning from ear to ear. "About time, by the way. Hey, Oaklee."

"Hey, Aiden."

Then there was Cait, who was standing at the massive kitchen island, tossing salad in a huge bowl. "Hi, Cait," Oaklee said, and Cait gave a friendly wave.

Moira came from another room, carrying a spare chair, and gave a big grin when she saw Oaklee. "I'm so glad you could make it," she said, putting the chair down and coming to give Oaklee a hug. "Do you know you're the first girl Rory's brought home since high school?"

"Mom," Rory said, his tone one of *you're embarrassing me*.

"I do know that. He's kind of weird that way," Oaklee said, feeling strangely at home even though this was far crazier than any event with her family.

Moira laughed. "Well, once in, never out," she quipped. "And I hope you like roast beef. John brought home a giant roast and decided we should have everyone over."

"Oh! Speaking of, I didn't know what to bring, so I brought some wine. There's red and white in here." She reached for the gift bag in Rory's hand. "I'm not much of a cook."

"If you're interested, you come see me. I spent twenty years cooking for eight people. Now that my girls are grown, I don't have anyone to teach until I have some grandbabies ready to take over."

Oaklee was blown away by the generosity. "Thanks. My mom's been giving me some pointers, too. I actually made a roast chicken that didn't poison us last night."

Ethan and Willow arrived with the boys, who were bouncing like crazy at the sight of the Halloween decorations. Finally everyone got a plate, filled it buffet style, and found a chair somewhere near the kitchen.

Oaklee counted. It was a simple family dinner and there were thirteen people crowded into the kitchen. And Rory said they did this all the time. How crazy and wonderful. She couldn't imagine what Thanksgiving and Christmas would be like.

John said a simple grace, and then everyone dug in.

When the roast had been demolished, the potatoes drowned with rich gravy, carrots, and peas consumed, and rolls had sopped up the remaining gravy from the plates, Moira cut a huge slab of carrot cake, slathered with cream cheese icing. Oaklee figured by the time she was done she'd be popping buttons off her pants, but she took a slice anyway. It melted in her mouth. And when the cake was gone, everyone pitched in to clear the table, even Ethan's boys. The twins worked side by side to put away leftovers, Moira rinsed dishes and put them in the dishwasher, and the boys took the leaves out of the table and put the extra chairs away. Willow, Oaklee, and Laurel washed the pots and pans and within half an hour, everything was spotless. Ethan and Willow bathed the boys and put them in pajamas for the drive home later, and everyone else gathered in the huge family room, where a hockey game played with the sound off. Oaklee looked up and realized Cam's team was playing, and a surge of pride and loneliness went through her.

"What's wrong?" Rory seemed to sense the change in her mood, and she looked up at him from her spot on a cushion on the floor.

"Cam's playing. I just got missing him, that's all. I think part of it is just being here tonight with your family. It's been so amazing, that it's made me miss mine a little bit."

"Then I have an idea."

"You do?"

"Yep. He can't often get away during the season, so maybe I can book a weekend off before the holidays and we can go to him. Take in a game and have a weekend away, just the two of us."

It sounded absolutely perfect. "Thank you, Rory. That sounds awesome."

They stayed until around nine-thirty. Ethan and Willow had taken the boys just before nine, and Rory stretched, saying he thought they should get a move on, too.

"Sure," Aiden said, a knowing tone in his voice. "Nine-thirty and you're pulling the plug? Riiiight."

"Aiden," Moira chided, while John merely gave his son a "really?" look.

"Actually, I have to go to the clinic. There's a pup there that needs some attention."

Oaklee looked up at him, reluctant to leave when she was having such a good time. "Do you have to be the one to check every weekend? Doesn't any of the support stuff do that?"

He shrugged. "I live there. It's not usually a big deal." He stood from his spot on the sofa and held out a hand to Oaklee. She'd been really comfortable, sitting on a plump cushion, her back leaning against Rory's legs while his fingers toyed with her hair now and again. But she got up and rolled her shoulders.

"Thank you so much for including me in dinner," she said. "It was delicious. And for making me feel so welcome."

Moira brushed off the thanks with a wave of her

hand. "You've made Rory happy, and that makes you family. You come by anytime. With or without my pain-in-the-ass son." She blew Rory a kiss. "You know I love you."

"Yeah, Mom, I know." He laughed, then went and kissed her cheek. "Best carrot cake ever," he added, and held out his hand again to Oaklee.

The drive to the clinic went by quickly and Rory parked his car by the back entrance. When he got out, he didn't make a move to go to the actual clinic part of the building, but headed for the stairs to his apartment. "Don't you have to check on a dog?" she asked, her brows furrowing.

"Yeah. Come on up first."

Hmm. Why did she get the feeling something was a little off? What was he up to?

She went inside the apartment. He'd turned on some lights, and as she put down her purse and took off her jacket, she heard the click of a door down the hall. "Where'd you go?"

"Bathroom. Hang on."

A strange sound touched her ears, high-pitched but faint enough she couldn't quite make it out.

But when Rory came back, it all became crystal clear, and Oaklee's hands flew to her mouth.

It was the most adorable puppy she'd ever seen, cradled in Rory's arms.

"Oh my . . . Oh Rory. He is adorable. It is a he?"

Rory nodded, a smile lighting up his face. "He's a lab terrier cross. A lot like Buster, though I think he's going to have darker fur."

"How old is he? Oh my goodness. Look at those

paws." She went forward and touched the soft puppy fur. The dog had floppy ears and big brown eyes and was utterly roly-poly. "The cuteness is just killing me."

"He's eleven weeks, and just weaned. Ready for adoption."

"So why are you having to care for him? Is he sick or something?"

Rory was quiet for a moment, and then his gaze settled on her. "Well, the other puppies in the litter were spoken for, and I figured he needed to be somebody's baby, so I thought he might be yours."

She stared at him, utterly shocked, beautifully surprised, and touched. She stared at the little face and melted. "You . . . you got me a puppy?"

"He's not a purebred or anything, and the owners already kept one from the litter. He needed a good home, and I happened to know where he could find one." He shifted a bit and put the puppy in her arms. "A place where he'd be loved even when he makes a mess or ruins a shoe. A place where he could find a strong but soft heart. You were so heartbroken when you had to give Buster up. I remember you saying the night he left, that you always knew he was somebody's baby, but you'd wanted him to be yours. This time, Oaklee, no one is going to come and tell you that you were wrong. That this love doesn't belong to you, or you don't deserve it. No one is going to make you feel like your love isn't worth having. And that goes for me, and this little guy right here."

She had never loved anyone more than she loved Rory at this moment. Her face was covered in little puppy licks, and he squirmed in her arms for a minute, but then seemed to find a comfortable spot and simply curled in, his velvety face tucked into the curve of her neck.

"I don't know anything about puppies. I'm going to need a lot of help."

"I thought that might be the case."

He leaned forward and kissed her, then put his palm on the pup's head. Oaklee had the strangest feeling that they'd just made a family. Didn't matter that it was a dog instead of a kid. It was love that mattered. Promises that mattered. Her heart, her life, was fuller than she'd ever imagined it could be.